DATE ME, BRYSON KELLER

♡

DATE ME, BRYSON KELLER

Kevin van Whye

Random House 🏠 New York

Text copyright © 2020 by Kevin van Whye
Jacket photographs copyright © 2020 by Howard Huang

Visit us on the Web! GetUnderlined.com

Educators and librarians, for a variety of teaching tools, visit us at RHTeachersLibrarians.com

Library of Congress Cataloging-in-Publication Data
Name: Van Whye, Kevin, author.
Title: Date me, Bryson Keller / Kevin van Whye.
Description: First edition. | New York: Random House Children's Books, [2020] | Audience: Ages 14 and up. | Summary: When Kai Sheridan, gay but not out, asks popular Bryson Keller on a date as part of a dare, both of their lives are transformed.
Identifiers: LCCN 2019028183 | ISBN 978-0-593-12603-5 (hardcover) | ISBN 978-0-593-12604-2 (library binding) | ISBN 978-0-593-12605-9 (ebook)
Subjects: CYAC: Dating (Social customs)—Fiction. | Gays—Fiction. | Sexual orientation—Fiction. | High schools—Fiction. | Schools—Fiction. | Family life—Fiction.
Classification: LCC PZ7.1.V3944 Dat 2020 | DDC [Fic]—dc23

The text of this book is set in 12.5-point Adobe Jenson Pro.
Interior design by Ken Crossland.

Printed in the United States of America
10 9 8 7 6 5 4 3 2 1
First Edition

Random House Children's Books supports the First Amendment and celebrates the right to read.

For my family.
Your belief, support,
and love are my everything.

PROLOGUE

It all started as a dare. Of course, at the time I didn't know the dare would change my life. But that's the thing about change, isn't it? Like love, it just happens, never seeming to announce itself. Instead, it's just one "oh shit" moment happening after the next. Or in my case, one capital "OH SHIT" moment, which, if I'm being honest, is what 95 percent of being a closeted gay teen is like.

It was a week before school reopened, and we were all at Brittany Daniel's New Year's Eve party. Brittany has been my biology partner since the start of senior year, and for once I'd actually been invited to the party by name, and not just as a tagalong for my best friends, Priyanka Reddy and Donny Duckworth. (I know, Donny's name is his cross to bear, but at least people *know* his name.)

I was standing in the corner near a bookshelf, trying to look casual as I scanned the spines for titles I recognized while secretly searching the room for my MIA best friends. I never know what to do at parties. Seriously, what do I do with my hands? Do I shuffle my feet to this song?

I didn't intend to eavesdrop, but Bryson Keller has a voice that carries, draws you in. He's the captain of the boys' soccer team and the most popular kid at Fairvale Academy, so it was no surprise he was holding court.

"High school relationships don't matter," he said. "We're in our senior year. Most of us are going to end up at different colleges, and it just feels like a waste of emotional energy to commit to something that is destined to end. Why even bother?"

"How romantic of you," Priya drawled.

Curious, I stepped into the kitchen to find my best friends among the überpopular crowd—the athletes and the wealthy.

It made sense for Priya and Donny to be there. Priya is captain of the girls' soccer team, and Donny is one of the richest kids in school, which means he doesn't have to play sports to be invited to things. I, on the other hand, am always their plus-one.

Priya took Donny's hand in hers. Their fingers interlocked. "You could very well meet the one in high school."

It's been six months since my best friends started dating. I'm still getting used to it. I'm happy for them, honest. It was clear to everyone but them that they were perfect for each other. They always had my blessing to take their friendship to the next level. But sometimes I end up feeling like a third wheel, standing at the edge of the crowd. Literally.

Bryson shook his head. His light brown hair looked a shade darker under the fluorescent lighting, and shadows danced across his sharp jaw. His pale blue eyes looked darker in this light, too.

"Well, my mom and dad were the 'it' couple of their high school," Dustin Smith said. He looked at his best friend. "You know, Bryson, it's funny that you're giving out hot takes on relationships when you've never even dated."

"Are your parents strict or something?" Donny asked.

"No," Dustin answered. "They would be fine with him dating."

"Yeah, it's my choice not to," Bryson explained with a shrug. He looked down at the red cup in his hand. "I just don't see the point in high school relationships."

"Maybe it's that he can't find anyone to date," Isaac Lawson teased, his white smile flashing. Isaac is also on the soccer team and happens to be the person I have had a very secret crush on since the start of junior year.

I edged farther into the circle.

Bryson snorted. "C'mon. No offense, but I could probably date someone new every week if I wanted." He took a sip from his cup as Priya rolled her eyes.

"Prove it," Dustin said. "I dare you."

"What?" Bryson asked.

There were *oohs* from the boys, and the girls around them laughed. Bryson shifted uncomfortably, not loving being put on the spot.

"Prove to everyone that you can date someone new each week," Dustin said.

"You're seriously daring me?"

"Yep," Dustin said. "Are you scared?"

"Fine. I'll do it." Bryson looked up and our eyes met. I looked away. "But if it's a game or dare or whatever, then there should be rules. Kai, what do you think?"

It took me a heartbeat to answer. I hadn't planned on participating. "Um, maybe it should only last the school week," I said nervously. "Monday through Friday."

"Nice." Bryson nodded. "I don't want to sacrifice my weekends for this."

"Nothing physical," Natalie da Silva suggested. "This is a game, and everyone's boundaries should be respected."

Bryson looked even more relieved. "And only seniors. I don't want to be gross about it."

"Agreed. Only seniors are allowed to play," Dustin said. He looked around. "Is that all?"

"You're not allowed to ask anyone out," Priya added. "Or else it's too easy."

"Wait, what?"

"The dare is this, Bryson Keller," Priya said with a wicked glint in her eye. "You will date the first person to ask you out each Monday until the final bell Friday. You are forbidden from asking anyone out. And if someone fails to ask you out, you lose."

"Oh, I like that," Natalie said. "Girls can totally ask boys out." She held up her hand for a high five, and Priya happily obliged.

"You also lose if you get tired of dating," Dustin said. "I

know you, dude. I don't believe you have this in you." He patted Bryson on the shoulder.

"And what happens if he loses?" I asked.

Bryson shot me a look like he'd been hoping no one would mention a punishment. I shrugged with a smile. How often would I get to see Bryson Keller squirm?

Dustin knew what would hurt the most. "You have to ride the bus for the rest of senior year."

Everyone laughed. We all know just how much Bryson Keller loves his white Jeep. It's arguably the cleanest car at school. He washes it at least once a week—I've seen the shirtless pictures on his Instagram feed.

"Shit, okay," Bryson said. "But there needs to be a time limit on this. I'll do this for three months and that's it. If I lose, then after spring break I'll start taking the bus. But when I win—and I will win—you won't doubt me ever again."

"Yeah, yeah, yeah," Priya said. "You will be a legend."

"Bryson Keller. The man. The myth. The legend. I like that," Bryson said. He chugged the rest of his beer. "Let the games begin."

"In that case," Natalie said, "date me, Bryson Keller!" She burst out laughing.

"Fine, even though it's not Monday. When school starts, Natalie, you'll be my first girlfriend." Bryson smiled. "But this will be the first and last time I ever break the rules. You've all been warned." He bowed gallantly to her.

And that's how it all started.

Two months later, the Bryson Keller dare is still going strong. And time is running out. A single school week is all anyone gets.

There have been no exceptions to this.

None.

Until me, that is.

OH SHIT.

MONDAY

1

Mornings in the Sheridan house are known to be loud and chaotic affairs—with Mondays being especially disastrous. Today is no different.

"Yazz, open the door!" I shout. I've been standing outside the door to the bathroom I share with my younger sister for the last ten minutes. I'm going to be late.

I love my sister, and aside from weekday mornings, we generally get along. I can't say that I'd kill for her, but I might be willing to help her bury a body. Right now, though, Yasmine Sheridan is the one I want to murder.

"I swear to God, Yasmine, if you don't open this door in the next two minutes, I'm going to kick it down."

"Kai!" Mom shouts from downstairs. "Don't use the Lord's name in vain."

I roll my eyes. As if that's what's important right now. I don't say this, though, because I really don't have time to get into an argument about religion with Mom—that's reserved for Sunday mornings, when I refuse to go to church.

I bang on the door again and it opens midknock. Yazz steps from the steam-filled room and fixes me with an exasperated look.

"If you got up earlier, we wouldn't have to do this all the time. Time management is key to living a successful life." Yazz is thirteen years old but has the personality of a middle-aged woman who yells at the neighborhood kids to get off her lawn. "When you head to college in a few months, you won't have me to help you. So let's work on that, shall we?"

She taps me on the shoulder as if to encourage me. By the time I think of an appropriate response it's already too late. She's closed her bedroom door, and I am left standing there like a scolded child. Who would believe that I'm four years older?

"Breakfast is ready," Dad shouts.

"I still need to shower!" I call back.

"You're going to be late, Kai. Donny will be here soon."

"I know, Mom!" Muttering under my breath, I enter the bathroom. I start the shower and find only lukewarm water waiting for me. I get that it's spring and this is California, but I like my water like I like my coffee—almost scorching.

Ten minutes later, I emerge a new man. There isn't time for me to shave, and I can only hope that the teachers won't punish me for it. With a towel around my waist, I race back to my bedroom and quickly put on my uniform—tan pants and a crisp white button-down shirt. Fairvale Academy is flexible on a great many things, but the dress code is something that the school isn't willing to budge on.

I look for my tie. I rifle through the piles of clothes that lie forgotten on my bedroom floor. I'm not the neatest person in the world, which earns me countless lectures from Mom and Dad. But I figure that within the sanctity of my own bedroom, I am allowed to be my true self—which encompasses my sometimes forgetting to put my dirty clothes in the laundry basket.

I find the crimson-and-white-striped tie. It's odd that the school emblem is two stylized eagles, given that our mascot is the cougar, but this is Fairvale Academy, so we don't question it . . . much. I transferred from a public middle school, and the private school uniform took some getting used to. I'd much rather wear jeans and a T-shirt.

I pick up my blazer from where I threw it Friday afternoon. I cringe at the wrinkles and try to smooth them out. But there's simply no saving this dull navy monstrosity.

I take the stairs two at a time. My house has a no-shoe policy, so my socked feet slip on the hardwood floors, and I only save myself from falling by gripping the kitchen island.

"One day you're going to end up breaking something," Mom warns. She's seated at the island, reading the newspaper on her iPad. Mom is dressed and ready for the day. Her bottle-blond hair is pulled back in a ponytail. There's a stack of Dad's pancakes on her plate, and my stomach growls at the sight.

"You better eat something quick, *boytjie*," Dad says. He's still got his South African accent despite having lived in the United States for almost two decades now. My mom is White, and my dad is mixed race. When I was younger, I didn't understand the stares that they got—the stares that *I* got—but now I do. People have an idea of what love should be, and my parents loving each other doesn't fit into everyone's perfect vision. Dad has always said that racists are sad people trying to make the rest of the world just as sad. Their hatred is something we should pity them for because it keeps them from living full lives.

My phone buzzes. I pull it from my pocket and open the three musketeers group chat with Donny and Priya. After finishing the Dumas book last summer, I convinced them to watch the movie with me. The whole "All for one and one for all" motto was so extra that it seemed perfectly made for us.

I scroll past the memes that Donny shared last night and find the text telling me that he's here.

"No time," I say as I head to the cabinet where Mom keeps the breakfast bars. She makes sure we always have some on hand because most mornings I tend to run late. I rip open the wrapper and take a big bite.

"He got the oversleeping from you, dear," Mom says to Dad.

"Well, I have an excuse. My body hasn't adapted to this time zone."

"It's been twenty years. I think that excuse is over."

Mom and Dad met when she was doing volunteer work with a church in South Africa. It just so happened that Dad attended that same church. They fell in love, and the rest, as they say, is history.

"Bye!" I call as I race from the kitchen. I stop at the door to put on my school shoes, grab my messenger bag from the hook, and gobble down the rest of the breakfast bar.

"Have a great day," Dad calls.

"Love you," Mom adds.

"You too," I say, my mouth still slightly full. I exit the house and walk toward the sports car that a teenager has no business owning. I climb into the back seat. Donny is driving and Priya is in the front seat.

"Donny, when you're at Caltech, please invent an alarm that will actually wake me up," I say by way of greeting.

Donny and Priya have both already been accepted into their first-choice colleges. In a few months' time, Donny will be off to Pasadena and Priya to UCLA. I'm currently waiting to hear back from Tisch. Every time I think about my dream being on the line, I feel sick. Any day now I will hear if I made the cut.

It's sad to think that these morning routines will be coming to an end soon. Donny and I met freshman year, and we've been best friends ever since. Priya adopted us several days later, insisting that without her, Donny and I would be lost little sheep. We'd never admit it to her, but she was probably right.

"There is a way," Priya says. "It's called willpower."

"You sound just like Yazz."

"The Force is strong in that one," Priya says.

"Priya made us watch *Star Wars* again." Donny catches my eye in the rearview mirror. "You should have come with."

"Nah, you guys need your date nights," I say.

"If a theater is showing any of the *Star Wars* movies, then it is a given that I must attend," Priya says. "It's a family tradition. My dad literally made sure it was the first movie I could ever remember watching. My father is nothing if not dedicated."

"Does your mom still want him to get rid of his figurine collection?" I ask.

Priya snorts. "I think that will only be possible if he dies. There are three things my father loves more than anything in this world: his family, his job, and his Star Wars collection."

"My dad's the same with Manchester United," I say. "Just this weekend he woke up at three a.m. to watch them get thrashed by Chelsea."

"I wish my dad had a hobby," Donny says. "Then he wouldn't be nagging me about my grades all the time. He wants me to be better at math."

"Impossible," I say. "Until you, I didn't even know someone could get such a high math grade."

Donny laughs. "Math skills and bad family names are Duckworth traditions." He twists to look at me when we stop at a red light. "Did you do the homework?" he asks. "I struggled on the last two equations."

"Please, Donald. Let's not ruin Kai's morning by asking him about math." My suckage at math is a longtime running joke among my friends, as is the legendary test on which I got one equation right and no more—that's a success if you ask me.

Priya is allowed to call him Donald, but no one, absolutely

no one, is allowed to use his full name: Donald Duckworth IV. I kid you not, the family name has been passed down from one generation to the next like some prized heirloom. Spoiler alert: it's not.

Priya looks at me. "By the way, did you finish your script? The deadline is today, right?"

I groan. "I have a bit left to finish at lunch today. I think I have a date with the computer lab." For each of the plays that we study, my drama teacher, Mrs. Henning, allows her students to audition to write a school play based on it. The deadline for the *Romeo and Juliet* one is after lunch today. I still don't have an ending. All my ideas blow, and I've spent hours staring at a blinking cursor, the blank page matching my blank mind. But it's now or never. Last year I came close to being selected: my modernized version of *Hamlet* was the runner-up. This year I want to be chosen. It's one of my goals for my senior year.

"That's cutting it close."

"You don't need to tell me that, Priya," I say. Priya only allows her friends to call her by her shortened name. She says it is a reward for all those who put in the time and effort to learn how to say her full name correctly. There is one thing that Priyanka Reddy doesn't tolerate, and that is laziness. Donny is just Donny to everyone—so he's the exact opposite. Maybe they truly are meant to be together.

"Still not going well?" Donny asks.

"Each word is like pulling teeth." I close my eyes. "I just haven't been inspired. Retelling *Romeo and Juliet* is tough."

Especially when I have no real dating experience is what I don't add. "But I'm determined. I have to win this year."

"Potential is what matters. I'm sure Henning is looking for that instead of perfection. You're talented. You'll do great!" Priya opens the glove compartment and finds her makeup bag. As much as this is Donny's car, it's also a part of our group. The Quackmobile holds little pieces of all of us.

The truth is, Donny's family has more money than they know what to do with. When the term *old money* is thrown around, the Duckworth family is definitely on the list. For Donny's birthday last year, his parents bought him this beautiful red Mustang—with racing stripes to boot. Donny was ecstatic at first, but then he saw the vanity license plate, QUACK IV, and outright refused to drive it. Of course, Priya and I convinced him otherwise, because who cares about some stupid license plate anyway? And from that day on, the three musketeers had a steed to ride.

We pull into the school's parking lot after a quick ten-minute drive. My house is the closest to school—not in a gated community—which is why I get picked up last.

"Oh, the latest issue of the *Herald* is out," Priya says, looking at her phone.

"For someone you hate, you follow Shannon's newspaper editorials pretty diligently."

"I can hate the person but appreciate their work." She glares at me. "I contain multitudes."

"Anything good?" Donny asks, changing the topic.

"There's an interview with Bryson's latest ex."

"Who asked Bryson out last week?" I ask.

"Isabella from my biology class," Priya says.

"Which one?" There are four seniors named Isabella.

We climb from the Quackmobile and Priya opens her Instagram. She clicks on #DateMeBrysonKeller and holds up a picture to us. It's of a brunette girl and Bryson.

"Isabella Mendini." Priya turns the screen back to her and sighs. "It should be illegal for Bryson to have this bone structure."

She isn't wrong. Of course, my admiration is only done from afar and in secret. My heart beats for another.

As if my thoughts have summoned him, my unrequited crush saunters into view. Isaac is tall with curly blond hair and blue eyes that remind me of the ocean. He has his blazer thrown over his shoulder, and he's holding a soccer ball under his arm. Why does he need a soccer ball to go to school? Who knows? But it's a common sight when it comes to Isaac.

We head toward the school entrance, studying the chaos that surrounds us. Ever since the dare started, Monday mornings have become a circus. A crowd lingers at the entrance, mostly spectators. Bryson has kept to the rule that only seniors can take part. It seems that they're all waiting for the arrival of the man of the hour.

"It's amazing how the dare has spread," Donny says. When it first started, it was mostly the girls from cheerleading and the soccer team who asked Bryson out. Then the girls from drama class. But now the dare is out there, and people with no real connection to Bryson and those activities are stepping up to ask him out for fun.

"I heard Eric say that if he could ask Bryson out, he would," Priya says.

I try not to react to the news of another boy wanting to ask Bryson out.

"Eric?" Donny asks. "The gay one?"

I'm pretty sure, like 85 percent sure, that Donny will be fine with me being gay. Generally, he seems really supportive. It's him saying stuff like this, though, that makes me hesitate.

Priya smacks Donny on the arm. "Eric Ferguson," she says. "That's his name."

I plan on telling both Priya and Donny ... after we've graduated from high school. I don't plan on coming out until then, because even in a school with out-and-proud students and an active LGBTQ club, "gay" is still a label. It doesn't matter that Eric is a state champion in chess or even that he's the vice principal's son. Those are all second to his sexuality. That's the thing with labels: they tend to stick to you like unwanted gum. It's why I'm so careful not to be labeled. More than anything, I do not want to be Kai Sheridan, "the gay one."

Donny shrugs. "I mean, we didn't really specify that a boy couldn't ask Bryson out, did we? So anyone could ask him out if they wanted."

All this talk about gayness has my warning sirens blaring. I try not to move, try to blend in with my surroundings.

"Either way, it doesn't really matter," Priya continues. "I'm pretty sure Eric has a boyfriend now. So I guess we'll never know." She looks down at her watch. "I need to stop at my locker before assembly."

Every Monday morning Fairvale Academy holds an assembly in the auditorium, and our principal delivers this week's announcements and recaps the glory that the sports teams have brought. I don't mind, though, because my first-period drama class is held in the same building, so I don't need to leave when the assembly ends. It's very convenient.

"Don't be late," I say.

"Right. I really can't afford detention for being tardy." Priya rolls her eyes. Anything that upsets the teachers means us forfeiting our lunch breaks as punishment—being late tops the list. For greater infractions, we earn demerit points—six and we get a Friday afternoon detention. And if you accumulate thirty, you'll find yourself at school on a Saturday with Vice Principal Ferguson.

"Well, I'll catch up to you guys later," I say. "I have an appointment with Big Bertha."

"No more soda. You drink too much of it. It's going to kill you."

"Yes, Mom," I say to Priya.

"Let a man live," Donny says.

"Enabling bad behavior is part of the problem." She turns to me. "We'll save you a seat." With that, Priya heads off.

Donny jogs after her. I'm envious of them. I close my eyes for a second and picture Isaac walking with me to my locker—doing normal, everyday things that straight couples get to do.

I open my eyes with a sigh. Judging from the crowd, it seems like Bryson is running late today. I walk over to the vending machine, which is sandwiched between two rows of lockers. Ever since the school board initiated the Great Sugar Culling, this vending machine has been the last of its kind. And I can't survive without my daily sugar fix.

The vending machine is old and in need of service, but all the students are too afraid to mention it for fear that Big Bertha will be next to receive the ax. As I'm waging war against it, Shannon Flockhart and Natalie da Silva stop by Natalie's locker.

"It has to be this week. I have to be the one to ask Bryson Keller out today," Shannon says. "The deadline's next week."

"And what if you miss your chance again?" Natalie asks. She looks down at her watch. "Maybe someone already asked him out."

"Not possible. Dustin says Bryson is coming in late today. So I just need to catch him after first period. I have it all worked out." Shannon sighs. She leans in close to whisper to Natalie, but Shannon's never grasped that whispering means actually lowering your voice. "And then I can have the finishing touches for my story. A firsthand account of dating the most popular boy: an in-depth look at private high school culture and the phenomenon of the 'it' boy. This will definitely get me off the waitlist for Stanford."

"You're doing this all for a story?" Natalie asks.

"I can focus on more than one thing. I can get my story, get off the waitlist, and win the heart of my dream boy. I have it all worked out."

"You do know this is supposed to be a game, right? He's specifically not looking for anything serious."

Finally, with a hard kick, Big Bertha releases my bounty. They turn to look at me—surprised. I blush and bend to pick up my soda. Deciding that I'm not a threat, they return to their conversation. I'm not eavesdropping, I swear.

"Love happens when you least expect it," Shannon says.

"So, what? You and Bryson are perfect for each other?"

"Yes," Shannon says. "I knew from the moment we kissed."

"As your friend, I feel like it's my job to remind you that that was during a game of spin the bottle, so I don't think it counts."

"It doesn't matter. All I need is five days to show Bryson Keller that we are soul mates."

Shaking my head, I leave Shannon to her fantasy. Everyone is entitled to one. After all, in mine Isaac and I rent a studio apartment in New York City, and we have a puppy named Dobby the House Dog—we're really very happy together.

The can opens with a satisfying click. I'm taking my first sip when Louise Keaton barrels into me, sending the can flying. Soda sprays everywhere, but mostly on me.

"Shit!" I say, looking down at my dripping, stained uniform.

Louise seems oblivious. She's chattering away on her phone. "What! You see Bryson's car? Where?"

Briefly, I wonder if this is personal, because Louise Keaton is my ex-girlfriend. I'm not even sure I can call her that, because our "relationship" lasted less than two weeks. Freshman year, I asked her out to fit in. Everyone was dating, and Louise said my freckles reminded her of the stars. I appreciated her poetic soul and so I took the plunge. Our relationship was fine . . . until we went to see a movie on Friday night. Having to lie to Louise when we were alone was too much. I broke it off. Now if anyone asks me why I don't date, I lie and say my parents are extremely strict.

I shout after her, "Thanks a lot, Louise!"

She's already bolted down the hallway, and I am left alone. The front of my shirt sticks to me and I can smell the soda. Everyone starts to stare at me, and I flush at the attention. With no other choice, I change direction and head to the nearest bathroom. The bell rings. I'll be late to assembly.

I can only hope that I won't get caught, because I can't afford to forfeit my lunch break—not today. I need to finish my script if I'm going to have any chance of meeting the deadline.

I peel off my blazer and loosen my tie. I try to wash off as much of the soda from my white shirt as possible. In the end I am wet, and the scent of the soda still clings to me. Staring at the damage in the mirror, I know that it won't get any better than this. Annoyed, I make my way to the auditorium.

"Missing assembly, Kai," Vice Principal Ferguson says. She stands at the auditorium door. She has the same bright red hair as her son. Her crimson lips are pursed in displeasure. She looks me up and down. "What on earth happened to you?"

"Sorry, ma'am. Someone bumped into me and caused this mess."

"Hmmm. You're late, untidy"—she scrunches her eyes and studies my jaw—"and unshaved. I'll have to write you up for this. Come along."

I groan. I know that I am about to receive my first-ever batch of demerits. As I follow Vice Principal Ferguson, I can't help but curse Louise Keaton and Bryson Keller himself.

This is not how I wanted my Monday morning to be going.

2

With a handful of demerits, I head toward drama. I'm late for this, too. The large metal double doors swing open with a screech, announcing my arrival. Mrs. Henning circles on me in a flurry of bangles and scarves to pierce me with her accusatory gaze.

"You're late, Kai." I can feel the blood rushing to my face. I hate being singled out more than anything. "You should know by now that the stage waits for no man. And excuses mean very little in the theater." Mrs. Henning shakes her head. "Hurry up and join us. You're disrupting the class."

"Sorry," I say.

"Very well." Mrs. Henning returns her attention to the rest of the class. "As you can see, everybody has already been paired up. But lucky for you, there is another latecomer this morning. Find the assignment breakdown on the chair up front. You and he will be partners. Be prepared to present on Friday. No exceptions."

I nod and make my way up to the stage. It's a long walk. The auditorium is large and was recently renovated. There are rows and rows of crimson seats to pass.

The rest of the class is already seated in a circle onstage. They have their copies of *Romeo and Juliet* open in front of them. We do have an actual classroom with desks and proper chairs, but Mrs. Henning believes that Shakespeare belongs in the theater and it must be performed instead of read. In her words, "it is a sin to do otherwise." So each class we take turns playing a role. She encourages us to use the space around us, to become the characters.

I find a spot and sit cross-legged, placing my ruined blazer next to me. I pull my well-used copy of *Romeo and Juliet* from my messenger bag and turn to the page where we last left off. The one perk of my being late is that I have avoided being assigned a role. This is my least favorite part of drama.

The only reason I even took this class was because of Mrs. Henning. She fought to have a script-writing course included in the curriculum, which is why she has always been my favorite teacher, that and because her tales of fame and fortune are hilarious. Mrs. Henning was "*the* leading lady of daytime television." She played the dual roles of identical twin sisters who were the hero *and* the villain in the daytime soap *My Face, Your Life*. I spent an afternoon on YouTube watching clips from the show. It had everything—rich people being terrible and murders and affairs and even alien invasions. Totally addictive.

I listen to the readings and find the right scene. It's the brawl scene: Mercutio has just died and we're leading up to the death of Tybalt. Isaac has been cast as Romeo, and I once more curse both Louise and Bryson for making me late. I almost missed out on having a legitimate excuse to stare at him.

Too soon, we reach the end of the act and Mrs. Henning holds up her hand to pause us. "Good work. I think we should stop for the day. Why don't you all break into your pairs and discuss the assignment?"

I study Isaac and his partner, wishing that I were lucky enough to work with him. At school I've never really spoken to Isaac aside from a few hellos here and there. It's the same with the rest of the soccer team. We don't run in the same circles. The soccer players are the kings of Fairvale Academy, and I am nothing but a lowly peasant, which has always been fine with me. I don't need popularity, because being anonymous is safest for me. I can exist with my secrets intact.

The doors open and we all turn as the man of the hour saunters into the auditorium. Bryson looks perfectly tousled—effortless and smooth. The sight irks me more than it should.

"Sorry I'm late, Mrs. Henning." Bryson stops at the front row.

"Welcome, Mr. Keller. Glad you could fit us into your busy schedule. I hope you're aware that you have a date with me at lunch. You too, Kai." Mrs. Henning looks between Bryson and me. I wish I were the type of person who could voice an argument about the unfairness of being punished twice for the same crime. Seriously, where's the justice in the world?

"Kai, please explain the assignment to Bryson," Mrs. Henning continues.

Not at all happy with these turns of events, I nod and stand. Grabbing my belongings, I head down the steps and off the stage. I sit on one of the fold-down seats and place my things next to me. Bryson's stealing glances at his phone.

Annoyed, I say, "Here." I hold out a copy of the assignment. "We need to choose a scene from a Shakespeare movie adaptation and perform it on Friday."

Bryson accepts the paper from my hand. "You okay?"

"Great. Just great."

Bryson picks up on my sarcasm, because he looks up. His blue eyes have a habit of looking through you. "Is something wrong?"

"No," I lie. "Let's just get this over with. We should make some time to get together. Let me know when works for you?" The sooner we make plans, the sooner I can try to convince Mrs. Henning to let me out of detention. I need to finish my script. This is my last shot. And I think an extension is out of the question.

"I have soccer practice tomorrow and Thursday, and I have a game Wednesday night." Before he can say anything else, his phone rings. I recognize the ringtone. It's a lesser-known song from my favorite indie band—the Graces. I'm surprised that Bryson Keller of all people knows such a deep cut. Bryson stares at the screen and I see the caller ID—*Dad*. He swipes his thumb across the severely cracked screen and ignores the call.

Bryson sighs. He picks up my blazer before taking the seat next to me. He rests his arm on the armrest and we end up touching.

"You free this afternoon?"

I look up from our arms. Our eyes meet and it's totally unnerving. This is the closest I've ever been to Bryson Keller. I jerk my arm away. Bryson frowns.

"Uh, yes. I'm free," I answer.

"Then how about we get together and at least decide on what movie we're going to perform."

"Okay. Where?"

"I know this great café," Bryson says. "We can go there if you want?"

"Sure."

"Meet me in the parking lot after school, then."

"Sounds like a plan." I stand.

"Where are you going?" he asks.

"To beg for my life."

Mrs. Henning is seated in the front row, flipping through some notes. As I approach her, I take deep, calming breaths. She looks up.

"What can I do for you, Kai?"

"Uh, actually, ma'am . . . ," I start awkwardly. "I was wondering if—no, hoping that—that you'd let me out of detention today. I can do it tomorrow?"

"Why would I do that?" Mrs. Henning asks. "You were late today. And so you must serve your punishment today."

"I was hoping to work on my script at lunch. I'm almost

done and just need to do a bit more work to get it ready by the deadline. If I don't, I won't be able to submit."

"Time management matters, Kai. I understand that life happens, but I can't give you any special treatment. On my way to audition for Elphaba, I broke my toe. But did I let that stop me? Of course not. I worked through the pain, made it on time, and was sensational."

There isn't anything I can do or say now. The one thing I wanted for my senior year is slipping away. I would have loved to write the school play for my final year at Fairvale Academy—a small way for me to leave my mark. It was important to me, and now it's all over—all because of Bryson Keller and this stupid dare.

I head back to my seat. "Why were you late?" I ask. I want to tell him why I was. I want to tell Bryson Keller just how much he has messed up not only my day but my year. I'm angry and annoyed at him. Maybe it isn't fair, but right now I don't care.

"Family stuff." Bryson's expression is clouded and heavy, and it almost dulls my anger, but then his phone vibrates with a text. "Everyone's wondering who I'm dating this week." He smiles then, showing perfectly white teeth.

"Who is it?" I ask. I swear to God, if it's Louise Keaton, I'll lose it.

"No one yet. It's nine-ten and I am still single," he says. "This hasn't happened in ages. I miss it."

That all this has happened for no reason pisses me off, as does his nonchalant attitude. I am drunk on anger and disappointment. It gives me confidence that I never had before.

"No, you're not," I say.

Bryson turns to me again. "Huh?" he asks. He's clearly confused. "What do you mean?"

"You're not single." I do it. I say the words that I never thought I ever would. "*I'm* asking you out. I'm first, so this week you're dating me."

Just then the bell rings, but Bryson and I stay seated. We're staring at each other. With each passing heartbeat, my confidence and anger shrivel up and die. Soon I am left with the aftermath of what I have just said, of what I have just done and what it all means.

Bryson bursts out laughing. It's too loud. It's clear that he thinks this is a joke. And I know it would be safer for me to laugh it off, too. I'm a senior, in my final year of high school. For these four grueling years, I've managed to keep it a secret that I am gay, and just like that, I've kicked the closet door open. As I listen to him laugh, I realize that I don't want him to think this is a joke. My being gay isn't a laughing matter. I want him to know that I am serious.

So I lean in close, our faces inches apart. His laugh tapers off.

"What are you doing?" He leans back, creating space between us, but I don't let that stop me. My face may be on fire, but so are all my insides.

I close the distance once more.

"I'm not joking," I say. "Date me, Bryson Keller!"

3

What have I just done?

It's a question that I repeat over and over in my head. Dread builds as I head toward English. I can't be late to second period, too, so even though it means facing Bryson again, I still run. Usually, this would be the last I'd see of Bryson for the day, but not today. I have lunchtime detention with him.

Oh God!

Why did I do that? It's another question that pounds in time with my galloping heart. What on God's green earth possessed me to out myself to the most popular boy at Fairvale Academy? I've never been very into the whole coming-out business—maybe because the one and only time I did it, my best friend back then ghosted me. The sleepovers stopped, as did the invites to swim. It was like I didn't exist anymore. Eventually we went to different high schools, but the scars of thirteen-year-old me ache even now, like a knee in winter.

So except for a few random boys I've chatted to online

since then, I haven't come out to a soul. Being a gay teenager stuck in the closet is so lonely and isolating.

Oh God, why did I do that?

I'm not overtly religious. It's not that I don't believe in a higher power or anything. I kind of like the idea of someone always watching over me, at least up until the point I do things that will make Jesus blush. But right this second, I would not refuse some sort of miracle.

Any sort of miracle, really.

For the first time I am openly gay to someone at Fairvale Academy. I want to throw up. I can't focus on any of this, not when the five-minute changeover is swiftly ticking away. I race from building A toward building B.

Fairvale Academy is divided into two main buildings, each consisting of three floors. Our classes, save for gym, are split between them. Aside from drama, my classes are held in building B.

I take the stairs two at a time and enter the large courtyard that divides the two buildings. I'm not the only student racing to beat the clock. I manage to sink into my seat just as the second-period bell rings.

There are twenty other students in the class, but there is only one I concern myself with. I pull my copy of *The Great Gatsby* from my bag and turn to the page where we left off. Bryson arrives just before the teacher does. He's not smiling, and his brow is furrowed. I make sure I keep my gaze trained on the words before me. He takes his seat, next to the window. Bryson and I sit in the same row. There's just one desk between us—and it's *still* empty. It seems that Mary-Beth Jones is out sick.

I curse her.

Our English teacher, Mr. Weber, is a barely-out-of-college type. This is his first official year teaching, so he tends to do everything by the textbook. Everything is the same, and everything is incredibly boring.

Mr. Weber reads from the book before pausing and looking up. "Focus, please, Bryson."

For most of the period I try my hardest to ignore Bryson. But then I lose the war against myself. I turn to secretly look at him, and end up looking directly into his eyes. For the second time this hour, I stop breathing.

Quickly, I turn back to my book while fighting the heat that colors my cheeks. Blushing makes my spattering of freckles stand out more. They are both my most distinct feature and the thing I hate most about the way I look.

For the rest of the period, I force myself to stare at the same page. While the rest of the class moves forward, I relive asking Bryson Keller out. I did what Eric Ferguson wanted to do. I wonder if I was brave or stupid. It's all too late now.

The end-of-period bell rings, and I shove my copy of *The Great Gatsby* into my bag without much thought. Leaving this classroom means leaving Bryson behind—at least until lunch.

I join the swarm of classmates feeding into the hallway and hope to lose myself in the crowd. A hand clamps down on my shoulder and instantly I know who it belongs to.

"We should talk?" Bryson says. His breath tickles my ear

and I fight a shiver. In the crush of students, Bryson bumps into me, creating a warmth at my back.

"Okay," I say. I try to calm my nerves. He just wants to talk. Bryson is known for being fair. Earlier this year, the school wanted to allow only seniors who are athletes to leave the premises for lunch. It wasn't the first time the teachers had outright shown that the athletes are truly the gods of this school. And as captain of the boys' soccer team, Bryson is on the highest pedestal. But he argued that all seniors should be allowed—and he won. It's one of the reasons why everyone loves him.

"Yo, BK." Dustin's voice cuts through the chatter that surrounds us. The bulky boy, who serves as a defender for the Cougars, pushes through the sea of bodies. His cocky gait is a sure sign that he's very much aware of the hierarchy at Fairvale Academy and he knows his place at the top.

I never thought that I would ever be thankful for the ball of testosterone that is Dustin Smith, but as he nears us, I can't help but feel relieved. At least 90 percent; the other 10 is disappointment, but that's easy to ignore.

Bryson greets Dustin in what can only be described as a bro-hug, and I stand there awkwardly as they talk. Halfway through the conversation, Dustin stops and looks at me.

"Why are you here?" Dustin looks from me to Bryson.

The lie is quick on my tongue. When you live in the closet, lies become easier to tell. "Henning paired Bryson and me for drama, so we need to plan a practice schedule." I don't look at

Bryson's eyes, because if I do, I know the lie will not be believable.

"Okay." Dustin must buy my words, because he says to Bryson, "Did Shannon finally get to you?"

Bryson shakes his head. "I haven't seen her yet." He sighs. "Why? Did you tell her I was going to be late today?"

"You should just get it over and done with. You know how she is. What Shannon wants, she gets. The more you avoid her, the worse it is," Dustin says. "So, who is it?"

I swallow hard and even though I don't want to, I turn to look at Bryson.

"Who's what?" he asks. Bryson may not be a good liar, but his feigning ignorance is something that I'm extremely thankful for.

"C'mon, man. Your girlfriend this week?"

Before Bryson can answer, my name is called. At first, I think I've imagined the saving grace, but I look up and spot Donny walking toward me.

"What are you doing, Kai?" Donny asks.

"Hey, Quack," Dustin says, using the nickname that the seniors gave Donny when we were freshmen. The name stuck at first, but it's mostly just Dustin who calls him that now.

Bryson smacks Dustin on his chest. And I'm thankful for the small gesture.

"Uh, I'll talk to you later, then, Bryson," I say.

I pull Donny along as the changeover bell signals the start of the next class.

Because math is just down the hall, we make it there before our math teacher, Ms. Orton, does. Donny pulls his workbook from his bag and caresses it like it is his most prized possession. For all the things that he and I have in common, the love of math is not one of them. On the list of things I hate, the subject sits snugly between phone calls and Leonardo DiCaprio and his Academy Award thirst.

I flip my notebook open to this weekend's homework. Already I know it's wrong. And already I simply don't care. But Donny has made it his mission to ensure that I don't fail. Thanks to him, I manage to scrape the bottom of a C grade.

"So what were you and the King talking about?" Donny asks.

I smile at our inside joke. "Uh, Henning paired us up for a project." The best lies are the ones built on truths. There is no way I'm telling Donny why Bryson actually wanted to speak to me.

"Unlucky," Donny mumbles just as the math teacher saunters into class. We all start to find x, but thirty minutes into it I give up. X is currently missing, presumed dead.

For the rest of class, I sit and watch the clock. Each ticking minute inches me closer to not only my punishment but also missing my deadline. Just as the bell rings, the intercom above the whiteboard crackles to life. The voice of the school secretary blares out, "Will Bryson Keller and Kai Sheridan please report to the auditorium. Thank you." As if I could forget. "Will Bryson Keller and Kai Sheridan please report to the auditorium. Thank you."

"What for?" Donny asks. "I thought you needed to write."

I swear. "That was the plan, but *stuff* happened." My anger from before is nothing more than an ember—small and dying. "I was late."

"Damn. That sucks," Donny says. He has no idea. We part ways, and with no other choice I head toward the auditorium.

I walk toward my hour alone with Bryson Keller.

4

I stop before the auditorium doors and take a deep, calming breath to prepare myself for what awaits inside. It doesn't work. I grip the strap of my messenger bag tightly. Exhaling, I take the plunge. The door swings open to reveal Mrs. Henning standing before the stage. She has a file clutched in her hands.

"Thank you for being on time now," she says as she looks down at her watch. I head toward her. "Well, when Mr. Keller decides to arrive, please have him help you."

"With what?"

"We need the props organized so we can start prepping for *Romeo and Juliet*," Mrs. Henning explains. "Please be careful with them. Some may be crafts made by you students, but others have been donated by my peers. And thus, they are holy." Mrs. Henning smiles. "Take care."

I nod. It's not like I have a say in the matter. She seems to realize this, too, as she purses her lips. She walks up the aisle but stops halfway.

"Please stay for the full lunch break. If you leave or mess around, I will know." There is no denying it. Among the students, Mrs. Henning is infamous for her uncanny ability to know everything and anything that happens within the auditorium—whether she's present or not. A few months ago, someone damaged one of the seats by running across the backs of them on a dare, and as soon as she came through the doorway, Mrs. Henning knew just who it was. Now there's an ongoing rumor that she may be a witch.

"Yes, ma'am." I watch her leave before heading toward the stage. I want to get this over and done with as soon as possible.

The prop storage room is small and located at the back of the stage. It's still a mess from our *Hamlet* production. I enter the crowded space, remove my soda-smelling blazer, and drape it across my messenger bag. I'm bent over, organizing a box of old shoes, when there is a tentative knock at the door.

Bryson leans against the doorframe and looks at me like he's seeing me for the first time—the real me. I can't decide if that's a good thing or a bad thing. I clear my throat awkwardly.

"Oh, you came." In hopes that I can ignore the very distracting presence across from me, I search for the partner to the shoe I'm holding. My heart's racing in my chest. We're alone and we still need to talk. Should I bring it up first? Should I stay silent? I'm torn about what to do, what to say, how to act.

"Sorry I'm late," Bryson says as he places his bag down next to mine. He's holding two sandwiches. "Here."

I stare at his outstretched hand. "What's this for?"

"I thought you might be hungry."

I hesitate, deciding whether I should accept the sandwich, but the loud growl from my stomach makes the decision for me. I reach for it with a mumbled thanks.

I sit with my back against the wall and take a bite of the sandwich—it's chicken and mayo. Did he know that's one of my favorites, or is it just a coincidence? Bryson sits down directly opposite me. He crosses his long legs and starts eating, too.

"So are you thinking of auditioning for the next play?" He points at the props around us.

"No. I *hoped* to write it," I say. "I'm not an actor."

Which is sort of a lie, considering I put on a performance every day. I've lied about crushes that I've never had, kisses with girls who don't exist. I've acted out my own dramas. But I don't say any of this. We seem to be talking about everything but the elephant in the room. And I'm okay with that.

"*Hoped?* Past tense?"

"The deadline for the play is the end of lunch. I still need to finish it, but I'm here instead."

"What happened?" Bryson asks. "Why were you late?"

"*You* happened," I say. The anger from before is mostly gone, though. The fear of what might happen between Bryson and me is demanding the spotlight now.

"Me? What do you mean?" He studies me, eyes narrowing.

I shake my head. "Louise Keaton was racing to ask you out and she bumped into me while I was drinking a soda." I motion at the state of my uniform. Even though it's dry now, it still carries the stain of the cola. "Which made me late for assembly. So I got busted for that and ended up late for drama, and, well, here we are."

"Oh," Bryson says. He runs his hand through his hair, a nervous gesture. "Your morning sounds worse than mine. I'm sorry about that. And I'm sorry Henning punished you."

I shrug. "She's still my favorite teacher. So I can't be mad at her too much."

"Don't be too mad at me, either, okay?" Bryson offers me a smile. "Henning's my favorite, too. You know, I spent an entire afternoon once just watching clips from that show she was on."

My eyes widen. "Really? I did that, too." I laugh. "It was an *experience*."

"That's one way of describing it," Bryson says with a shake of his head.

"What about you?" I ask. "Do you plan on auditioning for the play?"

"Maybe, if soccer allows it. I like acting. It's fun."

"Hollywood aspirations, huh?" Living within driving distance of the City of Angels means that there have been a number of Fairvale Academy alumni who have moved to LA with big dreams. Those who have been successful have been invited back to guest lecture by Mrs. Henning. I can't deny that Bryson Keller is hot enough to be a leading man.

"Not really. It's not my dream." Bryson stands. He crinkles the sandwich wrapper and places it in his pocket to throw away later. I smile—somehow, Bryson Keller not littering makes sense. "We should get this done before Henning has us repeating this all week."

I stand, too, relieved now that there's some distance between us. I busy myself with sifting through the bevy of foam props in all shapes and sizes. The silence deepens, and I try to ignore the growing awkwardness of this moment. Does Bryson feel the same way?

"So, you're gay?"

I still. I know that I can lie. By saying no, I can change my story. But I find that I don't want to. Kai Sheridan *is* gay. Why should I deny it? I am who I am. Honestly, I'm tired of holding this secret so close to my chest. It's like a ticking time bomb waiting to go off, and right now I want to watch the clock run out. See what happens.

"Yes."

Three letters that change everything. Now there really isn't any going back. Oddly, I don't feel the sheer panic that I thought I would whenever I imagined this happening. Maybe I'm numb, and this is me preparing for the judgment that's surely coming—if my ex–best friend couldn't accept me, why will Bryson Keller?

"Cool."

That one word has me sagging in relief. Even so, I find myself searching for the signs that my heart remembers. Bryson is standing next to a costume rack. He's stopped what he was doing, and all his attention is on me. I look up from the box I'm rifling through and our eyes meet.

I wait for him to turn *gay* into an accusation—an insult.

I wait for him to stop seeing me as Kai and to see me just as gay. I wait for all this while reminding myself that being gay is never a choice. If it were, why would so many of us choose to be shunned and spoken about behind our backs? The answer is simple: it isn't a choice.

It's all so unfair: because you're so-called different, you need to stand up and say that you're so-called different. What makes everyone else normal? Who gets to decide that?

Whoever it is can suck it.

"I take it you're not out." Bryson is leaning against the rack now. He's still looking at me, in a way that makes me feel like I'm the only one who matters. It isn't a question, but I answer anyway.

"Yeah. You're actually the first person at Fairvale Academy to know." I glance away.

"Really? Wow. I'm strangely honored," he says. "So not even Donny knows? Or Priyanka?"

"Nope. Not a soul." I shake my head in disbelief. Coming out was not on my agenda for today.

"What is it?" Bryson asks.

"Nothing. It's just . . . *weird*." In my best aged-theater-actor voice, I say, "Revealing one's soul should come with more grandeur, shouldn't it?"

A smile tugs at Bryson's lips. "I don't know about that, but I do know it's brave." He puts down the box he's holding and dusts his hands. "I'm sorry for laughing." Bryson chews on his lip. "I wasn't laughing at you being gay. I think I was just startled by you asking me out."

"I'm sure there are others who have thought about it." I recall Donny and Priya's conversation about Eric. "I think I just beat them to the punch."

"What made you do it?"

"Would you believe me if I said I don't actually know? It was spur-of-the-moment. And then when you laughed, I realized that I didn't want you to think I was joking. But I think I've used up all my courage for right now. Maybe a few lifetimes' worth." I turn to him. "So you can't tell anyone about me."

"I won't," Bryson promises. And he has a look in his eyes that makes me feel like he won't. "You'll come out when you're ready. This will be our secret."

"'This'?" Somehow it sounds like he's talking about more than just right now.

"Our relationship for this week." The silence stretches between us, and Bryson races to fill it. "I mean, that is, if you want to fake date me for the next five days." He rubs at the back of his head. "It's up to you. No pressure."

"You'll really date me for the next five days? I mean, you sound so cool about it . . . that we're 'dating' for the week. Two boys?"

"When you first asked me out, I really did think you were joking, but when you said you weren't, I was kind of shocked. A guy has never asked me out before. And I guess I've never really said that they couldn't." Bryson busies himself, starting to sort through a tangle of fairy lights. They were the makeshift stars that our Ophelia stared up at while reading the love letter from Hamlet.

"You were there when I was dared," Bryson says. "Everyone just assumed that this was limited to girls. It was simply 'the first person.' I've been thinking about the reason this wouldn't be allowed. And that reason is kind of shitty. You asked me out, and I'm saying yes, just like I promised I would. That's the dare. I . . . I really do believe love is love. And if I believe that, then I have to say yes . . . you know?" He stops working and looks at me. "Of course, it's all up to you. Let me know what you decide."

"And what happens if Shannon asks you out? She sounds very . . . determined."

"You noticed that, too?" Bryson asks, and I nod. "Well, I'll tell her that someone beat her to it." Bryson shrugs. "It's fair. It's how this game works."

I remember that Priya once said Bryson had refused to have his starting spot on the soccer team handed back to him after an injury. He'd torn a ligament and his replacement had been doing well, so he insisted that he ride the bench a few games while he won it back fair and square in practice. It's why he was unanimously voted captain this year. Bryson clearly believes in fairness.

"Thanks," I say, and I mean it.

The very idea of Bryson dating me for the next five days seems like some barely lucid fantasy. It doesn't make sense that the most popular boy at Fairvale Academy has agreed to date me—even if it is a fake relationship. Things like this just don't happen to boys like me.

We work in silence. My mind buzzes as I sift through a collection of handmade masks from the masquerade scene in our *Hamlet* retelling. I find the jester mask that I made.

It somehow seems fitting that I have these masks in my hands right now, seeing as how I just removed my own for the first time. My mask has been so tightly fastened on my face— it's been that way ever since I first realized I liked boys. I was thirteen years old and I had a crush on Colby Matthews—our class president.

It was so sudden. One day I found myself staring at him. I liked the way he scrunched his nose to lift his glasses up. When he smiled at me, my heart would race. And talking to him left me a sweaty, blushing mess. It was then I figured out that I was gay. I remember feeling sad and upset about the realization because it was almost three years after society had taught me that being gay is not okay.

At ten I had heard the pastor of our church condemn homosexuality. At the time I hadn't realized his sermon would affect me. Now I know that the pastor was saying I would be spending eternity in hell for something I had no control over.

The bell rings and our current punishment ends.

"Meet me in the parking lot after school?" Bryson asks as he picks up his backpack. My heart skips a beat. Those are the famous words that preface a fight, and for a moment I picture Bryson and me facing off. The one and only time I've hit someone was in kindergarten, when the kid next to me ate my blue crayon. But other than that, my record is spotless. And I hoped to keep it that way.

"What?" My voice comes out a squeak, and I clear my throat too late. "Why?"

Bryson neatens his tie and tucks in his shirt. I watch every movement, unblinking. He stops when he registers my panic. "We made plans to get together for our assignment, remember?"

I didn't. With so much happening between us, this morning seems so far away.

"Right," I say. I exhale my relief. Why was I so quick to think he was threatening me? "I'll meet you after school, then."

Before he leaves, Bryson turns to me. "I meant it when I said your secret is safe with me," he says. "You can trust me, Kai. I promise."

Bryson exits the prop room and I am left staring at where he once was. Staring after a boy who is willing to be my boyfriend for one school week.

If I play this game . . . will I win or lose?

5

The day ends without ceremony. I have spent the last few hours replaying my conversation with Bryson in the prop room.

"Earth to Kai? We're going to go, then," Donny says. We're standing just outside the doors that open onto the student parking lot. The afternoon sunlight has me squinting against the glare. "You sure you don't need a ride?"

Usually the three musketeers would head home together. Or, when Priya has soccer practice, it's just Donny and me. Often I spend the afternoon at his house and Mom picks me up after work.

"Yeah, it's best for me and Bryson to figure out now what we're going to perform on Friday. You know how I am with these types of things."

Priya pats me on the shoulder. "This is why I will never understand why you forced yourself to do drama."

"I've never heard of a person dying from blushing before, so Kai will be fine."

"Gee, thanks, Donny."

"You've got this, buddy." He pats me on the arm.

"See you." Priya offers me a wave.

"Later." I watch as they head off. Donny and Priya walk hand in hand toward the Quackmobile. Students mill about, some waiting for extracurricular activities to start, others talking to their friends. I spot Shannon and Natalie, and I can't help but wonder if Shannon asked Bryson out. I'm too far away to hear them, though.

I scan the space and spot Bryson's car. The snow-white Jeep is almost as popular as he is. It's become synonymous with its owner. It was a gift from his parents for passing his driver's license test. At the time, it was the most expensive car that a student at Fairvale owned. That is, until Donny and his fire-engine-red Mustang.

I don't see Bryson anywhere. I pull my phone out and look at my social media. There's nothing much to go through, so I close my eyes and try to calm my racing heartbeat.

"What are you doing?"

Startled, I trip over my own feet and Bryson reaches out to catch me.

"Are you okay?" he asks. He lets me go just as fast as he grabbed me.

"Yes." I step to the side to create some room between us. "Sorry," I mumble as the heat assaults my face.

Bryson studies me. He holds up his crimson-and-white school tie next to my face.

"Yup, it's a match," Bryson says. "I don't think I've ever met someone who blushes as much as you. It's fun." I can tell that he's teasing me . . . I think. He drops the tie. "Sorry I'm late. I needed to see Henning about something. Are you ready to go?"

I nod. Bryson starts to walk, and I follow him. No one stops to look at us because this is normal. We're just two guys hanging out together. The fact that Bryson and I actually have a reason to spend time together this week would be the perfect cover for our relationship.

Should I agree to it?

The Jeep unlocks with a loud chirp and Bryson opens the back door to throw his blazer and bag onto the seat. He pauses. "Do you want to put your bag here or keep it with you?"

"Uh, I'll keep it."

Bryson nods and bangs the door shut. He climbs into the driver's seat and starts the car. The sound of the engine roaring to life snaps me from my stupor. I open the passenger door and climb into the den of the lion . . . or rather, the Cougar. His gym bag is on the back seat. It's open, and pieces of his crimson-and-white soccer gear lie scattered about.

I place my bag at my feet and drape my messed-up blazer across my lap.

"Seat belt, please," Bryson says as he clicks his own into place. Just then his phone rings. That it's not on silent or vibrate surprises me. My own phone has been that way since the day my parents bought it for my birthday—two years ago. It was a much-needed upgrade from my previous one.

"Hello, Mom." Bryson smiles and it is dazzling. Up close, I get to see the dimple that's usually hidden. I didn't know about it until right now. It only lasts a second before it disappears. "Dad called you?" He sighs. "If he wanted to give me a ride to school, then he should have been on time." I can't hear his mother's response. "I waited for as long as I could. I was even late today." Bryson taps his hand against the rim of the steering wheel. "Saturday? Why's he talking through you?" He casts me a look. "You know what, never mind. I'll talk to you when I get home. I'll be home for dinner. I just need to work on an assignment with a friend." The conversation continues for two more minutes before Bryson says goodbye. He places his phone in the cup holder between our seats. "Ready?" he asks.

I nod. Bryson effortlessly pulls out of the parking lot. When he joins the main road, he switches on the radio. I instantly recognize the song: "Art of War" by the Graces.

"Oh, I love them." There are few things in this world that can make me talk excitedly to strangers. My love for this band is one of them. The Graces is an indie rock band that has been growing more and more popular each year. Some die-hard stans have started to question whether their rising popularity has made them mainstream. I don't care much for the politics of it, even though I've been their fan since the beginning.

The Graces are fronted by Ezra Grace. He's openly gay and, more than that, he's mixed race, just like me. To see someone who looks like me, who loves like me, living his life on his own terms has made this band special to me. They also make really great music.

"Really? Me too," Bryson says. "Their songs are the most played on my Anytime, Anywhere playlist." He sounds just as excited as I do. Almost as if my declaration has given him permission, he ups the volume. The vocals of the lead singer swirl all around us. Soon we are both humming and singing along to the chorus. The music makes me forget just where I am—and who I am with.

"I can't wait to see them this Friday," I say as the piano echoes out. "It's about time they come back to LA." The Graces are an East Coast band, with New York City as their base. They've performed here and there, and the last time they came to LA, my parents deemed me too young to attend. Finally I'm old enough, and finally I will get to see my idol in person.

Bryson smiles. "I hear they're amazing live." When we come to a stop at a red light, he plugs in his phone and clicks on his playlist. "Who are you going with? Donny and Priyanka?" Bryson asks as he hits play.

"No, alone," I admit. "Donny and Priya have date night on Fridays, so I didn't want to bother them. Plus, they don't really like the Graces."

"Oh, I'm in the same boat," Bryson says. "None of my friends like them, either. So I bought my own ticket." Bryson studies his phone, adjusts the volume. "We could go together? If you wanted? I can give you a ride?"

"Really?" I smile. I arranged to borrow Mom's car, but it would save me from night driving, which makes me super anxious in LA. Besides, no one wants to go to a concert alone. "I'd love that."

"Great," he says just before the opening chords of "Left Behind" start to play.

When the light changes to green, Bryson turns right, and we head toward the heart of town. Fairvale, California, is barely what anyone would call a city, and the lifestyle of this place lives up to its nickname of Sleepy Shores. The town is nestled close to the beach. Open any window and you'll be able to not only feel the sea breeze but smell it, too. We have all the popular franchises that any city has, and we even have a mall. The town is just big enough so that not everyone knows everyone.

In between songs I ask, "Where are we going?"

"Off the Wall."

Off the Wall is a café I've visited before. The last time was when Donny had begged me to accompany him on a double date. Priya was dating her ex-boyfriend then, and so Donny had wanted to get over his crush on her. The date was a disaster because Donny didn't stop talking about Priya. And of course I wasn't into the girl his date had brought for me. It was then that I vowed never to go on another straight date again.

Bryson parks the car, and we climb out of the Jeep. We enter the café, which is quaint and filled with various mismatched furniture. There's a warmth to the randomness of it all. Almost like this place is inviting you to relax and take a breath. Reminding you that you don't need to be so serious all the time. Bookshelves line the walls and soft music wafts through the space. Above all else is the intoxicating aroma of brewing coffee.

"What are you having?" he asks as we approach the counter.

"Iced mochaccino with lots of whipped cream, please." He looks at me with a frown and I shrug. "I like sweet things."

Bryson places our order: one Americano for him, and one iced mochaccino with extra whipped cream for me. Before I can find my wallet, he's already paid.

"Don't worry about it," he says as the barista hands him his change. Bryson puts it in the tip jar and heads to find a place to sit. We end up in a corner booth toward the back of the café. I scan the room for any familiar faces—not because I'm scared, just because I'm curious. My being here with Bryson for a school project is perfectly normal, so I'm not anxious about being seen by others. My being gay isn't written on my forehead. No one knows that I have asked Bryson Keller out this week.

And no one knows that he has agreed to date me, either.

I stumble as a thought occurs to me: *Is this a date?*

I sit down and Bryson digs free the drama assignment. He runs a hand through his hair, causing it to stand up slightly in the front, in a way that can only be described as cute. He places the worksheet down on the table, making it clear as day that this is not a date, not that I thought that in the first place—*I swear.*

"So we have to choose a scene from a Shakespeare adaptation and perform it," I say.

"Do you have a favorite Shakespeare play?" Bryson asks.

"Not really," I say. "You?"

"*Romeo and Juliet*. Not the play, but the movie. The old one, from the nineties."

"Well, we should choose a scene from that, then."

"No, we don't have to do the one I like."

I laugh. "It's not that. It's just that I know Mrs. Henning loves that movie, too. She mentioned it when we first started reading *Romeo and Juliet*."

"Oh yeah, nice catch," Bryson says. "It'll be smart to perform from the teacher's favorite movie." He makes the okay sign with his fingers. Just then the barista brings us our drinks. I take a large sip and savor the sweet chocolaty taste. I take another just for good measure.

"Bryson?" We both pause at Isaac's voice. Bryson looks over my shoulder and smiles at my crush. Isaac comes to stand at the edge of our booth. I look up and meet his gaze. He offers me a small nod, which I barely manage to return. "What are you doing here?"

"Drama assignment," Bryson explains.

"Oh, right, I need to start that, too. Having any luck?"

"Working on it," Bryson says. "You here alone?"

"Natalie's in the car," Isaac says. Just then an order is called. "That's me."

"I'll see you, then."

Isaac saunters off and I try not to watch him leave.

"You have something on your lips."

"Oh God, did I have it there this whole time?" I ask. Bryson nods with a smile as I roughly wipe my lips. Trust me to embarrass myself in front of the boy I like.

"Weird, Natalie said she hated the coffee at this place when we dated."

I look up. "Are Isaac and Natalie dating?"

"Yeah," Bryson says. He's looking at his phone, trying to hunt down clips of the movie. "It's pretty recent, though." He looks up when he feels the weight of my eyes on him. "Wait, do you like him?" Bryson whispers.

I've never had anyone ask me that question before. And it feels strange to have it be Bryson, but strange doesn't always mean bad. I simply nod.

"Huh, so that's your type?" Bryson's brow is furrowed, and his eyes are looking anywhere but at me.

"I don't think I have a set type," I say. "I just liked him."

"Past tense?" Bryson quirks an eyebrow. It's annoyingly cute.

"It's not like I ever stood a chance with him." I know that it was impossible for me to like Isaac, but his dating someone stings nonetheless. The fantasy of our future dissolves like a burning photograph. "That's the problem with liking straight boys. The story always ends the same."

I take another long sip from my drink. Bryson stares at me.

"What?" I wipe my lips. "Do I have something on my face again?"

"I'm just curious about something."

"What is it?"

"Why do you assume that everyone you like is straight?"

I shrug. "I mean, I don't always know. But Isaac probably is. He's dating Natalie now, so it doesn't really matter."

"Yeah . . . Isaac is straight. But I just mean in general, why are you so sure that the guys you like are straight?"

I bite on my straw as I think. I've never really thought about it. It's strange to be having this conversation with Bryson Keller. He waits for me to answer, and finally, with an exhale, I do.

"I think it's what society has made me believe. Everyone says straight is the norm. Look at our school. The number of out kids can be counted on one hand. I'm pretty sure there are other closeted people like me and maybe even a few who haven't figured out their sexuality yet." I chew at my lip. "Maybe assuming everyone around me is straight is a defense mechanism."

"Sorry, maybe I shouldn't have asked?" Bryson sighs. "It's just so shitty."

"Yeah, it is. But I'm glad I outed myself to someone like you." I laugh but it's hollow. "This could have ended badly for me."

He meets my gaze. "I won't tell, but on the off chance that anyone does find out about you being gay and gives you crap about it, call me."

"My personal bodyguard?"

"A friend," Bryson says with a wink. His phone rings again

and he moves to answer it. "You need me to pick up something?" He pauses. "Okay. Got it. I'll be there soon."

While Bryson talks on the phone, I finish off my mochaccino and study the boy before me. He's different than I thought, but not in a bad way.

Bryson hangs up the phone. "Sorry about that."

"Don't be. Do we need to go?"

Bryson nods. "That okay?"

"Sure. I don't want to miss dinner, either."

We leave the café, with my thoughts preoccupied by Bryson. In the car, one of the Graces' ballads thrums as I give directions to my house. I live about fifteen minutes from the café, but it takes us longer because of afternoon traffic. It feels oddly strange to have Bryson taking me home . . . but thrilling, too.

We come to a stop outside the two-story house that I have called home since I was three years old. The house is off-white brick with French windows and a dark wood door that I helped Dad stain. Ivy covers the side of the house, and from where we're parked we can just see the balcony that's off my parents' bedroom. There's a two-car garage, and above it hangs a basketball hoop that Dad and I use from time to time. We used to live in an apartment, but then Mom got pregnant with Yazz and my parents decided to take a leap of faith and invest in a fixer-upper. Over the years the house has grown and changed just as I have. It's not as large as the homes of some of the other kids at school, but it's special because we put the time into making it ours.

I turn to Bryson and say, "Let's do it. Let's date for the week."

Bryson's eyes widen before he offers me a small smile. "Are you sure?"

I'm a nervous wreck, and I'm positive my face matches our tie once more. But I've already taken the first step. I might as well continue walking. I nod, more for myself than for him.

"As long as we can keep it a secret, why not? This is only a game. Why should my being gay keep me from playing, too?"

Bryson smiles. It's tight-lipped and nervous. It's cuter than should be legal. "Well then, I, Bryson Keller, pledge to be your perfect boyfriend for the next four days."

With a matching smile of my own, I climb out of his Jeep. I start to collect my things.

"Leave your blazer so I can drop it off at the dry cleaner's."

"It's fine."

"It would make me feel better," Bryson says. "The only reason your blazer got messed up is because of me and this dare. So let me take care of it, please?"

Bryson leans forward and I think that he's reaching for my hand. I jerk back. Bryson stills. He's leaning over to the passenger side and his hand hangs there as I belatedly realize he's waiting for me to give him the blazer. I pass it over, berating myself for being so awkward.

Bryson folds my blazer so that it sits neatly on the passenger seat. He unlocks his phone before holding it out to me. "Save your number so I can text you. We can plan more about how you want this week to go."

Even though I was serious when I asked him out this

morning, I didn't think we would ever get to this point. Because of his phone's cracked screen, it takes me two tries to hit the final seven of my phone number. Satisfied, I hand the phone back to him.

"Sweet." He places his phone down. "I'll text you later."

I watch as he drives off. I stand there until his taillights become nothing more than a memory. It all catches up to me then. Like a wave crashing into the shore. Even though it's fake, I'm dating someone—a boy.

Holy shit, I have a boyfriend.

And it's none other than Bryson Keller.

6

The first thing that greets me as I walk into our house is the smell of something burning.

"Mom, I'm home," I shout from the entrance hall.

"I'm in the kitchen, Kai," my mother calls back.

"Why?" I head toward what I know will be a disaster zone.

My mother is not a good cook. She's skilled at a great many other things, like singing in the church choir, making sure we survive holidays with the extended family, and guessing who the killer is before the end of a movie or book. Cooking is not one of them.

"Thank God you found us, Kai," Yazz says. "I tried to stop her, but she wouldn't listen."

Every few weeks Mom gets it into her head that she wants to cook us a family meal. And every few weeks this familiar scene takes place. Truth be told, I blame all the cooking shows that she spends her time consuming. The television has been lying to people for too long. Just because you watch something does not mean you can actually do it. I seriously think that all shows should come with the warning of *Do not try this at home*, not just WWE.

"What's Mom burning?" I stage-whisper to Yazz as I lean against the large island in the center of the kitchen. There's a comic book open before her. She's been obsessed lately, which makes sense, though, given how much she loves to draw.

"It's meant to be a casserole. At least that's what Nana's recipe calls it," Yazz whispers back. "But I don't actually know what this is."

Pots and pans litter the granite countertops. Mom's armed with a very large knife, and chunks of potatoes lie massacred before her. Her bob is pushed back with a headband. Mom's wearing the WORLD'S BEST CHEF apron that Dad, Yazz, and I got her as a joke one day. In retrospect I think she missed the humor of the gift and sees it more as encouragement. We will never make such a mistake again.

"When will this torture end?" Yazz asks as Mom sends another potato off to its early grave.

"Dad's not home yet?"

"No," Yazz says. "If he was, do you think any of *this* would be happening?" She points at the mess and shakes her head exasperatedly.

"You two do know I can hear you, right?" Mom asks.

"Of course," I say, just as Yazz says, "That's the point." We turn to look at each other and smile.

"Other children try to encourage their parents."

"Mom, please, I've been encouraging you to stop all afternoon."

Mom walks to the fridge and removes some carrots. She returns to her chopping board. We watch as she dices them—poorly. They all end up different sizes. Yazz reaches for a few of Mom's victims. With no other choice, I take a seat beside my sister. I grab a piece of carrot and pop it into my mouth. The only thing Mom can't ruin is raw vegetables.

"How did your assignment with your friend go? What was it for?" Mom asks me.

"Drama." I groan. "I have to perform."

"Just try your best, honey. It may not be much, but it's something." Mom and Yazz share a look before laughing.

I know what that look means. I was once cast as Joseph in the Nativity play at church, and I spent most of it just staring blankly at the audience—and when I did deliver my lines, they were mumbled. It was a complete disaster. The one plus side of that was that Sunday school allowed me to be in the background from then on. Which suited me just fine.

"*Ag nee,*" Dad says from behind us. Sometimes he uses Afrikaans phrases, like this version of "Oh no." "I thought I smelled something burnt." He rests one hand on my shoulder and the other on Yazz's.

"Save us, please," Yazz says, her eyes never leaving the page of her comic book. She pushes her large black-rimmed glasses back into place.

Dad crosses the kitchen in long strides and hugs Mom

from behind. Even after twenty years, they continue to act like a young couple in love. The thought makes me think of Bryson. Are the dare's rules the same or different between two guys? Just how exactly will our relationship work? Granted, it will only be four days—a relationship shorter than the life span of a housefly. So it's not like it's real or anything.

Distracted, I pop a carrot into my mouth and end up choking. Yazz pats my back—hard.

"I feel the same way," Yazz says. "The sight is rather unpleasant."

With a final sigh, she stands and leaves the kitchen. Mom takes the vacated seat. She picks up a carrot and chews.

"Besides drama, how was school?" she asks. "Anything exciting happen?"

"No, what? Why would you ask that?"

She stares at me with her mouth open and half a carrot hanging there. "Is something wrong? Did something happen?"

"No," I say too quickly and too loudly. I am a murderer still holding the murder weapon. Before I can confess to Mom, I make a hasty retreat out of the kitchen and up the stairs.

"It's obvious that something happened," Mom calls after me.

"Maybe he's embarrassed," Dad offers.

"I wonder if it's a girl."

"You think so?" Dad asks.

I should say, *Actually, I have a boyfriend.* But the thought of coming out to my parents scares me. I've heard them discuss "homosexuality" and how it's a "sin" before . . . but that's always been about other people. Will their feelings change when they find out their son is gay, too? The uncertainty keeps me from saying the words.

Among all my family, I'm referred to as a late bloomer. My one saving grace has been that brief relationship with Louise Keaton. While my cousins have all been actively dating for years, I have feigned no interest. I often wonder how long my excuses will last. How long until the obvious truth will be revealed? *Sorry, Mom and Dad, it's never going to work out between any girl and me. In fact, dear family, I am very interested in dating—just not girls.*

Give me an Adam's apple and some stubble, and let's set the date, shall we?

My bedroom is at the end of the hall on the second floor. The wall color changes with each new year to a different shade of blue—my favorite color—and currently the walls are painted a very light blue. There are two large bookshelves that take up the left wall, and they are overflowing with all my favorite books—mostly fantasy and young adult. There are also a few of Mom's mysteries shoved in there because her shelf is too full.

My computer and desk sit before the window. The desk is littered with some of my yet-to-be-done assignments, and my idea journal is open to where I previously worked. Just last night I spent a good twenty minutes world-building for this fantasy book that I have been writing for the better part of the year. It's my goal to finish this draft before I graduate and head off to New York City for college.

I fall face-first onto my bed. I pull my phone free and scroll through my social media notifications looking for his name. When I realize what I'm doing, I stop myself. How did I get to the point of waiting for Bryson Keller to text me?

I type a quick note about my mom cooking tonight in the three musketeers group chat before opening up Instagram. One of the first posts is from the *Fairvale Academy Herald*. For the past two months, every Monday, the newspaper has updated the feed with who the belle of the ball is for the week. But now all we have is a very large question mark.

My eye catches on Shannon's username: *Seriously, who is it?*

It's the most liked comment on the picture.

I can't help but wonder what everyone would say if they found out that it was me. In a perfect world, no one would bat an eye and I'd be free to post about my "relationship" with Bryson—just like the girls before me.

I pull open my Thinking playlist. Almost instantly the latest slow-tempo song from the Graces comes to life all around me. The ballad is about feeling lost and insecure. My music choice has always been a point of teasing from my cousins. While they like hip-hop and R&B, I have always preferred rock or indie music.

Being mixed race is tough—it's like being caught between two races. I'm expected to look a certain way or act a certain way or like certain things. It's like there's a list of things I'm meant to be, and if I'm not, then I'm not authentic enough. I'm not Black enough for some and not White enough for others.

As the music plays, I lose myself in my memories of today. Coming out has always been this thing that I dreaded and feared, but now I feel a sense of relief. Even if Bryson is the only person who knows I'm gay, there is at least one person who knows me—the *real* me.

My today is worlds apart from my yesterday.

Sometime later, Mom calls me for dinner. The exchange from earlier seems to be forgotten, but I'm quiet and watchful. This happens whenever the talk of me dating girls comes up. Lying to those closest to me is exhausting, but at any hint at my possible sexuality, I become a knight protecting his kingdom—armed and ready to defend my secret until the very end, or at least until I'm away at college.

Even now when I close my eyes, I can perfectly recall the way Lee Davis started treating me after I told him that I thought I was gay. And every gay kid has heard the stories and watched the movies. We've been told we aren't normal for so long, been punished and ridiculed, that hiding who we are is second nature to us. Sometimes hiding is the difference between life and death. It's why the closet still exists. It keeps us hidden and, more important, it keeps us safe. Living your truth is important, but sometimes living the lie is what keeps you warm, fed, looked after ... *breathing*. Which is something a lot of people looking in from the outside don't get.

Oh, times have changed.

No one cares anymore.

Being gay isn't a big deal.

But it is.

For me, right now, at this dinner table, it is the thing I am most scared of anyone learning. I know that my family loves me, but I'm a puzzle that's incomplete. If they ever see the full picture, will they feel the same way?

Mom holds out her hand to me. This is a family tradition. We always eat dinner at the table and we always say grace before eating. I put my hand in hers, and Mom closes her eyes and starts to pray.

Saying grace has become a thing that I am conflicted about. I do it more out of habit now than belief. I'm still trying to figure out just where and how I fit into the religion I've grown up with.

"Amen," we all say before we dig in.

I pick at my food with no real appetite.

"*Ag man,* I promise I cooked, Kai," Dad says with a chuckle. "So it's safe to eat."

Dad was taught to cook by his mother from a very young age. He is the designated chef in the Sheridan household, and if he can't perform his sacred duty, then a stranger is chosen, and we order takeout.

"It's good, Dad." It's true. Somehow Dad has managed to rescue the casserole—and us—from certain death.

"Any news from Tisch?" Dad asks me. The impending arrival of my letter has become a daily topic. For me, though, it feels like I'm waiting for my very own letter to my very own Hogwarts. Magic and adventure await me, too, in a city where no one knows me, and where I can be my true self. It's a powerful fantasy.

"Not yet," I say. "I think I'll hear any day now."

"Even if it's a no, you can still achieve your dreams," Dad says. "You're talented and we believe in you."

"Ew," Yazz says. "Can we save the kumbaya stuff until after dinner?"

"You're too young to be this cynical," Mom says to Yazz. "Life is still meant to be about unicorns and rainbows for you."

"It's a dog-eat-dog world out there, Mom. Don't you read the news?"

"She has a point there, honey," Dad says with a dry chuckle.

"Why did we have to raise such smart children?" Mom asks no one in particular. "Oh, Kai, the concert is this Friday, right?"

"Yeah," I say. "But I don't think I need the car anymore. I have a ride."

Mom and Dad share a look. It's Mom who asks the question they both want to know the answer to. "With who?"

"A friend."

"Who exactly is this friend?" Dad asks, just as Mom says, "We'll have to meet them before we agree to let you travel with them."

"No, but seriously, who is it? It's not Priya or Donny, so who?" Dad asks.

Sometimes it's as clear as day that my parents' favorite

television shows are the ones about detectives. Their third-degree interrogations are expected. It's almost as if they're Sherlock and Watson.

"I have other friends, Dad," I say as I spoon some casserole into my mouth. "And I'll ask him to come in and say hi."

"Oh, it's a him," Mom says. "That's disappointing. I hoped it was a date."

I hold my breath. I don't want to show any reaction.

"Me too," Dad says. "I was about ready to give him some dating advice."

Mom meets my gaze. "If your father ever tries to advise you on how to date, please do the opposite of everything he says. He was truly terrible at it."

"It worked on you, didn't it? So it couldn't have been all bad," Dad quips.

"I was charmed by how bad and awkward you were."

"Then Kai won't have any problems," Yazz says. "We can all imagine just how bad and awkward he'll be at dating."

I force myself to join in on the laughter. For the rest of dinner, I just go through the motions. I analyze everything my parents say to me, looking for any hint that they suspect anything.

After dinner, with a mumbled excuse about homework, I retreat to my bedroom, closing the door behind me. Between these four walls is the only place in my world where I can let my truth fly free.

Are you there, Loneliness? It's me, Kai.

7

Bryson does text me.

I'm lying on my bed, reading the next few scenes of *Romeo and Juliet*. It's a habit of mine to read ahead. I always want to be prepared for the inevitability of being selected to perform. I'm still a bumbling mess whenever I'm assigned a role, but I am certain I'd be one hundred times worse without having done this preparation.

I spot a message from an unknown number and reach for my phone. Another one comes through. I swipe to unlock my phone and open the messages.

Sorry, I meant to message you earlier, but I had to cook.

It's Bryson btw.

Another message: *Keller, that is.*

I smile. As if anyone at Fairvale Academy would need the clarification.

I reply: *I know. You cook? Color me surprised.*

I take this opportunity to save his number. I start entering his name but stop midway before deleting it. Instead, I save him as *Kelly*. The CIA should seriously recruit teens living in the closet.

Bryson responds: *Yes. I am a man of many talents.*

I sit up and rest my head against the wall.

Huh. Who would have thought it?

Bryson replies two minutes later. Not that I am watching the clock or anything.

Well, I'll cook for you sometime.

I drop my phone.

Haha. You dropped your phone, didn't you?

Another message follows hot on its heels, and it sends more heat rushing to my face.

You're probably blushing right now. Haha. It's awesome.

I exhale. Here in my room I can be anyone. I can have the confidence that I never would have dreamed of when it came to Bryson Keller.

Why do you like me blushing so much? I ask. I add a tongue-out emoji for kicks. Let's see just how much Bryson Keller likes me flirting. Sometimes in life you have to give just as much as you get.

I don't know. I guess I like how honest it is. Your mouth may lie but your face can't. It's like a siren.

Well then, I promise to blush for you a lot. I'm not much for emojis, but sometimes one is required. That it's my second in such quick succession is unprecedented. The winking face mocks me as I hit send. Who have I become?

I watch the dancing ellipsis as I wait for his response. And when the dots disappear, I worry that maybe I overstepped.

Maybe I shouldn't have flirted with a straight guy. I move to lie on my back. I'm holding my phone above me when I see his reply. I drop my phone again and it smacks me right in the middle of my face. And only that pain proves that this is all real and happening.

On my screen is a selfie of Bryson Keller. His face is pulled into an overdramatic shocked expression. And he captioned it: *Are you flirting with me?*

Let's see if you're blushing. Send me a selfie. You have to give as good as you get. I read his new text and am surprised to find that they are words that I just thought. I start to type a response saying no but I stop halfway. When, if ever, will I be given a chance like this? Yes, this relationship is fake, but for a few days it can feel real. For these five days I am allowed to act cute with my boyfriend.

A boyfriend who wants a selfie of me.

With a pounding heart, I open my camera and tap the front view. Instantly I am assaulted by the sight of me. My curly hair sticks up in different directions. It's longer than I normally keep it, and in a week or two I will need to visit the barber with Dad. The galaxy of freckles on my face stand loud and proud against the redness of my skin.

Whoever thought that the front-view camera was a great idea was surely mistaken. Just as quickly as I opened it, I close it. This is a bad idea. There's a reason my Instagram only has fifteen photos total, and why only five of them are of me and my face.

Ticktock. His words mock me. They urge me on.

I open the camera again and extend my arm. There's a click and a flash as I take the picture. I turn to study it. It's terrible—a crime against humanity. For the next two minutes I try to perfect the art of the selfie, until finally I succeed. The last photo that I take before giving up isn't half bad. I'm posing with my arm behind my head, and my brown—almost black—eyes surprisingly don't look vacant and/or dead. I'm also smiling wildly—showing off perfectly straight teeth that are a result of years of braces and a great orthodontist. And before the shambles of my confidence scatter on the wind, I hit send.

I add a caption: *happy now?*

He responds not even a minute later.

See. I shall make a boyfriend out of you yet.

It's followed by a stream of confetti-cannon emojis.

And I know that it shouldn't, but my heart catches on the word *boyfriend*. On the fact that he has referred to himself as that. It's physical evidence of this, whatever it is, actually happening.

As we chat, it almost becomes like he's sitting next to me. So much so that I imagine him doing just that. There is no distance between us now, there are no phones and texts. It's just him and me here in my bedroom.

Bryson's light brown hair is damp from a shower. He's wearing a white tank top that shows off his toned and tan shoulders and basketball shorts revealing the light sprinkling of hair on his legs. His large feet are bare, too. Okay, so maybe I've had this exact fantasy one or two times before.

"So, we should talk about our five-day relationship," he says.

"Yes, we should," I reply nervously. The tension from earlier comes crashing back into me. It's always surprising that something so unseen can be so heavy.

"Well, the basics: I usually give my weekly dates rides to and from school. . . . Is that something you want? Or not?"

I think on it. I'm pretty sure that none of his previous "dates" have had to stress about something so trivial. And yet, one wrong move and I can have rumors spreading about me.

"I mean, just because two guys are together . . . doesn't make them gay?" I say. "So I'm pretty sure that will be fine. And if anyone does ask, we can use the drama assignment as our cover. Which isn't actually a lie—we do need to work on it. Besides, this is a once-in-a-lifetime opportunity for me." I laugh nervously. "When else would I ever get to date the most popular boy in school?"

"Haha, who, me? I don't know about that. Anyway, just let me know if it ever feels too much for you," Bryson says. "No dare is worth the risk of outing you before you're ready. You can end this at any time. If you feel like it's too much. The last thing I want to do is make you uncomfortable."

I'm pretty sure I swoon when I read that.

"Does everyone have this option?"

"Yes," Bryson says. "I'd never want to force someone to play this game if they're uncomfortable. It's why we have the rules. But on top of that, if at any time during the five days someone wants to break up, we can."

"Has that ever happened?" I ask.

"No. Not yet," Bryson says. "You know, you're strangely more talkative over text."

"That's because you can't see me. I'm a really anxious person. So on top of all that, I also have this huge secret that I would prefer no one knowing until I leave this place."

"You're going to be out in college?" he asks.

"That's the plan. Or should I say, dream," I reply. "I mean, I know Fairvale Academy is a pretty welcoming and accepting place on paper. We have the right clubs, but I've heard the jokes. The teasing that we're just meant to accept as light-hearted, even though it hurts. So I just don't want to put myself through that." *Not again* is what I don't say.

"So, it's those dickheads at school?"

I want to point out that some of the dickheads happen to be on his soccer team, but before I can type that out, another message comes through.

"I'm pretty sure *dickheads* describes most of the soccer team. I once brought up the jokes they make, and everyone teased me about being gay, too. I probably should try again. Sorry."

"Don't be," I say. "I mean, the dickheads are a big reason for me staying closeted, but I think the bigger reason is my parents."

"You don't think they'd accept you?" he asks. "You don't think they already know?"

I move to lie across my bed. "Maybe deep down a part of

them suspects. And maybe they'd rather ignore that suspicion so that they don't have to face that their son is gay. It's funny, just today I was feeling down about that very thing. My mom and dad are eagerly awaiting any news of a girlfriend."

"It'd probably be a huge shock to them to know that you have a secret boyfriend, right?"

"That's the understatement of the year. What would your parents say if they found out you were dating a boy for the week?"

"I mean, my mom is pretty cool. Her younger brother is gay and everyone is fine with it. So I think she'd be perfectly fine with a gay son. As for my dad . . . well . . . we aren't that close anymore, and I don't know enough about him now to know how he'd react. . . . And a part of me feels like he's lost the right to have an opinion on the matter."

I knew that Bryson's parents were divorced, but I didn't know the details. And before, I wasn't all that curious, but now I am. Talking to Bryson Keller like this makes him more real.

"Sorry . . . if I shouldn't have asked."

"Don't be," Bryson says.

"How would Dustin react to knowing you have a boy-friend? Even if it's only for five days?" I've never actually heard Dustin being homophobic, but then again, I haven't really gone out of my way to spend time with him.

"Dustin's really cool. Once you get to know him, he's a lot different from how everyone thinks he is. He out of anyone has always been there for me, so I know he'd be there for me . . . if I was gay."

I stare at those last few words: *if I was gay.* That's the truth of the matter. Bryson Keller isn't gay. This is all just a part of the dare.

"Makes sense," I say. "Well, anyway, thanks for being my first-ever boyfriend."

"Don't mention it," he says. "You know, I really can't believe how different you are right now."

"That's because right now I can be whoever I want to be. The real me. I promise to try to be like this in person, too. I mean, I only have four days left."

"Yes! Better make them count. I look forward to getting to know the real Kai Sheridan."

"Don't fall for me for real, Bryson Keller. I'm quite charming."

"Hahaha. I'll keep that in mind." He pauses, then continues to type. "Is this your first relationship—real or fake?"

"I mean, I dated a girl before."

"Really! Who? For how long?"

"Louise Keaton," I say. "It was freshman year and it lasted less than two weeks."

Bryson sends a series of laughing emojis. "So you have experience with short relationships?"

"Some would call me a master at them."

"You're funny."

"Those of us who don't look like models have to develop our personalities."

"What are you talking about?" Bryson says. "You're good-looking, Kai."

"You say as an impartial third party?" I add a teasing-face emoji.

"Sure. That's why you can trust my words. Besides, I'm a really bad liar. In part because I just suck at it but also because I hate lies. They can ruin things that were once perfect."

"That was deep," I say.

"I am a man of much depth. You should see my philosophy bookshelf." He adds a nerdy-face emoji.

"I'll show you mine if you show me yours. . . ."

A stream of laughing-with-tears emojis follows. "Nice one. High five!"

I send him a smiley-face emoji and switch to the group chat with my friends.

Bryson's giving me a ride to school tomorrow.

Priya: *Why?*

Donny: *What she said.*

Me: *We need to finalize our assignment, and with his busy schedule, this works out better.*

Makes sense, Donny texts. *If he flakes, let me know. I'll swing by.*

See you at school, then, Priya adds.

I exit our chat and head back to Bryson's message.

"I'll take you up on that ride to school," I say. "What time?"

"How does seven sound?"

"Great."

It's well past midnight by the time we both say good night.

As I plug in my nearly dead phone to charge, I realize that I can't fight the smile from my face.

I climb into bed and find that I can't sleep.

Maybe it's because for the first time in my life I'm actually fully awake.

TUESDAY

8

I open my eyes with a groan. I stare up at my ceiling for a few unseeing minutes before rolling over for my phone. Scrolling through social media before I do anything else is part of my morning routine.

The first thing that greets me is a text message from Bryson—*my boyfriend.*

Morning. I'll be there by 7.

So it wasn't all a dream. The realization both scares and excites me. I check the time and notice that it's just past six-thirty. School starts at eight sharp, so I have thirty minutes until Bryson arrives at my house. Only thirty minutes.

I scamper from my bed, race across the hall to the bathroom, and find it empty and waiting for me. Today I am the victor. While I'm in the shower, I hear Yazz knock at the door. The sound brings a smile to my face, and ten minutes later I saunter from the room, leaving a cloud of steam in my wake.

I pull on my school uniform and look for my blazer, before remembering that Bryson has it. All students are required to wear their blazers as they enter and leave the academy buildings. It's part of the school rules. Mine being at the dry cleaner's means certain punishment. I curse Louise Keaton once more, but this time I don't curse Bryson Keller.

I collect my school bag and phone before heading downstairs. There are just five minutes before my boyfriend is set to arrive. Will I get tired of referring to him that way? Probably not. Until Friday afternoon I plan to relish it. Because last night while chatting with him, I finally got why Bryson Keller's dare has become so popular.

"Morning," I say as I whiz into the kitchen. Mom and Dad are seated at the island, finishing off their breakfast before work. Dad works in IT and Mom is an accountant. How they ended up with two children who dream of being a writer and an artist is a mystery.

"What's the hurry?" Mom asks as she sips her coffee— black with no sugar. I often wonder who hurt her so much that she needs to torture herself by drinking such bitter sludge.

"I'm going to be late."

Dad checks his watch. It took me working part-time cutting lawns all summer to be able to buy it for him for his fortieth birthday.

"*Hayibo!* School starts at eight. Why's Donny so early?"

I check my own watch. The screen is scratched, but it does its job. There are only three minutes left.

"Actually, I have a different ride to school."

"Really?" Dad asks.

"Yes, Sherlock and Watson," I say. "We already established that I have other friends."

"Are you sure you're not dating?" Mom asks as she gets up from the island and takes her dishes to the sink. "Getting rides to school is the fun part about dating in high school."

"You sound well versed in high-school dating," Dad says.

"Of course." Mom flips her unbrushed hair from her shoulders. "I was very popular in high school."

Dad looks me up and down. "So are you saying Kai got his awkwardness from me?"

"Hey," I say around a bite of apple. "I'll have you know that I'm doing just fine, thanks."

"It's okay, honey," Mom says. "Most people peak after high school. Look at your dad."

This time both Dad and I exclaim, "Hey!"

Mom laughs. She has this unique laugh that makes watching movies with her an experience. I'm always thankful that theaters are dark because when Mom laughs, it's enough to make me want to hide.

My phone buzzes with a text from Bryson. It's 7:01. There is nothing I like more than someone who is punctual. Priya has a nasty habit of setting a meeting time and then arriving fifteen minutes later. It's her belief that good things come to those who wait.

"I'm going now. Bye." I take another bite of the apple. I make my exit before they can grill me further. On my way out the door, I offer Yazz a parting high five. She looks barely awake and will remain that way until she has her first cup of coffee.

Even though I knew he'd be there, I'm surprised at the sight of Bryson's Jeep waiting for me. I take a calming breath as I walk toward the passenger seat. I climb in.

"Morning," I say. My confidence from last night is nothing more than a memory, because now he is actually here and not just a figment of my imagination.

"Morning," he says back. He watches me as I try to settle myself, but my hands are full with the apple, my books, and my bag. Eventually he leans over. Bryson grabs the seat belt and pulls it across me. So close. His face is just a breath away from mine.

I feel the heat surge to my face, and his lips pull into a small smile. He clicks the seat belt buckle into place before leaning back against his seat.

"There was no rush, Kai. You could have taken your time."

"I don't like being late."

"I don't mind waiting," Bryson says as he starts the Jeep. He looks at me again. I'm in the same position that he left me in. My body hasn't caught up with my brain.

"Relax." He smiles at me. "Have you eaten breakfast yet?"

"Just this apple."

"Okay. Let's go." Bryson drives off and I finally let myself relax. We don't drive for very long, and soon we're entering the parking lot of a diner. I recognize Glenda's not only from the Date Me, Bryson Keller hashtag but also from Bryson's own

Instagram—I wasn't stalking, I swear. That's my story and I'm sticking to it.

Bryson climbs from the car and I follow him inside. Bryson offers greetings to those he sees, and everyone seems to know him on sight, too.

"You know everyone?"

Bryson shrugs. "I've been coming here since I was young. This diner used to be owned by my grandparents, but my dad sold it a few years back." Bryson's tone doesn't sound all that happy when he says that. He sighs before continuing. "Eating breakfast here was my family's routine. Now it's just mine."

He shrugs again and walks between the booths. We take one near the window. I've driven past the diner before, but I've never ever been inside. Glenda's looks like it's been ripped straight from the 1950s. The booths are done in black-and-white vinyl, which matches the black-and-white-checkered floor. There's even a jukebox in the corner. Aside from the booths, there's a long counter area where those who have come alone can sit. The kitchen is open and active.

An older man approaches us. He claps Bryson on the shoulder and grins. "Your goal this weekend was excellent."

"Thanks, Mr. Humphrey," Bryson says. He has his own smile to match. With the appearance of his dimple, I know that it's real. "I'm glad you could come watch us play."

"I'm sure we can take States this year."

"We're really hopeful, too."

"It'd be great for you to leave with such a big win."

"Fingers crossed," Bryson says. Mr. Humphrey says good-bye and Bryson watches him leave.

"I didn't realize soccer was such a big thing."

"We're the pride of Fairvale. No pressure." Bryson stretches and yawns. "You kept me up too late last night."

I find myself yawning, too. "It takes two to tango."

"I almost missed my morning workout because I over-slept." Bryson runs a hand through his damp hair. We both grab our menus.

"Their bacon and eggs are the best," Bryson says.

"Is that what you're having?"

"Yeah."

"Cool, I'll have the same, then." My stomach growls in anticipation.

The server comes.

"Morning, Alice," Bryson says cheerfully to the older woman.

"You doing well, kiddo?" Alice asks, and Bryson nods. She offers me a kind smile. "What will it be?"

We order.

"How would you like your eggs?" Alice asks me.

"Sunny side up, please."

"Same for you, kiddo?" she asks Bryson.

He nods. "And can I get an orange juice, please." He turns to me. "What about you?"

"Just a water for me, thanks."

Alice nods. "I'll be right back."

Bryson pulls out a folded piece of paper. He pushes it toward me.

"What's this? A love letter?"

"You like that sort of thing?" Bryson asks.

"No," I say too quickly. Redness paints my cheeks. "Yes . . . I don't know. . . ." I shrug.

"Did you and Louise Keaton write love letters to each other?"

"We didn't date long enough for any of that to happen."

Bryson studies me. He leans in close to whisper, "Why'd you date her? If you don't mind me asking."

"It seemed like everyone around me was dating. And I didn't want anyone to think of me as different. I knew Louise liked me, so I figured why not? But then I wasn't comfortable with how unfair it was of me to lead her on when I knew who I was." I look at the piece of paper between us. "Still, I mean, a little romance never killed anyone."

"I'll keep that in mind," Bryson says. My heart speeds up, and before I can react instead of simply staring at him, our food comes.

While we eat, I open the piece of paper and find a hastily scribbled list. Of all the things that Bryson Keller is good at, writing is not one of them. His handwriting is practically indecipherable. Maybe he'll be a doctor one day.

"It's a list of adaptations," he explains. "I know *Romeo and Juliet* is Henning's favorite, but I wanted us to have options. Do you want to perform something so romantic?"

"You said it was your favorite, too, right?" I look up. "Why?"

Bryson smiles, and his eyes light up. "My older sister used to have this huge crush on Leonardo DiCaprio, and so she watched it like it was her religion."

"Oh, I have a sister, too."

"Older or younger?"

"Younger in age, but older in everything else," I say. "I haven't seen the movie. I kind of hate Leonardo DiCaprio."

"Why?"

"Does there need to be a reason for me not to like someone?"

"Generally, yes."

"I guess it irks me that he only takes on roles that are bound to earn him an Oscar nomination."

"But it's good to have a goal, no?"

"Maybe . . . but it's annoying to me. Also, all his girlfriends are blond, models, and twenty-five or under—that seems odd to me. I mean, live your life, but also, really? That's how you're going to live your life?" I shake my head and hold up a finger. "Also, my dad is South African, and let me tell you that Leo's accent in *Blood Diamond* was terrible. I just don't understand why Hollywood doesn't hire actors from the region instead of giving us bad accents. Or, like, just don't do an accent that is offensively bad."

"You've thought long and hard about this, haven't you?" Bryson chuckles.

I hold up my thumb and finger an inch apart. "Just a little bit."

"So what else do you hate? I figure a good boyfriend should

at least know the basics." The air seems to change when he refers to himself that way. Bryson doesn't realize it, but I've dreamed of hearing those words from someone, and never once in my life did I think they would be coming from his lips.

"Well, the top five things that Kai Sheridan hates, including dear old Leo, are . . ." I hum in thought. "Phone calls."

"Now that I know you, that makes sense."

"Math."

"Join the club." He holds up his large hand. "Come on, Kai. Don't leave me hanging." I stare at his upheld hand for a heartbeat longer before bringing my own to smack it in a high five.

He grins. "What else?"

"Um, peas?" I say. "They're of the devil."

Bryson laughs. "Aren't you meant to, like, outgrow your hatred for peas when you turn, like, three?"

"I guess I missed the memo."

"And what's the final thing?" Bryson's been counting them off as I list them, and one finger remains standing.

"Deciding stuff," I say. "I'm probably the most indecisive person you will ever meet. So I spend a lot of time just day-dreaming about stuff instead of actually doing it. I always worry about what everyone will think."

"So, is deciding what to perform a nightmare for you?"

"More or less," I say. "But I'm happy to go with *Romeo and Juliet*. You know I suck at acting, so any bonus points we can earn from Henning are a good thing."

"Works for me."

"So if we do this, who's Romeo and who's Juliet?" I ask.

"Well, you can be Romeo, and I can be Juliet." He pauses, raises an eyebrow, and looks at me. "Or vice versa, whichever you prefer."

I choke on my eggs while trying not to laugh. "Nice one."

Bryson laughs, too. He pushes my glass of water closer to me. I grab it and our fingertips brush. In my haste to pull my hand away, I end up spilling some of the water.

"Shit," I say as I use napkins to wipe up the mess. Bryson helps. There's laughter in his eyes, and the right side of his mouth is pulled up.

"So, have we decided on the movie?"

"I think . . . so?" I finish weakly.

Bryson laughs. "Well, in that case, we should get together and watch the movie so we can pick a scene. Maybe one between the supporting cast? Just because it's *Romeo and Juliet* doesn't actually mean we have to be Romeo and Juliet."

"Okay." I smile, relieved. "I like the way you think."

"Well, I have soccer practice today, but if you're cool waiting, we can get together after and watch the movie at my house?"

"Sure, let me just text my parents quick. I have my shift in the library this afternoon and they usually pick me up," I offer by way of explanation. I pull open the family group chat: Sheridan Shenanigans, aptly named by Mom. I type a message explaining our plans.

"You work in the library?" he asks, genuinely surprised.

"Yeah." I take a sip of my water. "You would know that if you ever went there."

"Hey, it's not that I don't read. I just prefer comics over books."

"Really? You and my sister will get along."

Bryson takes a final sip of his drink. "Are you done?"

I nod.

"We should leave now so we're not late."

"Sure." We walk over to the counter to pay. "I've got it." Before he can protest, I open my wallet and hand over the amount due.

"Fine," Bryson says. He studies me for a moment. Eventually he smiles. "Tomorrow it's on me, though."

And just like that, getting breakfast together becomes a thing that we will do.

If the me of last week could see the me of right now, he would never believe that any of this is actually happening.

Hell, even the me of right now can't really believe it.

We leave Glenda's and head for school—*together.*

9

Bryson pulls into the school parking lot with five minutes to spare until the first bell rings.

"Thanks for the ride," I say.

"No problem."

We climb from the car and find Shannon waiting. She's scrolling through her phone but stops and casually smooths her jet-black hair when she sees us. She's a head shorter than me, but her large blue eyes are piercing and oddly intimidating.

"So, who is it?" Shannon asks. "Who are you dating this week?"

"It's a secret," Bryson says.

He manages to not look at me, and I'm relieved. It seems that he's taking very seriously his promise of keeping us a secret. I know that in a perfect world it wouldn't need to be a secret, but the one that we live in is far from perfect.

Shannon keeps pestering him, but Bryson doesn't budge. Eventually she storms off as I walk to class.

"Kai, wait up!"

I stop and turn to find Bryson holding out his blazer.

"Here. Take it." He doesn't give me much choice, because it's already being forced into my arms. So I do.

"What about you?"

"I have a game tomorrow night, so the worst I'll get is a lunchtime detention." Bryson shakes his head and sighs.

"True," I say as Bryson takes my books and bag. I slide into his blazer. It's a few sizes too big and smells like him—pine. It's probably some name-brand cologne, but as I inhale, I know that it is worth every penny.

"Let's go," Bryson says. He studies me one final time before handing over my belongings.

"Go?"

"To drama," Bryson says, chuckling. Then he leaves me standing there.

All I can do is watch as he walks away. Not that I'm complaining about the sight or anything. The bell rings and I race to catch up to him. I'm not in the mood to serve another of Mrs. Henning's detentions.

We walk to drama together, and by the time we arrive, everyone is seated. Bryson high-fives Isaac and sits down next to him. He twists to look at me expectantly and taps the empty spot beside him. I sit cross-legged and pull my copy of *Romeo and Juliet* from my bag.

Mrs. Henning enters the auditorium just as the start-of-period bell rings. Today she is wearing a faux-fur jacket, leather pants, and bedazzled heels. To top it all off, she's wearing a wig straight out of the French Revolution. All she needs to say now is *Let them eat cake*.

She comes to a stop at center stage and holds out a sheet of paper. "Good morrow, my thespians. Before we begin, please pass around this sign-up sheet. I'm allowing you all to book hour slots to rehearse for the performances this Friday. Also, I would like to inform all of you that I have decided to extend the deadline for the school play submissions. It, too, will be on Friday. Many factors led to this decision, so please use this extra time wisely. I want to be wowed," Mrs. Henning says. "Now, Mr. Keller, could you please fetch me a chair?"

Bryson nods and stands. He disappears backstage to find a chair for Mrs. Henning. I catch the drama teacher's gaze; she offers me a slight nod and there's a smile at her lips. Did she extend the deadline for me? Whatever the reason, I gasp in disbelief. There's a chance for me yet. I smile as I pull a pen from my bag and accept the sign-up sheet from Jessica Cho. A lot of the slots have already been filled, and given Bryson's busy schedule, I need his help to decide the best time for us to practice.

I turn to the person beside me. Isaac is talking to someone else. I reach out and tap him. He fixes his blue eyes on me.

"Uh, you can fill in your slot first. I need to wait for Bryson."

"Cool." He accepts the sheet and looks around for a pen. His eyes land on the one in my hand. "Can I?" He offers me a thin-lipped smile.

"Sure." Our fingers touch as he takes the pen from me and I feel myself flush. Even though I know Isaac is straight, it doesn't stop me from feeling some type of way about him. That's why one-sided crushes exist.

"Thanks." When he smiles this time, he shows teeth. One of Isaac's front teeth overlaps the other, but instead of detracting from his looks, that small quirk only adds to them.

"No problem." I watch as he leans forward and fills in the time he prefers. Unlike Bryson, Isaac does have good handwriting.

Isaac leans back and puts my pen against his lips. I watch every movement. He must feel the weight of my eyes because he looks up. His brow furrows as he does. I look away first.

"Here you go, Kai." It's the first time Isaac has spoken my name to me. And the sound of it from his lips thrills me. He holds out my pen and the sign-up sheet.

I reach for it slowly. Bryson sits down louder than necessary and plucks the pen and paper from Isaac's hands. He's studying me like I'm some math problem that he can't figure out.

"What's wrong?" Isaac asks.

"Nothing," Bryson says. But it doesn't sound that way, and before either of us can ask anything further, he turns to me. "When would you like to practice?"

I glance over his shoulder and meet Isaac's eyes. He shrugs and smiles again. I feel heat coloring my cheeks. Bryson holds up the sheet of paper and waves it. Effectively breaking my eye contact with Isaac.

"How about at lunch sometime?" I say, meeting his eyes instead.

"Tomorrow?"

"Sure."

Bryson smiles as he scribbles in our chosen time. As he does, a small part of me wonders what just happened. A small part of me, the one that lives in fantasyland, can't help but ask: *Is Bryson Keller jealous?*

It's an absurd thought, so I choose to ignore it.

• • •

When the lunch bell chimes, Donny and I leave our math classroom and head toward the cafeteria. Already it's filled with other students. Some stand in line waiting for their turn to be served, while others sit at the many rectangular tables that fill the space. Donny and I join the line. Soon I am greeted by the smell of grilled cheese sandwiches. Few things in this world are as pure and sweet as a well-done grilled cheese sandwich. Aside from pizza and books, it's the thing the human race can be proudest of.

I order and pay for my lunch and turn to find Priya already seated at our regular table. Priya spots me first and waves me over excitedly. With Bryson being my ride this morning, this is the first time that I'm seeing her today.

I cross the cafeteria and take my seat. Donny slides into his place opposite his girlfriend. I take a bite and savor the taste. Few places manage to get the right amount of cheese on a grilled cheese sandwich, and surprisingly enough, the Fairvale cafeteria does it the best. Well, second best—not even this can compete with Dad's.

"There you are, Kai," Shannon Flockhart says. I look up to meet Priya's gaze, but she isn't looking at me. She's staring at the girl standing at my back.

Shannon and Priya have been mortal enemies since last year. And in this feud, I have never been Switzerland. I have picked a side and it isn't Shannon's.

She is public enemy number one, and she knows it.

"No," Priya says.

"I'm not here for you," Shannon starts.

"I don't care."

At last year's Spring Carnival, Shannon wore a bindi. Priya tried to explain to her that it wasn't just a fashion statement, that what Shannon was doing was cultural appropriation, but the other girl wouldn't hear it. Instead, she started to cry and accused Priya of being a bully. In the end, both girls' parents were called to the school, and it became a matter dealt with behind closed doors. Of course, Priya told us everything. She even showed us the apology letter that Shannon wrote. The insincerity and victim playing were hard to ignore. Since then, there's been bad blood.

And once Priyanka Reddy has a grudge, she tends to it like a much-loved pet.

"I just—"

"Bye." Priyanka makes a show of chewing a grape—slowly. Her dark eyes bore into Shannon's. Eventually the other girl spins on her heel and leaves with a huff.

"What did She Who Shall Not Be Named want?"

I shrug. "I think she wants to know who's dating Bryson Keller this week."

"Why would *you* know that?" Priya asks.

Instead of answering, I take a big bite of my sandwich.

"She's so annoying," Priya scoffs.

Donny eyes the blazer that's between us. "Whose is this?"

I take a deep breath before lying to my best friends.

"Bryson's. He forgot it after drama. I've been meaning to return it, but I keep forgetting."

"Ah, no wonder Shannon thinks you're close," Donny says.

"That name, Donald. I've told you not to use it before. It upsets me," Priya jokes.

"Yeah, I'm really not that close to him. We're just working on our drama project," I explain.

Even though I'm totally not looking for him, I do notice that Bryson is missing when Dustin and the rest of the soccer team walk into the cafeteria. It's a rare occurrence for the Cougars to even be here. The team usually leaves school for lunch.

I pull my phone from my pocket and open my chat with Kelly. *Did you get detention?*

"Who's Kelly?" Donny asks. His eyes are trained on my phone screen. I angle it away from him as I read the reply.

Yeah. It's okay though. No big deal.

My eyes move to Bryson's blazer. He did end up getting into trouble because of it—because of me.

"Kai, who's Kelly?" Donny asks again.

"No one." I can feel both of my friends' eyes on me. "It's really no one."

My phone vibrates with a text. *You eating out?*

"No One seems to be texting you a lot," Priya teases.

"Is it Kelly Gold?" Donny asks.

"No."

"Kelly O'Brien?"

"Donny, be quiet." His rattling off of Kelly names is messing with my thoughts.

Where are you? I text back.

"Kelly De Palo?"

"Donny," I grumble. "Give it a rest." I know my words are futile. When Donny latches onto something, he doesn't let it go. He's like an untrained puppy that way. It's one of his charms, but also really annoying.

In the west quad. Why? Want to visit me?

I check my watch. The lunch break is almost over.

"Maybe Kelly is short for Kelsey?" Donny muses. "Maybe it's Kelsey Scott."

"Donald, learn to read the room. Jesus," Priya says. "Kai clearly doesn't want to talk about it." I watch as Priya gets up from her seat. "I need the bathroom."

"I need to go, too," I say as I gather my things. "I'll see you later."

I throw away my trash and run up to the lady at the counter

to place another order before the cafeteria closes. Two minutes later, my order is served. With no time to waste, I sprint to make it to detention before the bell rings.

Setting a new world record, I arrive at the west quad breathless and red in the face. I spot Bryson leaning against the wall. For most students, lunchtime detention means being sent to this quad and staring at a wall in silence. It's why we call it Purgatory. Other offenders stand around him. Bryson doesn't see me at first. His eyes are on his phone.

I approach him and clear my throat. Bryson looks up, surprised. He makes to hide his phone but then realizes that it's me. He smiles like he's happy to see me. Is he?

"You're here?" He looks at his watch and then at my heaving chest. "You didn't actually have to come."

"I did," I wheeze.

"Why is that?"

I hold out a warm grilled cheese sandwich and a bottle of apple juice. He looks from the offered items to my face, studying me.

"For me?" He smiles, showing his dimple.

"Yes."

He takes his lunch just as the bell rings.

"I always try to give as good as I get," I say.

10

The library is my favorite place in all of Fairvale Academy. Located in block A, it is large enough to house a very modern computer lab. Even though the end-of-school bell has just rung, the library is already bustling as I enter. To my right and walled off by glass is the computer lab, directly in front of me are various workstations and alcoves with a few comfortable chairs thrown in the mix, and to my left are rows and rows of bookshelves.

Someone bumps into me as they race into the library. Before I can complain, they throw me a whispered apology. I watch as they head toward the computer lab. Spaces are limited and it's often on a first come, first served basis.

"It's good to see you, Kai," says Ms. Tarkovsky, the head librarian. I move to put my belongings behind the counter.

"You too, Ms. Tarkovsky."

"You can work the front desk while I finalize our latest guest speaker." I nod and watch as the librarian heads toward her office. I love that the library invites authors for events. It's amazing to meet people who are living my dream.

I take up my post behind the computer, ready to scan books in and out. The first student who approaches me is none other than Shannon Flockhart.

"Jesus Christ, Shannon. Are you stalking me now?"

Shannon ignores my question. "You and BK seem to be really close lately?"

"BK?" I know who she means, but the jock nickname doesn't fit the boy I've spent time getting to know. I don't share my thoughts with her, though. If there's one thing Shannon is known for, it's her desire for a scoop.

"Bryson, silly." She pats my shoulder as if we're old friends. The overly chumminess is so fake that it sets my teeth on edge.

"What do you want, Shannon?" I ask, wanting nothing more than to end this charade.

"Tell me who Bryson's dating now. I'll even pay you," she says. "No one has updated their Instagram with evidence. We all want to know."

I sigh. "Not everyone updates their Instagram."

"*Everyone* who dates Bryson Keller does it. Check the hashtag."

It seems that I am not everyone.

"I seriously don't know who it is."

"Liar," Shannon says.

"Why are you so sure I know something?"

"Because you've spent the most time with him this week." Shannon cocks a perfectly plucked eyebrow. "You know I have a sixth sense about these things," she says. "I smell something fishy."

"Ask Bryson if you're so curious. I don't get what this has to do with me." I try to deflect and almost sigh in relief when another student comes to stand behind her. I smile at Eric Ferguson before turning back to Shannon. "Would you excuse me? I need to do my job, please."

Shannon steps aside but makes no move to leave. It seems that the aspiring reporter in her has awakened.

Eric walks up to return a book. "How was it?" I ask as I scan the spine.

"It's a good read. If you like fantasy, you should check it out," Eric says.

"I do, actually." I smile at Eric and set the book off to the side so that I can read it later. I've often wondered what it would be like to hang out with other gay teens like Eric. I haven't been brave enough to take that step yet. Eric offers me a parting smile. And as soon as he leaves, Shannon pounces.

"I know you know."

"You know nothing, Jon Snow," I mumble under my breath.

"What?"

"Nothing."

"No, you said something."

I stare her dead in the face. "I think you're imagining things, Shannon."

Shannon groans. "You're just as annoying as Priya."

The fact that she insists on calling Priya by her shortened

name, regardless of the many times she's been asked not to, irks me further.

"Proud of it," I say with a smile so sweet it could attract bees.

Shannon studies me. "I think you're hiding something. You have me intrigued." Before I can respond, Shannon leaves the library.

I sigh. The last thing I need is the aspiring journalist looking into me. I'll need to be careful. But I've been lying for years—I've become pretty good at it.

I'm finally able to work in peace. My shift passes in no time, and with five minutes left, I venture into the stacks.

I'm busy reshelving books when my phone vibrates in my pocket. Donny has linked the trailer of a movie that he wants us to all go see.

My phone buzzes with another text and I open the message from Kelly: *Where are you?*

"Oh! There you are." His voice surprises me. I turn to find Bryson standing at the entrance of the aisle. Bryson Keller with his cap backward should be illegal. It should be impossible for anyone to look this good, especially after they spent an hour and a half running on a soccer field.

"Kelly?" Bryson asks. He's staring at his message open on my phone. "Am I 'Kelly'?"

"I shortened Keller to Kelly," I explain. "I figured a girl's name would be easier to explain to prying eyes."

"That's really smart," Bryson says. "But also really shitty that you even needed to do that."

I turn to look at him and realize we're standing so close—maybe too close. God, it's unfair for someone to be this handsome. I step back and end up pushing the book cart by accident. Bryson reaches for it. I move to take it, but he stops me.

"I'll help you," he says. "I'll steer, you shelve. Deal?"

"Works for me." I take a moment to study Bryson. His hair is damp from the shower, and he's wearing gym clothes instead of his school uniform. Looking at him now, I realize that my fantasy of him last night wasn't that far off.

"What made you want to work in the library?" Bryson asks as he steers the cart.

"I've always loved books," I say. I decide to tell Bryson another of my secrets: my dream. More people know about it than they know about me being gay, but not many, too few to count on both hands. "I want to be a writer. And you really can't be a writer without being a reader first." I stop the cart and place another book back where it belongs. I turn to him. "Do you have a dream? Is it soccer?"

Bryson pauses and looks at me before answering. "It used to be," he admits. "Soccer was something I loved to do with my dad. But now I play it more out of habit than love." Bryson shrugs. "I'm hoping to find out my dream in college. Something that's only for me."

"Have you decided where you're going yet?"

"I got accepted to UCLA, but they want me to play soccer and I'm not sure if I want to yet."

"Oh, I got accepted there, too. Though not to play soccer." Bryson laughs at my lame joke and I'm thankful. I signal for him to steer the cart and he does. "I'm waiting to hear back from my dream school."

"Which is?"

"Tisch."

"I'll keep my fingers crossed for you." He smiles. "Let me know if you get in. Even if it's after this week."

"It's weird," I say. "This is the most we've ever spoken. I mean, we were friendly, but we weren't friends. Who knew we'd get along so well?"

"I know, right? You're a pretty cool guy, Kai." He grins. "It's weird how we all stay in our groups. Because I play soccer, it means everyone around me does, too."

"That's high school," I say.

"True." Bryson stops the cart when I tell him to, and I stack the next few books. One of them needs to go on the top shelf, so I stand on my toes to do so.

"Let me?" Bryson holds out his hand and I give him the book. With ease, he places the book in its rightful place. He pauses and whispers, "What's the point of having a tall boyfriend if you aren't going to use him?" He adds a wink before returning to his position at the book cart. The absurdity of it makes me smile.

We continue to work, and with Bryson's help, the books are reshelved in no time.

"You ready to go?" Bryson asks, and I nod.

"I've been thinking about our performance. Please let us pick something quick and easy?"

"Scared you're going to blush?"

"No, that's inevitable," I say.

We fetch my bag and his blazer. I follow him to his Jeep. Even though there are other students around, I don't feel any of the anxiety I expected to feel. Even though it's only Tuesday, it surprises me how comfortable I'm starting to become around him. Bryson has a way of doing that.

He starts the car and we drive out of the parking lot. Bryson removes his sunglasses from their storage space and puts them on. Instantly he goes from high school senior to model advertising shades. He faces me, and it's hard not to stare.

"What?" he asks, and from the hint of a smile that dances at his lips, I know that I have been caught checking him out.

"Nothing," I lie. I turn my attention forward. As we drive, I squint against the glare of the afternoon sun. At the next stoplight, Bryson reaches across me. He opens the glove compartment and fetches a glasses case.

"Here," he says as he hands it to me. I open it and find an identical pair of sunglasses. "They're my spare ones."

I put them on and turn to look at him. Bryson's staring at me.

"They look good," he says.

I laugh. "You really go all in on this boyfriend thing, huh?"

"What do you mean?"

"We even have matching sunglasses now."

Is this what boyfriends do?

I catch myself grinning and decide not to overthink things . . . for now.

11

We arrive at Bryson's house too soon. I'm certain that I blinked and missed the trip. Bryson lives in the same neighborhood that Donny does—I know Shannon lives close by, too. It's a gated community where the über-rich live. The top 1 percent of the student body of Fairvale Academy call each other neighbors.

Bryson's house has been taken from the pages of some architecture magazine—which makes sense considering that's what his father does. I only know this because my parents scoured his designs to use for inspiration with our own renovations.

The house is two stories, like mine, but so much bigger. Truthfully, *villa* is a more apt description for it. It's got sand-colored walls and white finishes. The windows are large and clean with white shutters. Bryson's house looks like it belongs somewhere more interesting than Fairvale, California—maybe Spain.

Even so, this house pales in comparison to the house of Donny Duckworth a few roads away.

"Are we getting out?" Bryson asks. His arms are draped across the steering wheel and his head is resting against them. It seems that we've been sitting there for a while already and he's been staring at me for I don't know how long.

I blush, and he smiles.

"Oh, uh, right." I unbuckle my seat belt and climb out.

Bryson follows me as we walk toward the house. Silence greets us when he opens the front door. We enter and pause in the foyer. He seems unsure for a moment, looking at his shoes, the house, and then me.

"My mom kind of has a no-shoe policy in the house." Bryson points to the slippers in the corner for guests. I smile as I hook my right shoe behind my left and pull it off. I do the same to the other one.

"My dad's like that, too," I say. "We grew up wearing different shoes inside and out."

Relieved, Bryson leads me through the house.

"Wow. This is amazing." It's like the family room was ripped from the pages of a magazine, too.

"My mom runs her own interior decorating firm," Bryson explains. I know this already. There was a profile about her in one of my mom's magazines once. She's a designer to the stars. And judging by the space around me, it's clear that she's very good at what she does. It is both showstopping and homey.

We don't enter the family room, though. Instead, Bryson

leads me toward the kitchen, which is large with white cupboards and white granite countertops. It's filled with state-of-the-art appliances. There's no doubt that this kitchen would be a chef's dream. Bryson walks over to the large double-door fridge and pulls it open.

"Do you want anything to drink?" Bryson asks. "We have water, juice, and soda."

"What juice?" I'm standing at the island, leaning my hip against the edge of the counter.

"Mango," Bryson says.

"Apple, orange, and grape are the only three juice flavors that deserve to exist in this world." I smile. "Water is fine."

Bryson takes two bottles of water from the fridge. He places his down on the counter and holds out mine. "You have the strangest opinions."

"Thanks," I say as I take it. Our eyes meet. It hits me then: I am alone with Bryson. I know our relationship is fake, but that doesn't stop my heart from racing as he looks at me. Wanting something to do, I open the bottle and end up drinking too fast. I choke, and Bryson moves to pat my back.

I freeze. We're home alone and there's hardly any distance between our bodies. He must realize it, too, because he quickly takes a step back.

"We should head up to my room." The words take a second to register. Eyes wide, he hurriedly adds, "To work, I mean." It seems to me that Bryson's just as nervous as I am. With a start, I realize that it's the first time I've seen it. He's looking everywhere but at me. And I can't help but wonder why. . . . Bryson's straight, right? He shouldn't be as bothered by me as I am by him.

Bryson laughs and seems to come back to himself, back to being the self-assured Bryson Keller that I've come to know. Maybe my doubting him is nothing more than wishful thinking. *This is just a game,* I remind myself.

"Lead the way," I say.

We leave the kitchen, and I follow Bryson up the flight of stairs to his bedroom. We enter.

"Uh, sorry about the mess," Bryson says.

"What mess?" I ask. I look around. Almost everything is in its place, save for one hoodie on the floor and a pair of dirty socks. The walls of Bryson's room are covered in pictures. I notice camera equipment sprawled across his desk. There's a camera, a tripod, and some lenses.

"I didn't know that you're interested in photography," I say.

Bryson smiles. "Isn't the whole point of being in a relationship getting to know one another?" He turns to me. "Come to think of it, there's a lot that we don't know about each other."

It's true. We've known each other for years, but when I think about it, there isn't much beyond the surface that I actually know about Bryson Keller. And for the first time in my life I find myself wanting to dive deeper, to get to know more and more about this boy with the easy smile and soulful eyes.

I study the collage of photographs that I assume Bryson has taken. Among them are several posters of Liverpool, an English football club that happens to be Manchester United's greatest rival. I can't help but wonder what my dad would think if he saw this. Picturing Dad and Bryson arguing about soccer makes me smile—will that ever actually happen? I pluck the thought out before it takes root.

I notice that some of the posters look worse for wear. Like they've been torn and were hastily repaired. I don't ask him about them. Instead, I shift my focus back to the photo collage.

"So, you like photography?"

"Yeah," Bryson says. "It's fun."

"You're good." I turn to him. "Maybe you should be a photographer?"

"Maybe," he says. "I guess I need to find what I really love."

"You have enough time," I say. "No stress."

"Tell that to my mom." He sighs. "She's in a full-on panic because I don't actually know what I want to do when I get to college."

"Well, knowing you, you'll probably excel at everything."

"Everything but math."

"Oh God, me too." Our eyes meet. "Give me words over numbers any day."

"What about math with letters?"

"I hate it, and I hate whoever invented it. Algebra is the worst."

Bryson laughs. He watches as I take a closer look at his photos. He's seriously talented.

"When was this taken?" I ask. I point at a picture where Bryson looks a year or two younger than he is now.

"I took those on our last family vacation," Bryson says.

In the picture there's a happy family of four smiling back at me. This is the one and only picture that Bryson has of his whole family. All the others are of just his mom and sister.

I turn to study the rest of the space. Bryson's desk is almost as full as mine, but instead of the chaotic mess, his is perfectly organized. He has a large desk calendar with his schedule on it. He has a game tomorrow. So does Priya. Maybe I'll surprise him by attending his match after.

Bryson moves to stand beside me and picks up his computer. "Shall we do it?"

"Do . . . *it*?" I quirk my eyebrow in flirtation.

Bryson shakes his head and smiles. "Watch the movie."

"Sure." My eyes snag on a box on his desk. It's the latest iPhone. "Holy shit, you have one?"

"My dad thinks he can buy me back," Bryson says. His voice gets colder as he speaks about his father. "My dad is trying to see me for the first time in over a year. He's the reason I was late for school yesterday. He offered to take me to breakfast before school. And like a fool I believed him. I waited around for nothing." Bryson stops himself. His eyes widen as he looks at me. "You're really easy to talk to. Not even Dustin knows that. Everyone thinks I had a dentist appointment."

"Well, I'm always willing to listen if you ever need that." I meet his gaze. "Even after we break up."

The last two words hang between us. The inevitable end to our relationship flashes before my eyes. I need to remember that this will all be over soon. I can't get too comfortable, too used to having Bryson Keller in my life.

We're staring at each other.

"Same," Bryson says.

He clears his throat and looks away first. He moves over to his bed. It doesn't take long for Bryson to find the movie online. He grabs his laptop and places it on the floor. We both take a seat with our backs against his bed. Bryson's leg taps into me and I try to ignore the warmth of it.

He stands. "I'll be right back," he says.

"Okay."

While he's gone, I tell myself that this is just for school. This is not a date. Watching a movie with my boyfriend has been a fantasy of mine. It may seem small and inconsequential, but it's something I've never gotten to experience.

Bryson returns with his arms filled with chips, candy, and recently popped microwave popcorn.

"Wow, that's a lot."

Bryson smiles. "I wasn't sure what you liked, so I brought a bit of everything."

"I'm sure you treat all your girlfriends this well."

He places the snacks down. "Actually, I hardly ever saw any of them outside of school." He looks at me. "You're the first."

"Well, it's only for school."

"Right." It's one word that I know I will spend countless hours trying to decipher.

He grabs a handful of popcorn and throws it into his mouth before sitting cross-legged and pressing play. The movie starts, and I prepare to watch a Leonardo DiCaprio movie in its entirety. Not just bits and pieces. And for the first time in my life I watch a movie with my boyfriend—even if he is just pretend.

"I think we should do this scene between Benvolio and Romeo," Bryson says.

I watch the scene and nod. It's short and has just enough lines for me to be able to manage.

"I'll hunt for the script and send it over to you tonight," Bryson says. He hits pause and heads for his desk. "What's your email address?"

"My name at Gmail dot com."

Bryson jots it down before sitting next to me. He's closer than before. To distract myself, I point to the screen and ask, "Who do you want to be?"

"Maybe Benvolio? He has more lines. And Romeo in this scene can be seen as quiet and shy, which might make you more comfortable."

I nod. "Maybe you should look into studying directing."

"I should hire you as my college advisor," Bryson teases.

As we watch more of the movie, my attention is split. I'm aware of every move that Bryson makes next to me. He adjusts his position, and I hold my breath as more of his leg touches mine. Bryson's not looking at me, though. He's still watching the movie. My heart hammers in my chest. When Leonardo DiCaprio and Claire Danes are in the pool and are about to kiss, I reach for the popcorn. Bryson does the same, and our hands end up brushing. For the second time I stop breathing. A smile dances at his lips as he eats a handful of popcorn.

I watch him chew, my eyes never leaving his lips. I turn my attention back to the movie. I force myself not to look anywhere but at the screen.

I'm finally focused on the movie when I feel a sudden weight on my shoulder. Startled, I turn to find Bryson's head there. His eyes are closed and he's snoring slightly. I watch the rise and fall of his chest.

He nuzzles closer to me, his head finding the perfect spot to rest. While he sleeps, Bryson's totally oblivious to the effect that he's having on me.

I watch the rest of the movie trying to stay still with Bryson tucked against me. When the credits start to play, I study his profile. I bring my hand up but pause. I let it hover there.

Maybe in another life I'd be brave enough to do it. Bryson looks so peaceful, which is the exact opposite of how I'm feeling right now. It's only Tuesday. Will I be able to survive this unscathed until Friday? I don't know, but I need to remind myself that this is *not* real, and it can never be . . . right?

But watching him sleep, I'm grateful that I have three more days left with him. Bryson's eyes open. We stare at each other. My panic multiplies. I jerk my hand back, but Bryson reaches out to catch it. Our eyes haven't left each other. His swirl with questions. I'm about to apologize when Bryson's face breaks into a smile.

"Let's go."

"Go?" Bryson stands and helps me to my feet. He lets go of my hand, and I'd be lying if I said I wasn't a little disappointed.

"It's almost seven." Bryson points at the large clock above his desk.

I follow him down the stairs to find a dark and empty house. "Your mom must be working late."

"Yeah. She does when she has a new client." Bryson shrugs. "I'm used to it now."

We stop in the foyer to put on our shoes. I bend to pull them on, and Bryson does the same. I have a habit of not untying my laces. The left foot goes in with ease, but the right one puts up a fight. I stumble and Bryson reaches out to catch me. I'm the first to react. I clear my throat and create space between us.

"Thanks," I say awkwardly. There's no doubt that my cheeks are red. Bryson smiles and opens the door. He waits for me to exit the house. He locks the house and turns to me. Bryson looks from my face to my hand again. It's almost like time slows down as he reaches for it. I don't breathe as he takes my hand in his. I steal a glance at him, and I can't help but wonder, *What is this?*

"Is this a part of your dare?" I ask.

Bryson's silent for a heartbeat. He studies our hands. I'm not sure what he's thinking and before I can ask, he nods.

"It's okay if you don't want to—" Bryson starts to remove his hand from mine.

"No," I say. If his previous dates got to experience this, then I want to as well.

Bryson smiles, and that's how we walk to the Jeep. He

opens my door and helps me get in, then races across the front of the car. Bryson settles into the driver's seat and makes a show of taking my hand in his once more. This time he even interlocks our fingers.

Bryson Keller and I hold hands the rest of the way home.

And I take my first step into quicksand.

WEDNESDAY

12

By the time Bryson pulls into my driveway the next morning, I'm already outside waiting—and wondering if last night was just a dream. I run another hand through my hair, hoping that it's all still in place. I barely stop myself from redoing my tie for the third time this morning. *I'm fine, I look fine.*

"Kai?" The front door swings open behind me and Yazz comes outside. "Here." She holds out money. "Dad said I should give you this for tonight."

"Thanks." I mentioned my plans to stay and watch the soccer game tonight, and Dad was more than thrilled to offer me money in support. It seems that he's still holding out hope for a son who will love soccer as much as he does.

Just then Bryson rolls down his window. He pops his shades up and waves.

"Is that—" Yazz starts. "Bryson Keller?"

"You know him?"

"I know of him," Yazz says. "He helps coach our school's soccer team." She makes a show of removing her glasses to wipe them clean on her nightgown before returning them to her face. "Huh, so it really *is* him."

"Of course."

"This is very strange. So very strange."

"What's so strange about it?"

Yazz scans me up and down before turning her attention back to Bryson's Jeep. "Everything." She spins on her heel and goes back inside.

I pocket the money and jog toward the Jeep.

"Sorry," I say.

"Don't be," Bryson says as I climb into the car and try to get settled. He looks at the clock above the dashboard. Bryson whistles as he watches it turn to 7:00. "This is different," he says.

"What is?"

"Me not having to wait for anyone. I'm so used to being late because of the girls I'm dating," he says once I'm seated in the car.

"That's why you should date boys," I joke. "Tell your friends."

"Eh, most of my friends are kind of douchey."

"I'm glad you said it." I buckle my seat belt.

"Was that your sister?" Bryson asks.

"Yeah, Yasmine," I say. "She told me you coach at her school."

"Yeah, I help out when I can."

"Huh, you're an onion, Bryson Keller."

"An onion?"

"Layers. You have layers." I shake my head. "I learn something new about you every day."

"Are you complaining?"

"No, I like it," I admit.

"Me too."

I know Bryson's words shouldn't affect me. This Jeep will turn back into a pumpkin soon. I know all this in my brain . . . but my heart is starting to feel like it's an entirely different story.

Bryson drives into Glenda's parking lot. We climb from the Jeep and head inside. I smile at Alice and follow Bryson to a booth. While we wait to be served, I pull my script from my bag. True to his word, Bryson emailed it last night. "Should we do a quick read-through?" I ask.

"Sure." He pulls his own from his bag. He's already highlighted his lines. Before we can start, though, Alice approaches.

"Morning, boys." She smiles warmly. "What can I get you?"

"I'll have some pancakes," I say. "And a milkshake." I'm in the mood for something sweet.

"And you, Bryson?"

"The usual." Alice nods and jots down our orders before heading off.

"Do you eat the same thing every day for breakfast?"

Bryson nods. "I like when things stay the same," he says. "Change scares me."

While we wait for our order, we go over our lines. Halfway through, our breakfast is delivered, but we finish the scene. Bryson is confident. He's also patient as I stumble over a few lines of dialogue. When we're done, Bryson gets up. "I need the bathroom real quick."

I nod and return my attention to the script. I'm reading my lines when someone slides into Bryson's seat. I look up and find myself staring at Shannon. I groan.

"So, you two even get breakfast together now?"

I hold up our script. "We have to practice where we can."

"Interesting." Shannon studies me. I don't like the look in her eye, so to distract her, I ask my own question. I'm tired of Shannon thinking she holds the power in this situation. Yes, I have a secret to hide, but I'm pretty sure she has one, too.

"Aren't you working a little too hard for this story?"

"What are you talking about?"

"I know why you really want to date Bryson."

"Duh. I like him." The problem with Shannon is that she believes that she is the most intelligent person in the room. There's no denying that she is smart, and maybe that's why she's so desperate to do whatever it takes to get off the waitlist. She's currently competing for the title of valedictorian, so her being on the waitlist must seem unfathomable to her. Is that why she's borderline obsessed with getting this story?

I give a dramatic shrug. "I just find that super interesting. If you really liked Bryson, why play the dare? You could just wait until it ends in a few weeks." I lean forward and take a slow sip of my milkshake, not looking away from her eyes as I do. "Something's just not adding up."

"Not that I have to explain myself to you, but I wanted to

prove that I could be the one to end this game. That I could make it real. Yes, it's in part for the story, but it's also because I really do think we'd be perfect for each other." Shannon shakes her head. "I wanted him to break his rules for me. To hold my hand for the first time—"

"What do you mean, hold your hand?" I sit up.

"Where have you been living?" Shannon asks. "Do you even know anything about this dare?"

"Unlike you, I was actually there when it started," I say. "But that's not important. Tell me about the hand-holding?"

"Bryson sticks to his rules. Nothing physical, not even holding hands, between him and his dare dates."

I think back to yesterday—to him holding my hand. What does that mean?

A takeout order is called, and Shannon gets to her feet. "See you around, loser."

I don't answer her. I'm too lost in my thoughts. Is Bryson Keller gay? This time I'm sure it's not just wishful thinking. He held my hand. Shannon said that was against the rules—rules he had never broken. But then I think back to his text—he said he wasn't gay. Do I believe what he's said, or how he's acted?

My mind races with the possibilities.

"Kai?" Bryson sits back down. "You okay?"

"Yeah. Fine," I lie. But the words taste bitter. I know that I can get the answers to my questions if I just ask. But am I brave enough to hear them? Do I even have the courage to ask? It's Wednesday, and a part of me realizes that I've become too comfortable with someone who will walk away from me come Friday.

I don't want Bryson Keller to break my heart. I don't want to be the cliché of a gay boy falling for a straight boy. But he held my hand. Bryson Keller held my hand, so what does that mean for me? What does it say about him? And what does it say about us?

Maybe it's already too late, a small voice whispers at the back of my mind. Because looking at Bryson, as I am now, it's hard to deny that I'm starting to like having him around. I like having him as my boyfriend.

And I'd be stupid not to know just how dangerous thoughts like that are.

"Really, are you sure you're okay?" he asks. I can tell that he's genuinely concerned, and that makes it even worse. "Something happened. Did Shannon say something to you?"

It surprises me that he actually notices these things. The Bryson Keller that we think we know and the one that you get to know if you take the time to are two different people. He isn't some überjock stereotype at all. He's just . . . Bryson.

I look down and make like I'm reading our script. As I do, I say, "Yeah, everything's fine." He doesn't get to see my face. He doesn't get to see that I am lying.

"You sure?"

"Yes."

I have to be.

13

When we get to school Bryson hands me back my blazer. "I picked this up for you yesterday," he says.

"So soon?"

"I paid extra so I could give it to you sooner." Bryson runs a hand through his hair. "Neither of us can afford a lunchtime detention today. We've booked the theater to practice."

"Right."

Bryson moves to get his gym bag from the back seat, and I bring the blazer to my nose. I expect to smell soap, but instead, it smells just like Bryson does. When he faces me, his lips are pulled into a small smile—like he's holding back a secret. Did he see me? I look from Bryson's face to the car and catch sight of my reflection in the window. I pull on my blazer and try to ignore the reddening of my cheeks.

I look at my watch and realize that there are ten minutes left until the start of first period. "I'm going to see Donny and Priya before class," I say. I need to give my face a chance to cool down.

"No problem," Bryson says. "I'll see you in drama."

We go our separate ways. I pull my phone from my pocket and open up the three musketeers group chat.

Where are you guys?

At school, Priya replies. *Where are you?*

Me too. I'm heading into block A.

Meet us in purgatory.

It takes me five minutes to reach them.

"What's wrong?" I ask as I approach. Priya is standing with her arms folded and her mouth pursed, whereas Donny's ears are redder than our ties—a sure sign of his emotions. "Are you guys fighting?"

Ever since they started dating, I've been trying to figure out my place in their relationship. As their mutual best friend, do I involve myself? Do I pick a side, or do I stay neutral? This isn't their first argument, and this isn't the first time that I've felt this way.

"Donald's being ridiculous," Priya says.

"What did he do?"

"Leave it, Kai." I turn to Donny and swallow whatever I was going to say next. I nod. I'm not sure what happened but I don't think I can help. They need to work this out on their own. I'm starting to have my own relationship woes—like the fact that I think I'm starting to like Bryson Keller for real. This is how crushes start: first you can't stop thinking about the person, then you just can't wait to see them, and finally you want to spend all your time with them.

"Uh, I just remembered I need to do . . . something," I say. "I'll see you guys later."

I hurry away from them and enter the auditorium to find Bryson already seated. He has his bag and blazer occupying the space next to him. When he sees me, he smiles and waves me over. Bryson moves his belongings to make room for me and I feel a warm glow in my chest.

While I wait for Mrs. Henning to arrive, I lean back and support myself with my hands behind me. I look up at the stage lights.

Bryson leans back, too, almost mimicking my pose. He positions his hands to support him, and his finger touches one of mine. I inhale sharply. I look at him out of the corner of my eye, but Bryson is talking to Isaac. He isn't paying me any mind and he certainly isn't obsessing over something as small as our fingers touching.

What's wrong with me? This shouldn't bother me. That I'm paying such close attention to Bryson means I'm starting to like him . . . for real. Mrs. Henning climbs to the stage and I sit up straight. Bryson remains in his position. Us touching definitely wasn't intentional, but my foolish heart doesn't seem to care about that.

I'm not assigned a role to perform today, but both Bryson and Isaac are. I try to listen to the boy I've liked for the better part of a year, but my attention keeps getting pulled to Bryson. Bryson is every bit the distraught Romeo in Friar Laurence's cell. When he pleads with the Nurse for news of Juliet—the girl he loves—our eyes meet. Is this him embodying his character or is it something else? Bryson smiles, and it is dazzling.

The bell rings, and Bryson and I head toward English. As I study the boy next to me, I know that I need Bryson to believe that this is all fake. I can't let on that I'm starting to like him. This wasn't part of the rules.

God, who knew a fake relationship could be so complicated?

By the time the lunch bell rings, I'm confident that I can practice with him without any problems. I've liked other straight boys in secret before, and it's never been a big deal. I know I can do it with Bryson, too.

As I take my seat at our regular table, I notice that both Priya and Donny are still sulking messes. We sit and eat awkwardly.

"Whoa, whoa, whoa. Who died?" Bryson asks as he slides into place next to me. He looks from me to Donny and then to Priya. "Seriously, what's up with you guys? Did you guys fight?"

"Why are you here?" Priya asks.

"Kai and I have the auditorium booked to rehearse our scene." He looks from me to Priya and then to Donny, and then to me once more. A frown crosses his face and he asks me a pointed question with his eyes.

I shrug. I don't know what's going on, either. They'll tell me when they're ready. We sit in heavy silence for a moment longer before Bryson speaks.

"C'mon, Kai, let's go. These two clearly need to figure some stuff out," he says.

I nod and stand. Bryson and I exit stage left. We push through the hustle and bustle of the Fairvale Academy cafeteria.

When we're in the hallway, Bryson says to me, "Weird. They were so confident about high school relationships lasting."

"I mean, every couple fights. It's what happens afterward that matters. I'm pretty sure that by the end of school, they'll be A-okay." We walk in silence for a bit before I ask, "Do you still believe they're a waste of time? High school relationships, I mean."

"Why do you ask?"

"Just curious," I say. "Isn't that the whole reason you agreed to the dare in the first place?"

"Well, partly. But also because it provided the perfect distraction from the mess of my home life. When the dare first started, I'd just found out that my dad was planning to get remarried. So it happened at the right time. I guess these past few weeks I've been glad to have something certain. It's been sort of a comfort. Exhausting at times, yes. But also, I really liked that there would be no hurt feelings, no expectations—nothing. After one school week, I'd be able to move on." We stop outside the auditorium door. "I guess I'm starting to see the appeal of having something real," Bryson says. "Especially with the right person."

I swear he looks at me when he says that, but it happens so

quickly that when he pushes the auditorium doors open, I'm left feeling like I imagined it. Like I saw what I wanted to see and nothing more.

Bryson Keller, are you gay?

As I watch him walk toward the stage, I can't help but wonder that very thing. The auditorium is empty, and it's funny that my week with Bryson started right here. This was where I first asked him out, and in the prop room was where I first came out to him.

"Kai?" he calls out again. "Earth to Kai."

"What?"

"Where'd you go?" Bryson asks. "You seemed to be thinking really hard about something."

"It's nothing." I shake my head. Now is not the time for me to be reminiscing. I need all the practice I can get. I join Bryson onstage and turn to look at the sea of empty seats. Even though there isn't a soul out there, I feel my heart start to race and my hands grow sweaty. I feel sick. The thought of performing onstage is enough to turn my stomach. Now that I'm standing here, it feels all the more real.

Bryson rushes over to me. "You don't look so good."

"I don't like acting."

"Everything's going to be fine," Bryson says. "Trust me. Now as we rehearse, and Friday when we perform. Just trust me, and it'll all be okay." He rests his hand on my shoulder to reassure me. "You can always depend on me."

Bryson takes his place and holds his script up before him. "You ready?"

I nod, even though I don't feel at all that way.

We run through the scene, both using our scripts. When we finish, Bryson stops and offers suggestions. We do it again, and when I mess up, Bryson continues to be supportive and calm.

By the third time, Bryson is off script. He moves with confidence, and as he delivers his lines, I find myself relaxing into the role. I'm nowhere near as good as he is. But when his character throws his arm around my shoulders, I don't react like Kai would. I accept that I am Romeo in this scene, and he is my best friend.

I deliver my last line and turn to look at Bryson. We're in our final position, so we're close. We both pause at the sound of clapping. We turn to find Dustin standing there.

"That was so gay." He laughs. My face reddens and I tense. Bryson must feel it because he puts some distance between us. I hate that I'm embarrassed right now. Angry not only at Dustin but at myself, too.

Bryson faces Dustin. "What are you doing here?" he asks.

"Coach wants to see you." Dustin laughs. "Nice acting, dude."

"Can you stop?" Bryson asks.

"Stop what?"

"Being an asshole." Bryson shakes his head. My heart lifts. His words are the ones I want to say.

"Wow. I was only joking. No need to get touchy, man."

"I'm not being touchy. I just hate that you said something stupid like that. You're better than that, D."

"You okay?" Dustin asks. "Did something happen?" He looks from Bryson to me.

I shrug.

"Anyway," Dustin says. "Coach wants to see you, if you have time?"

Bryson turns to me.

"You can go. You basically know all your lines. I just need to memorize mine now," I say.

He nods. "I'll see you later."

"Okay." I watch as Bryson and his best friend leave. I can see Bryson talking to Dustin, but I can't hear about what. I've never had someone stand up for me. Being closeted has meant that I've always just had to listen and ignore the homophobic stuff because I've never wanted to put the spotlight on me. I'm thankful for Bryson, and more than that, I don't want to stop spending time with him.

What happens next week when our relationship has ended? Do we go back to just passing each other in the halls and offering a smile here and a hello there? It's a worry I'm starting to have.

The truth is, I really don't want to go back to how it used to be between us. I want this, I want what we have now. I'm also starting to want it to be real. My heart is longing to forget that this is all a game. That thought both terrifies me and excites me. It's so sudden, so soon. I've never believed that there's a set amount of time before you can like someone.

When it happens, it happens.

And I can already tell that I am on the precipice of falling for Bryson Keller—my fake boyfriend.

14

Donny and I are standing amid a sea of crimson and white. I'm doing my part to fit in. I'm wearing black jeans and the only red T-shirt I own. When you blush as much as I do, it's best to avoid the color. The sun has just set behind the soccer stadium. I occasionally come to watch Priya play, but Donny comes to every game. He is energy personified. Every time Priya touches the ball, he screams his heart out. His face is red not only from the shouting, but also from Priya's number seven painted on his cheeks. I feel a pang of jealousy. I also want to date like this—out in the open and free.

Whatever tension there was earlier in the day seems to be forgotten. Just like I knew it would. Donny is the ever-supportive boyfriend. Still, he's a nervous mess next to me. He's been chewing his thumbnail ever since the away team leveled the score.

"We can't afford to lose this one. We really need the points." I smile at my friend. It's cute how he refers to Priya's activities as his own.

"What is it?" Donny asks when he catches me looking at him.

"Just . . . you practically have hearts in your eyes."

Donny laughs. "Is it that obvious?"

"Only to me, because I'm your best friend. And I know you."

"The same goes for you," Donny says. "I know you."

Before I can ask what he means, Priya scores. Donny practically jumps into my arms, and I barely manage to stop us both from falling. When we pull apart, I'm laughing. For the rest of the game, Donny and I are Priya's very own cheerleading squad. It works—we win two to one.

After the game, Donny and I go to grab a drink from concessions. My throat needs it.

"Wasn't she amazing?" Donny has been talking about Priya nonstop. I know I shouldn't, but I feel a pang shoot across my chest. I long to be able to talk openly about who I like, not just with my friends, but with the rest of the world, too. It's unfair how heterosexuals get to love, laugh, and live so freely, while we second-guess everything. Our actions are always cautious.

As if my thoughts have summoned them, I spot Eric and his boyfriend. They're crossing the parking lot, heading for their car. They look happy, oblivious to the few people who have stopped to judge.

Or perhaps not so oblivious. They stop and deliberately stare at those very assholes. My stomach sinks—I hope they don't cause a scene. For every step that I take toward wanting to come out, these moments hold me back. It's a mix of fear and anger that my coming out means dealing with stuff like this. Eric smirks and pulls his boyfriend toward him. They kiss and give the homophobes something to talk about. The group scurries away, and Eric laughs.

I laugh, too.

"What?" Donny asks. He's missed the boldness—and bravery—of this out and proud gay couple. Eric catches me looking.

He offers me a nod, and I find myself returning it. I decide that when I grow up, I want to be just like him.

"Nothing." It's our turn to order. "I'll just have a Coke, please."

Donny buys snacks for him and Priya, and I help him carry them to the Quackmobile. Priya arrives a short while later. She's showered and changed, and her wet black hair is braided down the length of her back.

"You were so great," Donny says.

"Thanks." She smiles and kisses him on the cheek. "I'm glad we won. It was tough."

I offer her a thumbs-up. Priya laughs. "Did you follow any of the game, Kai?"

"Hey, I at least know the basics."

"Your dad must be so proud," Priya teases.

I take a sip of my soda.

"You sure you don't need me to drop you off?" Donny asks me.

"Yeah. Dad will come get me. It's fine, go."

"It's really no problem," Donny says.

"I know, but it's fine."

"You sure?"

"Donald, Kai said it's fine. We should trust him." Priya pops a handful of candy into her mouth and chews. She heads around to the passenger seat and climbs in. Donny joins her in the car. I wave as I watch them leave the parking lot.

I finish my soda and throw the can away before returning to the stands. I scan the crowd for Bryson's family, but I don't see them. The Cougars are warming up as I make my way to an empty seat. Almost instantly my eyes find Bryson. He's talking excitedly to Dustin. Bryson laughs and his whole body shakes. I find myself smiling at the sight.

Bryson continues some stretches. His jersey pulls tight against his broad shoulders as he holds one arm across his body and then the other. He spins to look at the stands. I can feel the moment Bryson's eyes find me among the sea of people. His blue eyes widen with surprise at first, but then his face pulls into a wide grin. He waves and he could be waving at anyone around me, but I know that it's for me. I wave back. I'm just another face in the crowd. Bryson adds a wink to punctuate the gesture.

I watch as he jogs to join the rest of his team to finish off their warm-up. My eyes scan the rest of the team and I barely bat an eye at Isaac. *Who have I become?*

Everyone takes their positions and the referee blows his whistle. It's clear Bryson is the star of the team. He's a forward who always seems to have the ball. Bryson nimbly bypasses the opposition. He is sure and confident. And only ten minutes into the game, Bryson scores.

His team tackles him, and I can't help but feel a little jealous at the sight. Bryson pulls away and runs to the corner, and he slides toward me. Everyone around me goes wild, and I join in. Bryson spots me cheering him on. He smiles, and if I were closer, I'm sure I'd be able to see his dimple.

The home crowd starts to cheer even louder. I pay them no mind. My eyes are stuck on Bryson. Just before halftime, Bryson is roughly tackled in the penalty area and awarded a free kick. My heart's in my throat as I watch him climb to his feet. He limps for a bit and shakes his ankle. Only when everything seems to be okay do I release the breath I'm holding.

I take a bathroom break at halftime. When I'm rinsing my hands, I get a text from Kelly.

I didn't know you were coming. He adds a series of confetti-cannon emojis.

I smile as I type my response. *I wanted to surprise you. I guess it worked.*

I was the one who promised to be the perfect boyfriend, Bryson texts back.

Fair is fair.

What am I going to do with you? Bryson asks.

What do you mean?

Aaah. Got to go. Coach is calling. Talk later. I'm not sure if he's hit the emoji by mistake because he's in a rush, but my heart hammers in my chest as I stare at the kissing-face emoji.

I return to my seat but distractedly watch the second half.

My mind is on the text, on that kissing face. What does it all mean?

I pull my phone from my pocket and reread our conversation. My eyes snag on *What am I going to do with you?* Is Bryson as confused as I am? This can't go on. We need to talk.

Soon.

The final whistle blows, and the Cougars win four to two, with Bryson scoring three of their goals. I can't help laughing as Bryson is picked up onto Dustin's and Isaac's shoulders. As the crowd cheers, I realize my voice is one of the loudest.

As I'm leaving the stands, my phone buzzes—another text from Kelly.

Wait for me. I'll give you a lift home.

I planned on calling Dad to pick me up, but this is easier.

Okay, I text back.

I make my way to the school parking lot. It doesn't take me long to spot Bryson's Jeep, but I don't walk toward it. With so many people around me, it's best not to draw their attention. I don't need people questioning why I'm here and, more so, why I'm here with Bryson. I'm not sure I have a believable excuse to offer them. Instead, I head to the stairs that lead into block A and take a seat. I can still see and hear Bryson from here.

I watch as the parking lot starts to empty. Soon the vehicles that remain belong to either the stragglers or the team. Bryson jogs into view a short while later. He scans the parking lot but doesn't see me. I watch as he pulls his phone from his pocket.

Where are you?

Instead of typing a response, I stand. He spots me and his frown morphs into a smile. Before I can walk toward him, though, Shannon, Natalie, and Isaac approach him. I sit back down. This is how I've lived my whole life—hidden and in the shadows. And the longer I stay here, the more tired I'm getting.

"We're heading to my place to celebrate the victory; do you want to come?" Isaac asks.

Bryson shakes his head. "I'm beat, man."

"You should be. You were on fire tonight," Natalie says.

"That's why you deserve to celebrate," Shannon says. I watch as she slides up to Bryson. "Come with us. It'll be fun."

"I'm really not in the mood," Bryson says. He very subtly creates space between them. I can't help but smile at the gesture.

Dustin runs up to them. "So, is he in?"

"No," Shannon whines. "He says he's tired."

"I told you he's become a real buzzkill lately," Dustin says. He pats Bryson on the back. "Must be old age."

"You're older than me," Bryson points out.

"Well, we should get going, then," Isaac says. He takes Natalie's hand in his. And the sight should make me feel a little jealous. Just last week it would have.

It doesn't take long for them to climb into Isaac's car and drive out of the parking lot. Bryson waves them off. I stand and walk toward him once more.

"I hate that you had to hide," Bryson says when I approach.

The smile that was on his face is gone. He even curses as he unlocks the Jeep and climbs in.

I join him. We don't go anywhere, though. "I'm sorry," Bryson says to me.

"For?"

"I don't think it's hit me until this week how scary it is to think about coming out. How cautious you have to be." He sighs. "Even when you like someone, you can't just outright show them. Everything has to be subtle. Or announced. There's, like, no middle ground. You're either in the closet or you have to *announce* that you're gay and dating. You can't just do it." Bryson starts the Jeep. "It's such bullshit."

I offer him a small smile. "I admire people like Eric Ferguson who just live their truth."

"Yeah, I'm starting to understand just how brave Eric is."

Bryson scrolls through a playlist on his phone before hitting play. He pulls out of the parking lot, and soon we are surrounded by one of the Graces' ballads. It's a song about liking a boy for the first time. The song choice feels deliberate. I study the boy next to me.

"You know, I haven't scored a hat trick since sophomore year," Bryson says. "I think you may be my lucky charm."

"I should come to more of your games, then."

"I'd love that," Bryson admits. "It was kinda cool knowing my boyfriend was there to support me." He laughs. "I guess I'm starting to get the perks of dating in high school."

"I know I'm not the first of your dates to watch your soccer games."

"You're not," Bryson says. "But it's the first time I've felt *this*."

"Felt what?" My heart's in my throat.

Bryson doesn't speak. As I watch him drive, I keep playing over and over all the times that have made me question if Bryson Keller is straight. I want to ask him about it. I need to, for my own peace of mind, and for the sake of my heart, which will be breaking come next week. By the time we pull up to the front of my house, I've finally worked up the courage to speak. I clear my throat, ready to ask the question that needs to be asked.

"Are you—" Just then, his phone rings. Bryson looks from me to the ringing phone.

"It's my mom. She's away on a trip until Saturday. So I should take this."

"Go ahead."

Bryson answers the phone. "Hey, Mom. How—what?" Bryson's frown deepens as he listens to his mother. "What kind of accident?" Two minutes later, he hangs up. He turns to me. "My sister's in the hospital."

"What happened?" I ask.

"She was in a car accident on her way home from college."

"Is she okay?" I reach for his shoulder. Bryson leans into my touch.

He nods. "Mom says it's just minor injuries. But I should head over there."

"Do you need me to come?"

"No," Bryson says. "I'll be fine. Thanks for offering, though."

"No problem." I grab my things and reach for the door handle.

"I promise we'll talk more." Our eyes lock. "Soon."

"Okay," I say as I climb from the Jeep. I watch as Bryson drives off. He stops in front of the neighbor's house and reverses. Bryson rolls down the window and I bend to look into the car.

"To answer your question," Bryson says. "Yes, I think I might be."

And with that, he pulls off, leaving me breathless and full of even more questions.

THURSDAY

15

I won't get to see Bryson at all today. Which makes me want to simply just roll over and stay in bed. I blink the world into focus and reach for my phone. I reply to a message in my group chat before checking out Instagram.

I scroll through my feed and stop on one of Bryson. It's a selfie of him in his sister's hospital room. There's a small smile on his face, and even without a filter he looks good.

Babysitting today, the caption reads, with a doctor emoji. Already there are over fifty likes, even though the picture was only posted about fifteen minutes ago. I double-tap the picture and smile at the red heart.

My phone buzzes with a text from Kelly mere heartbeats later.

You're up? Yay!

I smile and respond: *How'd you sleep?*

Eh, not good, Bryson says. *Very tired. I was here at the hospital until late. My sister's getting discharged in a few hours. Concussion and whiplash. She'll be stiff, but nothing too serious.*

You should get some more rest.

Haha do I need some beauty sleep? Bryson adds a winking face.

Is it even possible for you to not look good?

You flirt you.

A few seconds later, another text follows.

Got to go. Chat later.

This time the kissing face that follows is intentional—I'm sure of it. I think back to last night and Bryson's confession. We need to talk about it, but it's the type of conversation that needs to be had in person, face-to-face.

I lock my phone and climb from my bed. I walk to the bathroom and begin my morning ritual. I've become used to being done by seven o'clock because of Bryson, so by then I'm already dressed. I realize too late that I've done everything too quickly.

With a sigh, I head downstairs and find Dad making waffles. Mom sits at the island as usual with her iPad open to today's news. She scrolls through the articles but stops at the sight of me. Mom fake gasps when she sees me taking a seat next to her.

"Is it really you?" she asks.

"It has to be a mirage," Dad adds.

"Maybe a hallucination."

I'll be the first to admit that I haven't been spending as much time with my family as I normally would, but it's only been three days. If this is how they're reacting now, how are they going to handle it in a few months' time when I head off to college?

"Are we tripping right now?" Mom asks.

"Funny," I say.

Dad laughs. "Are you eating with us today?"

"Yeah." I reach for the coffeepot. I pour myself a cup and add two sugars and some cream.

"How was the game yesterday?"

"Priya scored, so we won." I take a sip of my coffee. As I drink, I find myself missing what has become my routine with Bryson. He was right when he said the bacon and eggs at Glenda's were the best. "The boys won, too."

"You watched that game, too?" Mom asks.

"Yeah, I wanted to see what all the fuss was about."

"Baby steps," Dad says. "I might make you a soccer fan yet."

Mom shakes her head. "I don't need to find two people asleep on the couch. Why even bother waking up if you're just going to fall asleep instead of watching?"

Yazz rolls into the kitchen. "Oh, you're still here." She looks me up and down. "I hate to admit this, but I miss our morning altercations."

"I don't," Mom says.

"I'm pretty sure the neighbors don't, either," Dad adds.

"We aren't that loud," I say.

Yazz pours herself some cereal and adds milk. "We're loud because we love each other."

"*Jislaaik*, you two fight all the time but are so similar," Dad says as he takes the final vacant seat. He piles his plate with his own share of waffles.

"Most parents would be thrilled to know that Yazz and I are so close."

"Well, most parents did not raise you and Yazz," Mom says. Dad holds up his hand and she high-fives him.

Yazz and I roll our eyes. Sometimes our parents' corniness is too much to deal with. Thankfully, Donny sends a text that he's arrived.

"I'm off," I say. I grab my bag and pull on my blazer. I inhale and am thrilled to discover that Bryson's scent lingers.

"Enjoy your day, *boytjie!*" Dad says.

"Bye," Yazz says in between bites. "Congratulate Priya on her goal for me."

I race from the house and head for the Quackmobile.

"No morning practice with Bryson today?" Donny asks.

"No. He's out today."

"Oh, right, I saw the post in the hospital this morning," Priya says.

"Bryson's in the hospital?"

"No," I say to Donny. "His sister is. You seriously need to get Instagram. Stop living in the Dark Ages."

"Donald refuses to succumb to my peer pressure and get Instagram. And so my feed alone is filled with our cute-couple selfies," Priya says.

"Uh, I'm pretty sure you're meant to let other people call your pictures cute," I say.

Priya shrugs. "I call it like I see it."

"Are you saying Priya and I aren't cute?" Donny catches my eye in the rearview mirror.

"I plead the Fifth."

"It's not too late to make you walk to school," Donny says.

"I'd just take the bus."

"Oh, right. That reminds me"—Priya twists in her seat so that she can look at us both—"I heard that Bryson might be losing his dare this week."

"What do you mean?" I'm happy that Donny asks the question that I wanted to.

"Well, the soccer team was talking about how his girl-friend hasn't posted on Instagram this week. And even She Who Shall Not Be Named doesn't know who it is. And you know that's a mission of hers every week: to find out just who Bryson is dating." Priya lifts her phone. "I checked the hashtag and it's truly barren."

"Maybe they want to keep their relationship secret," Donny says.

"Everyone knows this is just for fun. So why?"

"Maybe the person lives in the Dark Ages like Donny and doesn't have Instagram," I say. My face starts to redden. I can only hope my blush won't be a dead giveaway that I know more than I'm sharing.

"Huh, maybe." Priya nods. "That makes sense."

Donny pulls into the school parking lot and we all climb from the Quackmobile. Even though I know the white Jeep won't be there, I find myself scanning the space for it. Even arriving at school without Bryson feels strange.

"I need to talk to my lab partner about something," Priya says. "So I'm off. I'll see you later."

"Will you be okay by yourself?" Donny asks me.

I nod. "Go be the dutiful boyfriend that you long to be," I tease.

Donny salutes. "Aye, aye, captain." I watch as he runs after Priya. He catches up to her and grabs her hand in his. The sight takes me back to when Bryson held my hand.

We seriously need to talk.

A soccer ball rolls to a stop against my leg. I look up and find Isaac jogging toward me.

"You okay?" Isaac asks. "You look dazed."

"Yeah. Fine," I say. And I don't even blush. Any other time, Isaac Lawson talking to me would have left me breathless and a stuttering mess. Instead, I pick up the ball and hand it to him. When our fingers brush, I feel nothing. The space that Isaac once occupied in my heart currently has a new tenant.

I head to the auditorium and take my seat. To distract myself while I wait for the start of class, I pull out my lines for our performance tomorrow. I can almost recite them all, but I need to be completely off script for tomorrow to be a success. I don't want our pair to get a low grade because of me.

The start-of-period bell rings, and Mrs. Henning climbs the stairs onto the stage. Today she looks like she's about to play in a polo match. She's wearing white pants, with black riding boots to complete the ensemble.

"Good morrow, my thespians. Just a reminder not only that your performances are tomorrow but also that tomorrow afternoon is the new deadline for you to submit the writing samples. I will not extend it again. So if you'd like to be considered for the position of cowriter for our next production, please submit your pieces by lunch tomorrow."

I finished my script last night. Finally wrote the ending that I didn't get the chance to write on Monday. And I hate it. It isn't my best work, and I'm not sure how to fix it. I sigh. I need inspiration, but I just have too much on my mind to find some.

While Mrs. Henning goes about assigning the roles for this class, my phone buzzes. I pull it from my pocket and see a text from Kelly:

I miss you, is that weird?

I take a deep breath and decide to be honest.

No, because I miss you too.

16

After school, I'm sitting in my bedroom at my desk, staring at the blinking cursor. It mocks me and my failure. I've been trying to fix this ending for the last hour. I sigh, get up, and throw myself face-first onto my bed. The words are just not coming. They're being held hostage somewhere in my brain, and I don't even know where to begin to rescue them.

My phone buzzes with a text. I pull it from charge and roll over to read the message. It's from Kelly.

What are you doing?

I was trying to write.

Write what? he asks.

My sample for Henning. I don't want to miss the new deadline.

Maybe you need inspiration, Bryson says. He sends a waving emoji. And a minute later a picture comes through. It's a selfie of him making a funny face. *Hello, my name is Muse. I am at your service,* the caption reads.

Haha. You must be bored. What are you doing?

I am incredibly bored. Crystal's friends are over, so I don't have much to do.

I sit up. Bryson and I need to talk. I'm currently home alone. If this isn't a sign, then I don't know what is. *Do you want to come over?*

For the first time in my life, I invite a boy I like over. I don't count that time I invited Colby Matthews over under the guise of wanting to show him my superhero action figure collection. Colby Matthews had been really into superheroes, and so I, too, had shown an interest in them. That visit was an awkward disaster and I refuse to have history repeat itself. This time I will not suggest we play any sort of game that may result in a broken window.

I look around my room and see it through Bryson's eyes. My room is a mess. I rush to pick up all the old—and new— clothes strewn across the floor. I try my best to neaten my desk, which is always littered with notebooks filled with half-baked ideas and scenes that need to be developed more. The pages of my sample mock me as I shut my computer.

I'm in the bathroom styling my hair in a way that will look natural and cool, and not at all overthought, when Bryson rings the doorbell. My heart pounds in my chest as I race down the stairs. When I reach the door, I pause and take a calming breath. What we started to discuss yesterday plays over and over in my head. Will we finish what we started? Will we confirm what is real and what is not between us?

I open the door and find a grinning Bryson. He's wearing

shorts, a golf shirt, and designer sneakers. I look down at my own outfit. I'm wearing a blue shirt with the word UNIFORM in bold across the front, brown shorts, and black socks. I changed just after inviting him over. I look somewhat semi-decent, I think.

"Hey, come in," I say. "How's your sister doing?"

"Fine. A bit bruised and blue. Her arm's in a cast, but she'll recover soon."

"That's good," I say. "I'm glad." Bryson pauses at the entrance and takes off his shoes. His socks have Pokémon drawings on them. I laugh. "Nice socks." I turn and lead him toward the stairs.

Bryson stops at the foot of the stairs, his attention caught by the large family portrait that hangs on one of the walls.

"You look like your dad," Bryson says. He looks at me and then back to the picture.

"Not everyone thinks so," I say. "I remember when I was about twelve, Dad and I were returning from visiting our family in South Africa when some random stranger at LAX stopped my dad to ask whose child I was. Even at that age I remember the awkwardness of the situation and the hurt that crossed Dad's face as he needed to explain that I was his child. Like it's so absurd that because my dad has dark brown skin, he can't possibly have a child that looks like me." I shake my head. "You wouldn't believe how many people actually question whether or not I am mixed race. It's like they have this idea of how I'm supposed to look, and I clearly don't, so to them I'm less authentic."

"That's such crap," Bryson says. "People really and truly suck major donkey balls."

"Yeah, it's been tough having to deal with the race policing."

"I'm sorry," Bryson says.

"It's not your fault." Bryson follows me up the stairs and we enter my bedroom.

"They say you can tell a lot about a person from their bedroom," Bryson says. He walks around my room. I mentally pat myself on the back for trying to clean up. Posters of my favorite bands and musicians line my walls—a lot of them are of the Graces. Bryson pauses in front of the biggest of them all. It's a picture of Ezra Grace. "This is a great shot of him."

"I bought the physical album just to get it." I point at the never-before-played CD. "I already owned their album digitally, but I wanted the poster."

Bryson walks over to my desk and looks on the wall above it, which is covered with notes for the fantasy book I'm working on and pictures of my life. "When was this taken?" he asks. He points at a picture of me in a long wig and a pirate getup. In the picture, I'm standing between Priya, who's dressed up as Rey from Star Wars, and Donny, who's wearing a plain white T-shirt that announces him as the comment section—truly the scariest place. He actually came in second for the costume.

"Last Halloween. I was Jack Sparrow before Johnny Depp became a mess."

"Cute." He moves toward my bookshelf. "You have a lot of books."

"It's the way to my heart," I say before I catch myself. "I mean, my friends and family know what I want for presents."

"When's your birthday?"

I startle at the question. "April fifteenth. Why?"

"That's soon. I better get book shopping."

"Do you plan to still be dating me by then?" I mean it as a joke, but Bryson fixes me with a look, and when he answers, he's dead serious.

"Yes."

"We should stop," I say, suddenly panicked.

I can't fall any farther. Bryson Keller and this five-day relationship are quicksand. The more time I spend with him, the more I find myself sinking deeper and deeper. I'm not sure if he means the words he's saying or if he's simply playing the part of the perfect boyfriend. Delivering the lines that the role requires.

"Stop what?"

"This, whatever this is," I say. "It's getting too hard to figure out. Why are you doing this? Saying all these things?"

"Because I mean them," Bryson says. "You may not believe me yet—hell, a part of me doesn't believe it, either—but I've decided to live in the here and now and trust myself." The sincerity in Bryson's words is impossible to ignore.

We stare at each other. This is it. This is the whole reason I invited him over.

"Please, trust me," Bryson says. "I need you to trust me. This is all scary and new for me, too."

"What do you mean?" I ask. I need him to say it. Is that unfair of me? I don't know.

"I don't think I'm straight. I mean, I never really had a reason to question it until I met you." His brow is furrowed. "Surely I should have known this about myself from the start?"

I'm surprised by how easily he's admitted it. "How are you so comfortable with all this?"

"It's hard to explain, but for the longest time something has felt off. I didn't know what it was until this week, until you. It's like spending time with you and listening to you talk about being gay made sense to me. Everything finally clicked. Like a puzzle." Bryson shakes his head. He rubs his hands on his shorts, almost like they're sweaty. Bryson's standing near my bookshelf, and I'm at the foot of my bed. Even though there's distance between us, this is the closest we've ever been.

I'm nervous, and I can only imagine what Bryson's heart must be doing.

"I don't know if it's weird that I didn't know this about myself," Bryson continues. "I was on Reddit reading about first-time experiences with guys and I came across this one post. He shared how all through high school he thought he was straight, and then he got to college and met this guy who was gay and found himself attracted to him. Is that what's happening with me?"

"It's different for everyone. There are no hard-set rules," I say. His words bloom in my chest. They are everything I wanted to hear from him . . . needed to hear. I close the distance between us. I could reach out to touch him if I wanted. Our eyes lock.

"I guess you're right." He runs a hand through his hair. "The truth is that I don't know if I'm gay. Yes, I like you, but does that mean I'm gay, too? You're the first guy I've liked. The only one so far. Maybe I'm bi?" He throws his hands up. "I don't know. Shouldn't I know? But, I mean, I've always believed love is love."

"It doesn't have to make you anything. Besides, you can figure it out later. It's been less than a week. Trust me, it took me a couple of years before I understood that I was gay. And a bit more time to accept it."

"Can . . . can I figure it out with you?" he asks. Bryson leans against my bookshelf for a heartbeat before standing straight. Bryson looks unsure what to do with himself. He shuffles on his feet, and it's clear that the confidence that is synonymous with Bryson Keller is gone.

"With me," I say. "Let's figure this out together."

He smiles then—it's part relief, part joy.

"Good." Bryson exhales loudly. "Because this is all kinds of scary." He holds up his thumb and finger so that they are inches apart. "But you make it a little less scary."

"You've been putting on a brave face."

"I was worried that you would run away. It's a lot of pressure for me to say to you that because of you I'm starting to think that maybe I'm not straight."

"I won't run," I say.

"Well then, we should celebrate," Bryson says.

"What do you want to do?"

"Let's go on a date. It's Thursday afternoon. I doubt any-one we know will be around. I think it's the perfect time." It's clear he's put thought into this.

This week I've already spent so much time with Bryson. We've gotten breakfast together before school and he's driven me home. We even watched a movie together. Those could all be considered dates, but Bryson doesn't seem to feel that way.

"We don't have to—" I start to say, but he cuts me off.

"Why not?" he asks. "We're boyfriends. Going on dates is what we should be doing."

17

If anyone had told me last Thursday that this time next week I'd be on a date with Bryson Keller, I would've smacked them in the face and called them stupid. And yet, here I am.

Here *we* are.

In recent years this boardwalk has become a hot spot in Fairvale, but given the time of week, it's emptier than usual. I scan the people around us and find no one I know. Bryson was right: no one really goes on a date on a Thursday afternoon.

The Duckworths bought the pier from the previous owners and revamped it to be what it is today. It's almost the perfect replica of the Santa Monica Pier. Being best friends with Donny meant visiting this place so much when we were younger that I now know it as well as the back of my hand.

The beachfront has a variety of stores that cater to almost every need. For those craving something sweet, there's Candyland. There's also a variety of smaller stalls that sell cotton candy, popcorn, and even candy apples. The latter is a family favorite of the Sheridans'. Sometimes Dad buys them and brings them home—we don't even need to visit the board-walk.

Whenever I come here to eat, Angelo's Pizza Emporium is at the top of my list. Angelo's serves the best thin-crust pizza in Fairvale. It also doesn't hurt that last summer Isaac started working there part-time. It felt like fate then, but looking at Bryson next to me, I now think it was just a stop on the journey.

I try to hide my smile, but Bryson's words from before replay in my mind. It feels like I'm dreaming. Maybe I need someone to pinch me, but I'm too scared. I don't want to leave this place just yet, to leave this feeling behind.

"We should ride the Ferris wheel before we go," Bryson says. He points at the ride in the distance. It looks empty.

I shake my head. "Hard pass."

"What's wrong?"

"I'm not a fan of heights," I tell him. "I'm told the view is amazing from up there, and I choose to believe those people."

"Noted." Bryson smiles. "Well, there's plenty of other stuff to do." We head toward the crowd. We're walking next to one another, close enough to touch, but not. Everything feels different between us now, like everything we do or say matters more than it did a day ago.

Whatever this is, it's something.

It's real.

Tangible.

Unexplainable.

But it's all happening to me—and it's all happening with him.

We join the surge of people, and almost instantly I'm assaulted by laughter and joy and the smell of freshly popped popcorn. Bryson and I line up at the ticket booth and purchase a strip of tickets that will allow us to play some of the games.

"What should we do first?"

"Let's try that," Bryson says. He points at a game stand to our right. It's big and green and in the shape of a dinosaur, but the dinosaur has different-sized holes cut into its body. The thrower needs to put the balls through those cutouts.

We push our way there and Bryson hands the attendant a ticket for his chance to take aim. Bryson throws, and he misses.

"That was just for practice," he says.

He throws again, and it's another miss.

Another one follows soon after.

"Still practicing?" I ask.

Around us the crowd snickers. Even when we're not at school, eyes seem to follow Bryson wherever he goes. It's the burden of looking like Bryson Keller does. But it's more than just his good looks—Bryson exudes a charisma that draws you to him, so attention sticks to him like clothing on a hot summer day.

As I watch Bryson throw his final ball and miss, I know

that whatever happens in the future, I don't regret spending this time with Bryson. Come what may, I'm all in.

"How are you so bad at this?" I ask as we walk away from the crime scene of Bryson's epic failure.

Bryson laughs. It's a sound so deep and pure that I want to bottle it up and keep it with me forever.

"There's a reason I play soccer and not baseball," he says.

"So you're saying that if you could use your feet you'd win?"

"Yes." Bryson pumps up his chest. "I have the highest goal count in California, three years in a row."

"Really?" I smile. I lean closer to him. "My boyfriend's pretty cool," I whisper.

Bryson smiles, too. "Smooth, Sheridan. Real smooth."

"I told you I give as good as I get."

"I'm glad," Bryson says. "Come on, let's go find something I can actually win at. I need to redeem myself."

It takes us three tries and three more failed attempts until we find something that Bryson is good at. My cheeks hurt from all the laughing, and my heart is so full that it feels like it's going to burst at the seams. We're standing in front of the hammer to test how strong you are. Bryson makes a show of preparing. He rubs his hands together and fake spits on them before he picks up the hammer.

Bryson brings it down with as much force as he can muster. We both watch as the points shoot up. When it sets a new record, Bryson drops the hammer and starts jumping in place.

"People watching would think you won the lottery."

"In life you need to celebrate all victories, big and small."

"But you didn't actually win anything," I point out. All the other games that he played and lost had prizes in the end. This one does not.

"I got to look cool in front of my boyfriend," Bryson says. "That's winning."

The attendant in charge gives us a thumbs-up. He's big and bald with tattoos running up the length of his arms. He's scary-looking, but the smile on his face isn't at all. "You two make a very cute couple."

"Thank you," Bryson says. "I also think my boyfriend is the cutest."

I choke on my own spit and Bryson ends up patting my back.

"You okay?" he asks.

How can I be when he's said something like that?

"Fine," I lie.

"Let's get something to drink." I follow him as he heads toward a stall, and we buy something to drink and two corn dogs. We walk along the boardwalk and lose ourselves to the sounds of waves breaking and seagulls crying overhead.

"This is fun," I say. I turn to him and notice a mustard streak at the side of his mouth. Without thinking, I reach for it and wipe it off. We look at each other, and I pull my hand back. It hangs there between us.

Bryson smiles again. "Amazing."

"What is?" I ask nervously.

"This." Bryson looks around us. "Being here with you. You meant it when you said you were going to trust me."

I nod. "Well, yeah." I shrug awkwardly.

"Thanks."

"For what?" I don't look at him as I take the final bite of my corn dog.

"For not running away." It sounds like he's talking about something other than me. I think of the little bit Bryson's told me about his father. I want to ask him about it, to delve deeper into Bryson Keller, but I don't think it's the time yet. For now, this is enough. Later, I will explore the layers that make up this boy next to me.

A stall to my right catches my eye. The lady is selling small trinkets. I scan what's for sale and my eyes land on a bracelet. It calls to me like a siren song.

I buy it and return to Bryson's side. He's standing on the pier, looking over the railing at the sea below. I hold out the bracelet to him.

"What's this?" he asks.

"It's for luck."

"Luck?"

"Well, you said I was your lucky charm at the game yesterday, so consider this my proxy for when I can't be there."

Bryson holds up his arm, and with shaking fingers I tie the bracelet into place. It's nothing fancy, a simple deep blue string with a metal anchor that glints in the sun. But the way that Bryson's looking at it makes it seem like it's worth so much more.

Bryson smiles. "You keep surprising me, Kai Sheridan."

"I keep telling people I'm special," I joke.

He looks from the bracelet at his wrist to my eyes.

"Yes. You are," Bryson says. And I can tell that he's serious.

Afternoon bleeds into evening as we wander from stall to stall. I'm eating a candy apple when my eyes catch on a claw machine standing all alone. It lures me toward it with its cartoonish song.

"These things are impossible to win at," Bryson says. He stands next to me as I fish out one of the last of my tickets. I straighten the ends before feeding it into the machine. It gives me a cheerful hello.

"Watch and learn," I say. There are few things in this world that I am extremely confident in. Winning at the claw machine is one of them. During freshman year, when Priya was dating her ex-boyfriend, Donny and I would spend countless hours here, and this game became my specialty. I use the joystick to maneuver the claw machine until it hangs over the prize I want—a bear holding a soccer ball.

There's no real trick to winning at this game. It is all about timing, and having practiced so much, I'm good at judging the exact moment I need to hit the button to release the claw.

I tap the button with more force than is necessary and watch as the claw opens and descends. Bryson's face is almost pressed against the glass as he watches. The metal claw grips the stuffed animal by the leg. It's not a perfect grip, but the bear doesn't fall as the claw pulls it up. We hold our breath as the claw moves to drop the bear into the hole.

Thank God.

Bryson turns to me, eyes ablaze with wonder. "I'm impressed," he says.

He claps for me and I mock bow. Then I bend to retrieve the stuffed animal. "Here." I hold it out to him.

"You won it," Bryson says. "It's yours."

"I won it for you, though," I say. "It has a soccer ball—see." I shove the bear toward him. He accepts it and smiles, revealing his secret dimple.

"Thank you." Bryson looks from the prize to me. "Is there anything else you want to do?"

I scan the boardwalk behind us and the photo booth catches my eye. It's another thing that I've fantasized doing with my boyfriend. I've seen Priya and Donny do it—couple snapshots in a photo strip. I've always been more than a little jealous about it. Sure, we've taken pictures as friends, but I've always dreamed of doing so with my boyfriend.

"What is it?" Bryson asks. "You just thought of something."

"Nothing."

"Tell me."

"I just . . . I've always wanted to take pictures in a photo booth." I don't look at him as I say the next words. "With my boyfriend."

"We can if you want," Bryson says. "Are you sure you'll be okay having proof of this date?"

"Are you?"

Bryson shrugs. "I'm more worried about you."

I think of not doing it, of just ignoring that it's something

I've always wanted to do. It would be safer for me to do that. But at what point do I start living for me? When do I get to do simple things that are meant to make me happy?

All around me people are living their lives free and happy, and here I am stuck in a dark and cold closet. The constant second-guessing is exhausting. So for now I choose to live in this moment. Today is what matters. Tomorrow will have to take care of itself.

I walk past him and, over my shoulder, call out, "Let's go."

Bryson jogs to catch up to me. He cradles the bear under his arm as we walk toward the photo booth. It's empty so we don't have to wait our turn. We step into the photo booth and close the curtain behind us. The space is small, forcing us to be pressed together.

Bryson works the machine. "Ready?" he asks. I nod. He hits the button and on the screen the countdown starts.

Three.

Bryson throws his arm over my shoulders.

Two.

He puts two fingers up above my head.

One.

I smile.

The camera flashes, taking the first picture. We alter our poses goofily for each one. With one more left to take, Bryson leans in toward me. I feel his lips on my face just as the camera flashes.

"All done," he says. He opens the curtain and steps out, leaving me behind to bask in my surprise and happiness. With a big smile on my face, I exit and find Bryson holding the strip of photos. My eyes snag on the last one.

It's tangible proof that Bryson Keller likes me. My eyes are wide in surprise, and there's no denying the flush in my cheeks. Bryson's eyes are closed as he pecks me.

"Perfect," he says.

I look from the photo to Bryson and realize that yes, he is perfect. I pocket the strip of photos. I'll hide them so that no one can find them.

Bryson looks at the stalls that surround us. "How about some cotton candy before we leave?"

"Sounds good." We head toward the stall and join a long line. The boardwalk is getting busier. We've timed our exit just right.

We're standing at the cotton candy stand when I spot two familiar faces. They see me just as I see them. Priya and Donny.

"What are you doing here?" Priya asks.

"I could ask you the same thing." I look at them. "It's a Thursday afternoon."

"It's a makeup date," Donny says. "We needed to clear the air."

"So you guys finally made up," Bryson says. He looks from me to my friends. "You guys talk." He points to an empty space by the pier railing. "I'll stay in line."

We walk toward the railing. I look over at the crashing waves. We're silent for a while before Donny speaks.

"Since when are you and Bryson so close?" he asks.

"We're not," I lie. I turn and lean against the metal railing.

"Kai, you know you can tell us anything, right?" Priya says. She meets my gaze, and I can see the knowledge there.

My heart starts to race, and I feel my face redden. My panic threatens to overwhelm me because I can tell that she knows.

I can deny it. I can act like I don't know what she's talking about, but just like that time with Bryson in the prop room, I find that I don't want to. This week with Bryson has changed me. It's made me greedy for the same acceptance that everyone else gets. Besides, I'm simply tired of lying to the people I love.

I exhale. "How long have you known?"

"Known what?" Donny asks. He looks between us. "Oh, that Kai's gay?"

Priya punches him on his arm, and he groans in pain.

"What?" I ask. "You know that I'm gay, too?"

"We're your best friends—of course we knew," Donny says as he rubs at his biceps. "We were just waiting for you to tell us."

"Yeah. I had hoped to handle this all with a bit more tact, but you know Donald." Priya looks at her boyfriend. "He's like an untrained puppy."

"Totally lovable, right?" Donny blinks his eyes dramatically, which earns him another smack from Priya, but even she can't hide her smile. Donny has a geeky cuteness about him.

I frown as I remember the conversation in the cafeteria a couple of days ago. "If you knew that I was gay, why did you want to know who Kelly was?" I point out.

"That didn't mean I thought you were straight." Donny

smiles. "Priya made me promise that we'd act like we didn't know until you were ready to tell us."

Priya looks from me to Bryson. We all turn to watch him then. He must feel our eyes on him, because he looks up from his phone and offers us a small wave. He's smiling, but it's tight-lipped. It's the smile he uses when he's nervous.

"So, what, is this a date?" Donny jokes.

When I don't answer, both Priya and Donny turn to me.

"Don't tell me—" Priya says just as Donny says, "Wait! It's true—" They stop speaking and look at one another. Then they shift their attention to me.

"Seriously?" they ask in perfect unison.

I smile.

"Dude!"

"Tell us everything."

And for the first time in my life, I do. I talk openly and freely to my best friends. And it feels so good.

It feels just right.

FRIDAY

18

My leg won't stop shaking. It moves up and down without my having any say in the matter. Bryson and I are seated in the back row of the auditorium. We're waiting for Mrs. Henning to call us to perform. Right now, Isaac is onstage, but I'm too nervous to care.

Bryson places his hand on my knee and I stop moving.

He grips it tightly. "It's going to be okay," he says. "Just look at me, only me, and trust me."

I exhale a nervous breath. We're one of the last groups waiting to perform.

"I don't think anyone's going to believe our performance."

"Why?"

"I'm Romeo and you're Benvolio." I turn to look at him. "How does that make any sense?"

"Why not?" Bryson asks.

I snort. "Because you're the leading man in almost every sense of the word, and I'm just a supporting character."

Bryson leans in, closing the distance between us. His next

words are just for me, just for my heart. "Don't ever say that again," he says. "You're every bit as much the leading man as anyone else. Never forget that, and remember that I like you just the way you are."

Before I can say anything or even react, Mrs. Henning calls for us. "Bryson and Kai, you're next," she says. Today she's wearing an ensemble that looks to be Victorian inspired. She even has a cane.

But how can I go anywhere when Bryson Keller just said he is attracted to me? How does moving from this spot make any sense? I should live here now, never moving, never budging. Please forward all mail to this address.

Bryson grabs my hand and pulls me to my feet. He lets go and makes his way toward the stage. I follow, my stomach twisting.

We take our places on the stage. I blink and everyone in the class comes back into focus. Those who have already performed occupy the first two rows of seats. Mrs. Henning sits at the center.

"What have you chosen to perform?"

"We selected a scene from *Romeo and Juliet*," Bryson answers.

"Wonderful," Mrs. Henning says. "In my youth, Baz Luhrmann, the famous director of the 1996 movie, considered casting me in it. Of course, at the time of shooting, one of my characters on *My Face, Your Life* had just returned from being abducted by aliens, so I wasn't in the right place emotionally to commit to a role in such a film. You know as actors it's about living your role. I was nominated for an Emmy that season." Mrs. Henning straightens her black skirt and rests her hands on the top of the cane. "So this movie has always held a special place in my heart. I can't wait to see your interpretation. Who will you be performing as?"

"I'll be Benvolio," Bryson says. "And Kai will be Romeo."

"Very interesting choices," Mrs. Henning says. "I look forward to being dazzled."

I don't know about being dazzling, but I'm going to try my best. Bryson and I did a run-through last night before he dropped me off at home after our date. And then this morning at Glenda's, we worked through the scene again. I know that I am as prepared as I possibly can be.

"We can do this," Bryson mouths. I nod.

"Whenever you're ready," Mrs. Henning says. She taps her cane on the floor to silence some of the whispering around her.

I'm so nervous that I'm numb. I try to ignore my racing heart and quickly reddening face as much as I can. Bryson delivers his first line. And I react like I've practiced. I turn to look at Bryson and find that he's looking at me. No, it's Benvolio looking at Romeo.

Everything fades away. I imagine that we're performing with no one watching. Bryson embodies the character of Benvolio. At first I'm stilted as Romeo, but soon I get carried away on the wave of Bryson's performance. The scene unfolds in a blur, and I'm sure that later I won't be able to remember any of it. Not the words I mess up, or the awkward way I move across the stage.

At the end, Bryson takes my hand in his and we both bow. He squeezes my hand once before letting it go and we stand up straight to await our critique.

"Bryson, please, I beg you to try out for the next production. Your talent should be shared with a wider audience. What I truly love about your performance is your confidence. You aren't afraid to go for it. Which is a must as an actor. There were many times on my show where my characters did things that I thought were absolutely absurd, but if you act with confidence, that is when real performances are born."

Mrs. Henning looks down at her notes briefly before turning her attention to me. "Kai, this is probably the best you've performed in this class. You and Bryson work well together. The chemistry between your two characters felt real. I believed them, and that's what I want to see as an audience member." Mrs. Henning applauds in that special way of hers, where she taps only the tips of her fingers together. "This was a successful performance. Bravo!"

The rest of the class claps politely as we leave the stage to take our seats.

"You did great," Bryson says. He smiles and all I can offer him in return is a sigh of relief. It is over. Finally. My knees feel weak, and my face is hot to the touch. For the rest of the period, I try to fan my blush away.

When the bell rings, I finally feel like myself. We both stand, but then I remember something. "I need to give my sample to Henning," I tell Bryson. "I'll see you in English."

I pull out my reimagining of *Romeo and Juliet*—a gay love story. Last night when I returned from our date, I felt inspired, so I sat down to write, and everything poured out of me. I started from scratch, so it's rushed and not perfect, but it's something. I'm confident in the potential. Even if I don't get selected this round, I'm happy that I at least tried. This week with Bryson has changed me. It may be a small act of bravery, writing a story like this, but it didn't even cross my mind last week.

Mrs. Henning is talking to Michael Donnelly, so I wait my turn.

"What can I do for you, Kai?" she asks when she's done.

I hold out my sample. "I'd like to enter this."

"I'm glad to have it," Mrs. Henning says.

"Thank you for extending the deadline." I smile. "*Romeo and Juliet* was tough for me to try to reimagine. I'm not sure if it works, but I'm glad I got the chance to submit this."

"That's the attitude you need to have to make it as a creative. Whether it's acting or writing, you have to always try. *Nos* will often come, but it takes only one *yes*." Mrs. Henning smiles at me. "I believe in you, Kai. As does Mr. Keller."

"Bryson?" I ask.

"Yes. He paid me a visit to ask for an extension. His passionate plea played a small part in convincing me to extend the deadline." Mrs. Henning chuckles. "He's a great friend to have."

I remain silent. Stunned that even before Bryson and I

became what we are now, he had done this for me. Bryson Keller is so much more than a friend to me—and I wouldn't have it any other way.

"Before you're late, you should hurry along to your next class," Mrs. Henning says.

"Thank you, ma'am."

I race from drama to English and make it there just as the bell is ringing. Mr. Weber shoots me a look, and I offer an apologetic bow of the head as I slide into my seat.

English and math pass without much happening, and soon I'm sitting at the three musketeers table. I realize that this is the first time that the real me is having lunch with my best friends. I feared coming out to them, and I am so relieved to know that my fear was in vain.

I lucked out when Priya and Donny became my friends.

"What?" Priya asks when she catches me staring at her. "Do I have something on my face?"

"Just beauty," Donny says before I can respond.

"You're ridiculous," Priya says.

I laugh. Everything is absolutely normal, as it should be. My being out doesn't make me any different from the Kai they have always known. I'm the same. We're the same. The only thing that's different is how I feel inside. It's like a knot that I've been carrying around has finally untied. I've waited my whole life for this.

Now with Donny and Priya, every breath, smile, and laugh belongs to the real me.

This is Kai Sheridan.

19

I'm staring at the clock when the final bell rings on Friday afternoon, and with it my fake relationship with Bryson Keller ends. It's officially over. At least those were the rules, but I'm hoping they don't apply anymore. Even with the memory of yesterday fresh in my mind, I still feel a flash of anxiety.

My phone buzzes with a text from Kelly.

You sure you're going home with Donny?

Yes. I'll see you later though.

Of course. I'll pick you up at six.

Please ignore any and all embarrassing things that my parents will say.

I am ready. Bryson texts a series of grinning emojis. *See you tonight.*

Bryson is coaching the team at Yazz's school, so I'm standing at the Quackmobile, waiting for Donny and Priya.

"Sorry," Donny says as they rush over. "I had a math club meeting."

"Why is my boyfriend such a dorkus?" Priya asks.

"Math is cool. Math is fun," Donny starts to chant. He pumps his hands in the air like a cheerleader. "Math is cool. Math is fun. Math is for everyone."

"I think we should walk," I suggest.

"Agreed," Priya says.

Our comments only make Donny chant louder. He unlocks the car and walks over to the driver's side.

"Math is cool. Math is fun. Math is for everyone!"

We climb into the Quackmobile and Donny pulls out of the parking lot.

"Should we go somewhere?" Priya asks.

"We can," I say. "I just need to be home by five so I can get ready for the concert."

"What time are you leaving?"

"Bryson said he'd pick me up at six." Almost as if it were planned, both Priya and Donny say "Ooh-la-la" at the exact same time.

"You know, now that you have a boyfriend, we can totally double-date," Priya says.

"So is Bryson officially your boyfriend?" Donny asks.

"Well, I mean the dare ended today." I shrug. "We haven't really discussed it further than that."

"You need to define the relationship," Priya says. "Knowing you, if you don't, you'll be an anxious mess about it."

"Yeah, ask him what's up," Donny says. "Don't be scared."

"I'm very surprised that you, Kai Sheridan, asked Bryson out for the dare." Priya laughs. "When I think about it, I can't believe that we were all at the party when the dare started."

"Weren't you the one who said Bryson had to be asked out first? And he had to agree to whomever it was?" Donny asks.

"Yes. That was me," Priya says. She looks at me. "I'm like your very own fairy godmother. Cinderella who?"

"It's funny the Friday afternoon school bell is meant to be my clock striking midnight."

"Wait a minute. Does that make me a mouse?" Donny asks. "I don't think I like this."

"In some lights you do kind of look like a mouse," I say.

"Ooh, burn," Priya says.

"Hey, I'm your boyfriend. You should be defending me."

I laugh.

"Squeak, squeak, where are we going?" Donny asks.

"I'm hungry. Let's go eat," Priya says.

"Aye, aye, captain."

"How about . . ."

"Pizza," we all say at the same time. Donny drives toward the boardwalk, where Angelo's Pizza Emporium awaits. We find parking and climb from the Quackmobile. As soon as we enter Angelo's, we are assaulted by the smell of all things good and pure in this world.

"God, that smells great!" I say.

"If they bottled this scent, I'd probably wear it."

"No thank you," Priya says. "No matter how much I love it, I do not want my boyfriend smelling like pizza."

Angelo's has a few booths that line the walls, as well as freestanding tables. We slide into one of the empty booths.

A server approaches us and hands out menus. They are

green, white, and red—the colors of the Italian flag. The same colors are everywhere at Angelo's: white walls, red chair cushions, green-patterned tiles.

"Would you like something to drink?"

"I'll have a banana milkshake," I say.

"That's kinda gross," Priya says. "But you do you, Kai. I'll have a Coke, please."

"Make that two," Donny says.

By the time the server returns with our drinks, we're in a heated argument over toppings.

"We do this all the time," Priya says. "But I am telling you pineapple does not belong on a pizza. This is my hill and I am willing to die on it."

"But it's so good," Donny whines. "Kai, please, for once back me up."

"You know where I stand on this." But I smile at Donny and say to the server, "We'll have a half and half, please. Half Hawaiian and half Margherita."

Priya gasps and Donny looks up, surprised.

"What?"

"Traitor," Priya says.

"You know you love me," I say with a wink.

"Debatable."

Donny holds up his hand for a high five.

It doesn't take long for our pizza to come. Priya makes sure to keep away from the side with pineapple, and so do I. The only reason I ordered it was because of Donny. I just feel really thankful and grateful to them both for treating me like they did last week before they knew.

I love my best friends.

• • •

By the time I get home, my cheeks hurt from smiling.

"Oh, you're back," Mom says as she heads toward the family room. I trail in after her to find the rest of my family sprawled in front of the television.

"Yeah," I say. "But why is everyone else here so early?"

"We got called to Yazz's school."

"Again?" I look at my sister. She's lying on the carpet, a sketch pad open before her.

"What did you do this time?"

Yazz sits up. "It really wasn't my fault," she says. "I kept telling Monica not to touch my hair, but she kept insisting on it. I don't need to hear how surprised she is to find that it's soft, and so I told her as much." Yazz shakes her head. "I'm about this close to making a large sign to wear to school to tell people not to touch my hair."

"Did you hit her?"

"No."

"Then why were you called to the school?" I ask Mom and Dad.

"Because Monica started to cry," Yazz answers instead. "I know my words can feel like a beatdown, but I was very patient with her. I didn't want it to be this whole thing, but she had the nerve to cry."

"Good job," I say. "You have to nip these things in the bud."

"Yes, well done, Yazz," Dad says.

"Did you have fun, Kai? What did you do?" Mom asks me.

"We just hung out," I say.

"With Bryson?" Yazz asks. She's back to lounging on the floor.

"No. I was with Priya and Donny." I study her. "Why'd you ask?"

"Oh, Bryson posted a picture on Instagram, and the comment section is blowing up. Everyone wants to know who bought him the bracelet," Yazz says. She looks up at me. "It's a mystery."

Yazz is smart—sometimes too smart for her own good. But it's impossible that she's figured it out, right? No one in this room knows what's happening between Bryson and me.

"Bryson is who you're going to the concert with, right?" Mom asks. She's flipping through channels. I watch as she settles on the Food Network. Someone needs to change it before Mom gets inspired again. These are dangerous times.

"It's truly hard to believe that Kai is friends with Bryson Keller now," Yazz says. "The world as we know it is upside down."

"Is he popular?" Dad asks.

"Very," Yazz explains. "He's the 'it' boy of Fairvale Academy."

"Then, what's he doing with Kai?"

"Hey!" I say. "I have my charms."

"That may be true, honey, but you're also incredibly awkward," Mom says. Her words are matter-of-fact.

"So awkward," Dad chimes in.

"It's embarrassing just how awkward," Yazz adds.

"Well, there goes my self-esteem," I mutter. "Thank you very much." I turn to leave my family behind. They laugh in my wake.

"You know we love you, Kai," Mom calls out as I climb the stairs to my bedroom.

What picture is Yazz talking about? Behind closed doors, I pull out my phone and open Instagram. It's a selfie of Bryson, and he's showing off the bracelet that I bought. *Call me lucky 24/7*, the caption reads. I smile at how cheesy it is.

I open a text to Bryson and type: *Nice pic, Mr. Cheese.*

He responds a while later: *That's Mr. Grilled Cheese to you, sir.*

I laugh and put my phone on charge. I walk to the bathroom and shower. It doesn't take me long to get ready. I settle on black jeans, a band T-shirt, and my leather jacket with a black beanie. Soon it's ten to six. I head downstairs and find Mom putting on lipstick.

"Where are you off to?" I ask.

"Choir practice, Kai," Mom says.

"Oh, right."

"I have a solo this Sunday." She looks at me expectantly. "Will I see you there?"

I groan. "I don't know."

Mom sighs. "How did I end up with a son who hates church?"

Before I can respond, the doorbell rings. I use that as my excuse and go open the door. Bryson is standing there. He's wearing black jeans with rips at the knees, boots, and a bomber jacket. There's a backward cap on his head, too. Effortlessly hot.

Bryson must catch me checking him out because he smiles. I blush and stand aside to let him in.

"Cute," Bryson whispers as he passes me by the door. He stops to take off his shoes, and I lead him to meet my parents and Yazz.

"It's nice to meet you," Bryson says to my parents. He offers Yazz a wave and a smile that shows his hidden dimple.

"So this is Bryson Keller?" Dad asks.

"Wow. He's handsome," Mom muses.

"You do know he can hear you, right?" I ask my parents, even though I can't help but agree with Mom's comment, at least silently.

"Our parents can be somewhat embarrassing," Yazz says. She pushes her glasses up. "Forgive them."

Bryson laughs.

"We should head out," I say. They've seen him, they've met him. It's time to escape before Sherlock and Watson take over.

"You have your phone, right?" Mom asks.

"Yes, Mom," I say.

"Is it fully charged?" Dad asks.

"Yes, Dad." I pull it from my pocket and show them. The battery's at 98 percent. They both nod.

"Don't do anything stupid," Mom says.

"Or reckless," Dad adds.

"I won't. I promise."

"No drinking or smoking."

"You can trust me," I say, holding in my exasperation.

"It's not you we don't trust. It's everyone else." Mom follows us to the door. "I love you. Call me if anything happens."

"Nothing will. But I promise."

"Drive safe, Bryson," Dad says.

"I will, Mr. Sheridan." Bryson smiles at my parents, his dimple on full show. He's genuinely enjoying this . . . meeting my family. "It was great to meet you both."

My secret boyfriend and my parents having just met is almost too much to wrap my head around.

Kai Sheridan, what has your life become?

20

As we drive out of Fairvale, Bryson tells me about the game he coached after school today.

"So did you win?"

"No, but we improved by a lot. So I'm happy."

I reach for the bracelet on his wrist. "I guess this didn't bring you that much luck."

He holds up his arm. "Well, I feel lucky wearing it, so that's enough."

Bryson turns onto the freeway. It's a straight road now all the way to LA.

"You've made it very famous," I say. "Everyone on Instagram is talking about it."

Bryson shakes his head. "People need to get lives. Who I date or like shouldn't matter."

"If only the world agreed with you."

Bryson looks at me and starts to sing one of the Graces' ballads. "'It's the closed-minded views on the way things should be. On what is right or wrong. On what is normal and what isn't. But who are you to tell me how to live? Who are you to tell me how to live?'"

"'We all just want to be loved . . . ,'" I sing.

"'Loved, loved, loved,'" we sing together.

"Wow, you'd better stick to being a writer," Bryson says.

"Excuse me, at least I can hold a tune. You do know you were off-key, right?"

Bryson laughs and switches on the radio. By chance the song we were just singing starts to play. Laughing and joking and singing make the trip pass by quickly. Soon we're in downtown LA and driving toward Echo Park.

"I'm glad we left on time," Bryson says.

"I like punctuality."

"Me too."

Bryson pulls up to the curb. Sunset Boulevard is busy. "Save our place in line and I'll find a place to park," Bryson says.

The show won't start for another hour, but judging by how many people are already lined up outside the Echo, we're in for a wait. I unbuckle my seat belt and climb out the door. I pull my leather jacket into place and fix my beanie. I lean down and smile.

"See you in a bit."

I close the door and watch as he pulls off into traffic.

The evening air is chilly. My breath escapes me in clouds of fog. I study everyone around me. Like me, some wear their official Graces merchandise. The beanie I'm wearing is from their online store, and it has the band's official logo on it. I'm also wearing a T-shirt with Ezra Grace's face on it.

With nothing else to do, I pull my phone from my pocket and reply to the three musketeers group chat.

How's the date going? Priya asks.

I don't think this is a date. We made these plans before . . . everything.

As long as you're with the person you like and they like you, it can be considered a date, Donny says.

Then, by that logic you and Priya have been dating since freshman year.

Touché, Priya texts. *Ten points to Gryffindor.*

You know I'm a Hufflepuff. Hugs for everyone.

Donny texts a meme with Professor McGonagall as the background, and in large, bold text, it reads: *"Ten points to Hufflepuff," said no Hogwarts professor ever.*

Priya sends through a series of crying-from-laughing emojis.

You Ravenclaws are the worst.

You know you love us, Priya says.

I should go. I'm standing in line.

Well, have fun, Donny says.

I close the group chat and head to Instagram. I scroll through my feed. Bryson has uploaded three new posts. The first is of him surrounded by the soccer team he helps coach, the second is of him getting ready for the concert, and the third is of him trying to find a parking spot.

I like them all. And this time I smile at the red heart without second-guessing myself. The flash of a camera causes me to look up from my phone. I startle at the person in front of me. I stifle a groan. It's Shannon.

She smiles in a way that sets my alarm bells off. "Interesting meeting you here."

"I could say the same about you." I look her up and down. "*You* like the Graces?"

"Of course not," Shannon says. She barely stops herself from scoffing.

"Then what are you doing here?"

"Research for a story I'm working on. I figured I'll kill two birds with one stone. I know that this is Bryson's favorite band, too." She scans the crowd. "Where is he?"

"You're kind of obsessed."

"Dedicated," Shannon says. She flips her hair from her shoulder. "I know that he wouldn't miss this for the world."

"Do you even really know Bryson?"

"Duh. Of course. Everyone knows Bryson Keller."

I shake my head.

She must not like the look on my face. "What? Do you think you know him?"

"Well, yeah." I shrug. And it's true. This week has been a window into who Bryson actually is. "Bryson's so much more than what everyone makes him out to be. He's more than his status. More than a jock. I don't know, maybe if you looked beyond all that you'd get to know the real him. And maybe then you'd stand a chance with him." Not that I ever want that to happen.

"Oh, please—" she starts to say, but her words taper out. Shannon looks just over my shoulder and her eyes widen. "Bryson," she says, softly at first, then louder. "Bryson."

Startled, I turn and come face-to-face with Bryson. His pale blue eyes send a shiver down my spine. He places a steadying hand on my arm. Seeing the look on my face, Bryson glances over my shoulder and spots Shannon. He quickly removes his hand.

"I finally found parking."

"You came together?" Shannon asks.

"Yeah," Bryson says. "We both really love this band. So it made sense just to come together."

She pushes past me, adding an elbow just for my benefit. "You could have told me."

"What are you doing here? You like the Graces?"

"Of course," Shannon lies.

I snort, which earns me a glare from Shannon. The three of us end up standing in line together. With Shannon as our third wheel, we aren't able to talk freely. So instead, we spend most of the time just stealing looks at each other.

The line moves forward, and soon it's our turn. Bryson and I hand our tickets to the attendant, and she gives us our bracelets to let us enter. Then Shannon hands over her ticket.

"I'm sorry, but you can't enter," the attendant says.

"What do you mean?" Shannon asks.

"This ticket is fake." The attendant holds the ticket up to the light overhead. "Where'd you buy it?"

"Online," Shannon says.

"When?"

"This week."

"I think you've been duped," the attendant says. She hands the ticket back to Shannon. "Next, please."

"This isn't fair," Shannon says. She looks from the attendant to us. But there isn't anything Bryson or I can do. With no other choice, we wave goodbye and enter the venue.

The Echo is small, so it's already full of people. My eyes scan the crowd. Ahead of us there is a gay couple. They walk hand in hand proudly. Bryson sees the same thing I do. He looks at me. The Graces fandom is very LGBTQ friendly, and all around us that shows.

"We're in a city where no one knows us," Bryson says. "We can be whoever we want to be." He takes my hand. I see other same-sex couples and smile. Bryson's right. I turn to smile at him.

"Let's go." We meander our way to find a place to stand. No one looks at us; no one says anything. We're all just here to have fun and watch the Graces. For the first time in my life, I hold another boy's hand in public. This is what life should be.

Bryson pulls out his phone and takes a picture of the stage. He uploads it to Instagram: *Let's rock.*

And when the Graces take the stage, we do.

• • •

Three hours later, we file out of the Echo. We're sweating and smiling. My throat feels sore from all the singing out loud. We both carry our jackets and caps now, the high from the concert keeping us warm.

"We should get something to drink. When I was parking, I saw a café that's open till late." Bryson points in the direction and we start walking. The café, Stories, reminds me a lot of Off the Wall. It's a bookstore and coffee shop. We manage to order something just before it closes for the night. We get something cold, and I pay. Bryson doesn't even bother to argue, because he'll pay next time. And that I know there will be a next time fills me with joy. Even though it's Friday night already, I don't think I have to dread the end of this. With each moment I spend with Bryson, I'm growing more certain.

We leave Stories behind.

"There's a park not far away from here," Bryson says. "Want to check it out before we go home?"

"Okay," I say. We head in that direction. I take a sip of my drink and my throat rejoices. The cool liquid does wonders for my strained vocal cords.

"I think I might lose my voice," I say.

"You were very loud," Bryson says. "You surprised me."

I hold my hand up in the classic rocker symbol. "I had the rock spirit."

Bryson bumps into me on purpose as we walk. "You're cute."

"Stop it. You're going to make me blush."

"I know," Bryson says with a laugh.

We walk so close that our shoulders touch. It's all I think about in the silence that follows. *He's so close to me.*

When we reach Echo Park, we stop walking and turn to study the view. The downtown lights are reflected on the lake before us. This moment is picturesque, it's perfect. This whole night has been. Bryson clears his throat nervously. He looks around to see that we're alone before turning his full attention to me.

"There's something I want to do," Bryson says. "Something I think I need to confirm for myself. I feel like it's the only way that I'll know for sure." He doesn't sound sure about himself at all, though. He's nervous, and it's cute. Butterflies spring to life in my stomach.

"What is it?"

His eyes move from mine, down to my lips. He studies them before meeting my gaze again.

"I want to kiss you," he says. "I've wanted to for a while now." His voice is low, gruff, nothing more than a whisper. "Can I?"

We're in a city where no one knows us, standing at the cliff, waiting to jump. My eyes move to his lips. Right now there is nothing more that I want in this world than for Bryson Keller to kiss me.

"Yes."

One word that changes everything. He closes the distance between us. Bryson's lips meet mine. The kiss is tentative at first. It's a test, a question seeking an answer. Soon, though, it deepens. His mouth moves against mine.

Bryson pulls back and his eyes open. He looks at me, then smiles. It's not tight-lipped and nervous. It's big and genuine. It's the smile you want to get after kissing someone.

"I just broke all my rules." He sighs.

"Sorry." My voice is breathless and not even a little apologetic. My heart hammers in my chest. I'm barely keeping myself standing upright.

"Don't. Don't apologize," Bryson says. "Not for that kiss, never for that kiss."

"Really?" I feel my face reddening. "This was my first kiss . . . like, ever."

"Well, this feels like my first real kiss, too," Bryson says. "I feel like everything finally makes sense now. You. Me. Us."

We stare at each other, and I can tell that neither of us is really looking at the other's eyes. We're looking at each other's lips.

"Should we?" Bryson asks.

"Yes," I say again, this time on a groan.

Bryson leans his head down. It's slower this time. His lips touch mine once more, and I feel like they belong there. There is no hesitation. Bryson Keller is sure. I feel braver, too. I reach for him. My fingers run through his hair. Bryson pulls me closer, and I moan into his mouth. This is what I've been waiting for my whole damn life.

On this Friday night, we are just two boys kissing because we want to, because we like each other.

And there is nothing at all wrong with that.

Because love is love is love.

SATURDAY

21

I don't sleep at all. I have too much going on in my head, too much going on in my heart. I'm thinking too much, feeling too much.

I roll over and bury my head in the pillow. I'm smiling, and I'm pretty sure I have been the whole night. I reach for my phone on the nightstand. I have messages in the group chat, and when I open it, I find a link to a YouTube video that Donny thought was funny. I scroll through my other notifications but find none from Kelly yet. Maybe Bryson's sleeping.

We got home pretty late last night. Neither one of us had wanted the night to end. Even after he drove me to my house, we spent almost an hour just sitting there and talking. Holding hands with our hearts full, a cloud of giddiness swirling all around us. I decided then that the night was a date, because it was everything I've fantasized about—and so much more.

I'm not saying that I'm in love with Bryson. But the idea doesn't seem all that impossible. It hasn't even been a full week, but there's no denying that I like him more and more with each day that passes. And what completely blows my mind is that he likes me, too.

His kissing me is the undeniable proof that my skeptical mind needs.

With his lips, he cleared my doubts and stilled my anxiety about us.

Last night he did it again and again and again.

There's a knock at my bedroom door. I roll over just as Yazz pops her head in. She's wearing the wrap that she swirls her hair in to sleep. Dad's sisters gave Yazz the hair 101 on her last visit. Both of us have super-curly hair. I'm lucky that I keep mine short, but Yazz's hangs down her back.

"Mom sent me to check if you were alive," Yazz explains.

I'm not. I've moved on from the land of the living. Last night was enough to kill me—the murder weapon: Bryson Keller's skilled mouth. I smile to myself. I'm sure to Yazz I look like a fool, but I don't care. I'm too happy to care. Nothing can go wrong today, not when I feel this good.

"What's with you?" Yazz asks.

"Nothing," I lie.

For once my secret doesn't feel like a burden.

"Are you going to see Bryson today?" Yazz asks.

"No, why?" There's something strange about her question, or rather the way she's asked it. Maybe if I weren't love-drunk over Bryson and me making out last night I would press her on it. In the end I don't. Sometimes willful ignorance is best.

"Just curious." She closes my door then, leaving me alone with the memory of last night. I am riding a cloud of euphoria. No wonder pop stars are constantly saying love is a drug. It may be cliché, but it also happens to be true.

I climb from my bed and walk to the bathroom. Fifteen minutes later I emerge dressed and ready to take on the day. I run down the stairs and enter the kitchen.

Mom and Dad are seated at the island, both with their laptops out. It seems that today is a Saturday for working at home.

"Good afternoon, sleepyhead," Dad says. He's being dramatic—there's over an hour to go before it's actually the afternoon.

"Did you have fun last night?" Mom asks.

My heart skips a beat. Just briefly I think she's asking about Bryson and me, but then I remember the concert. Something I was looking so forward to was completely eclipsed by my kissing Bryson Keller.

I turn to hide my blush and busy myself with pouring a glass of orange juice. "Yeah, the concert was great." But what happened after was even better. I tell them none of this, though.

"You should invite Bryson over sometime," Mom says. "We barely got to know him yesterday."

"You mean you couldn't interrogate him like you wanted."

Dad laughs. "I'd love to have someone to talk soccer with. Do you know which team he supports?"

I recall the posters on Bryson's bedroom wall. "Liverpool."

Dad sighs. "You must invite him over, then. I need to have a serious talk with him."

I imagine Bryson coming over and meeting my parents, as my boyfriend this time. I introduce him as such, and Mom simply asks if he's eaten. True to his word, Dad talks to him about soccer, and we spend the afternoon laughing and joking. There isn't a third-degree interrogation; there aren't any tears or disappointment or prayers for their gay son. There isn't any heartache or pain. Instead, we go about it as if everything is normal.

Because it is.

My having a boyfriend *is* normal.

I head to the fridge to find a snack. I see my breakfast covered and smile. I love my parents. I warm the food in the microwave and go back to my bedroom.

I pull out my phone. Totally by accident, I end up stalking Bryson's profile. He hasn't uploaded anything since yesterday. Actually, he's been oddly quiet all morning. No texts—nothing. A small part of me worries that last night overwhelmed him.

As I'm scrolling through the many pictures of Bryson, my phone vibrates, not with a text but with a phone call. Only a handful of people bother to call me, and all of them belong to my family.

But it isn't any of them. Kelly's name flashes on the screen. Immediately, I swipe to answer and bring the phone to my ear.

"Kai?" Bryson says. He sounds odd. "I'm sorry I'm calling. I know you hate phone calls."

"Bryson, what's wrong?"

"I wanted to talk to someone, and you came to mind."

"Why? Did something happen?"

There's a few seconds of silence on the other end of the phone.

"I saw my dad today," Bryson says. "He's having a baby." Another long pause. "He's having a son with the woman he had an affair with."

"Where are you?" I ask.

"Melody Beach." That section of the beach used to be popular before the boardwalk got revamped. Now it's deserted, with few people going there because it's a no-swim zone.

"I'm coming," I say. We hang up. I grab my wallet and go downstairs.

Dad is the first parent I see. "Dad, can I borrow your car?"

"For?"

"I have plans with Bryson today." My parents have met him now. I don't need to hide anything. It isn't weird for two boys to hang out, so why lie?

"Sure," Dad says. "You know where the keys are."

"Thanks." I walk to the foyer. There's a small table with a glass bowl that we use to keep our keys in. I find the ones for Dad's car.

I pull on my shoes and exit the house. Dad drives an SUV. Just after I got my license, every time I borrowed this car, the vehicle would come back either scratched or dented. To this day I swear that it was the tree's fault the first time. And the second time, the fire hydrant jumped out in front of me.

I was banned for a while after those accidents, but I argued that the only way for me to get better was to practice. My parents allowed me to use Mom's car instead. Now, though, I'm a much more confident driver, so Dad doesn't have an issue with my driving his car.

Melody Beach is on the outskirts of town, and the fastest way to get there is to cut right through the heart of Fairvale.

Soon the sound of traffic gives way to the sound of the ocean. I turn right, and the tree line breaks to offer me my first view of the glittering sea. I turn into the parking lot at Melody Beach. Bryson's Jeep is the only car there.

I pull into the space next to the Jeep and climb out. I peer through the window. The car's empty. I scan my surroundings and spot Bryson sitting in the center of the basketball court.

He doesn't see me at first. My shadow announces my presence. Bryson twists to look up at me. He smiles, but it's not the one that I have come to know—the one I've come to expect.

"You came?" His eyes are red, and so are his cheeks. It's clear that Bryson's been crying.

I nod and sit next to him. "Of course I came. I was worried about you."

I place my hand on the back of his neck, stroke his hair there. I wait for him to talk some more. There's no rush. I just want him to know that I'm here for him.

"You're the first person I've told about the affair other than Dustin." Bryson shakes his head. "My dad cheated on my mom. That's why they divorced." He looks at me then, and I see how much he's hurting over this. It breaks my heart. "I caught them once, you know. Sophomore year, when he was still married to Mom. I needed to ask him something, so I went to his office and I saw them. He spotted me before I could run away. He chased me down, and instead of trying to explain or make excuses, he told me not to tell Mom. I wasn't sure what to do. So I kept quiet, kept it a secret even though I knew it would destroy Mom. Even though I knew it would rip my family apart. The secret almost killed me. For one whole year he made sure I kept his secret. Mom caught him at the start of junior year. If I'd had to keep his secret any longer, I don't know what I'd have done."

"I understand," I say. "I know what it's like to carry a secret that could rip up the world you're used to."

It's unfair that Bryson's dad asked him to carry such a burden. He was meant to protect Bryson, not the other way around.

I reach out and cup Bryson's cheek. He leans into my touch and closes his eyes.

"She's pregnant. He says he wants us all to be a family again. But it feels like he's replacing us now. Replacing me with a new son." Bryson's eyes open. "I know he's my dad, but I kind of hate him. I hate him for all the nights he made Mom cry alone in her bedroom when she thought I was sleeping. I hate him for destroying a perfectly good family. For being so selfish. But I also feel guilty because a part of me loves him. He's my dad, after all. And I miss him."

There is no right or wrong in this situation. And all I can offer Bryson is my shoulder. The chance for him to break down without judgment. I pull Bryson's head to my shoulder. It isn't much, but maybe, just maybe, it's what he needs.

He breaks then. Whoever says that boys don't cry—or

shouldn't cry—needs to walk off a very short pier into a shark-infested ocean. As Bryson cries, I slowly rub circles on his back. We stay like this as the sun shifts and Bryson's heart empties. After a while, he sags against me. I maneuver us so that we're lying down and his head is resting in the crook of my arm. I close my eyes to the sun and hold him close.

"Thank you for coming," Bryson says. "After Dustin, you were the only person I wanted to see. I wasn't sure you'd pick up if I called. Dustin didn't."

"Well, from now on you can always call me," I say. "I'll always try to pick up."

I'm not sure how long we lie there. Just two boys forgetting the world.

22

"I have an idea," Bryson says eventually.

He gets up, and I sit up, too. The sea breeze rustles my hair. I follow Bryson as he walks to his Jeep. He stops at the trunk and opens it. Clothes and other sports equipment lie scattered there. He digs for a while before finding what he's looking for.

A basketball.

"Let's play."

Staring at the basketball under Bryson's arm, I realize just how long it's been since Dad and I last played. With me being distracted by senior year, time has passed so fast and both of us have just been too busy with our own lives.

Bryson throws me the ball and I catch it. It's so well used that most of the lettering has disappeared from the surface of the rubber.

"Will this make you feel better?"

Bryson nods. "Yes."

Of course playing sports is how Bryson Keller cheers up.

We head toward the basketball court and I throw the ball back to him. He catches it. Bryson starts to spin the ball on his finger.

"First person to get to ten points wins," he says.

"And the winner gets one wish," I say. "Deal?"

Bryson laughs. "Fine. Deal. I should warn you, I've been told I'm a sore loser."

"Me too," I say. "I've never been a fan of losing. My parents have even placed a board game embargo in our household."

"Cute."

I bounce the ball toward him, and he returns it. I dribble around him. I'm so focused on the ball that I don't think much about Bryson's presence at my back. I fake right but turn left. I jump and shoot. The ball circles the rim before going in.

"Not bad, Sheridan," Bryson says. "You have some skills."

What few skills I do have pale in comparison to Bryson's. Soon he's up 3–1. When I manage to win the ball away from him, I waste no time in shooting. The ball bounces off the backboard and I hold my breath as I watch it finally slide through the net.

Adrenaline courses through my veins. As we play we forget everything. We become just two boys on a court, each one trying to best the other. Each of us trying to win.

The sound of the ball bouncing on the asphalt becomes a mirror to my own pounding heart. I lose myself to the rhythm, and soon we are 8–9, with me in the lead. I can taste victory. It's so close.

Bryson delivers a jump shot, effectively squaring us up. He

catches the ball on the rebound. His hair is damp with sweat and his skin is red from exertion. Yet somehow he still manages to look good.

"I'm impressed," he says.

"I'm more than just a pretty face," I say.

Bryson bounces the ball between his legs and smiles. "There's the Kai Sheridan I've come to know." He dribbles the ball around me, teasing me. "The Kai Sheridan I'm falling for."

By the time I look up, the ball has already left his hands. I turn and watch it swish through the net.

And just like that the game is over.

I've lost.

I turn back to Bryson.

The grin on his face is wild and uninhibited. It is the smile of a victor. He throws his hands in the air and begins a victory dance that consists of a lot of hip thrusting and fist pumping.

Watching Bryson Keller like this, I wonder if maybe *I've* won.

"That's cheating," I say, resting my hands on my knees. A stitch flickers in my side, a clear signal of just how unfit I am. "You distracted me on purpose."

Bryson laughs. He mirrors my pose now. Sweaty and out of breath, we stand and stare at one another.

"That was fun," Bryson says. We head back to the Jeep. "Here." He holds out a bottle of water. It's a little warm but it goes down smoothly. I sigh with satisfaction.

Bryson drinks his own bottle, and when he's done, he takes both of our empty bottles over to the trash can at the edge of the parking lot. I watch as he bends to take off his shoes. Bryson pulls off his socks, too. He wiggles his toes and gives me a wink before stepping onto the beach.

I bend and remove my own shoes, then follow Bryson onto the sand as he walks toward the water. We come to a stop at the water's edge and watch as the ocean ebbs and flows.

Bryson takes a step into the water and laughs. The sound—pure, undiluted joy—warms me. He runs deeper into the water and I chase him. I splash water at him, but he easily avoids it. Not willing to let him get away, I continue my assault. Bryson shrieks when the water hits its mark.

"Okay, okay, okay," Bryson says with a laugh. He holds up his pruned hands in surrender. "I give up."

With my chest heaving and a smile spread across my face, I bask in this feeling. Normally I would be nervous about the way my wet shirt clings to my body, but with Bryson I'm not ashamed. Closing my eyes, I hold my face up toward the sun.

"Thank you for today." Bryson's voice makes me open my eyes. He's closer than he was before. Standing next to me. We both smile.

"You're welcome." I leave the water behind and sit down on the sand, warm in the afternoon sun. Bryson joins me a short while later.

"So, when do you want to use your wish?" I ask.

"I just got it and you want me to spend it? I consider it an investment." Bryson looks around us. "Besides, I think I have everything I want right now."

"For someone who had to be dared to date, you really are romantic."

Bryson sighs. "I know I said I didn't date because of me not wanting to put in the time and effort, but the real reason was my dad. I was scared I'd be like him. I'd hate to hurt someone I supposedly loved. You know, he blamed my mom for the affair. Said that he was unhappy and that's why he cheated." Bryson blinks back tears. "If he was so unhappy, why didn't he just leave? Why did he have to hurt us all with his lies? It's one of the things I don't think I'll ever be able to forgive him for."

"I'm sorry," I say. It's the only thing I can say. I move closer to him so that our shoulders touch. We sit like that in silence, both of us lost in our own thoughts but just happy to have the other there.

Bryson eventually breaks the silence. "What are you thinking about?" He lifts his finger and taps at my forehead. "Your forehead is all wrinkled."

"Just deciding not to worry about tomorrow when I have today right in front of me."

"Damn, Sheridan. Are you writing a book?"

I laugh. "This all feels like a dream to me, you know?"

He turns to look at me. My words hang between us heavy like rain clouds just waiting to burst. His face is serious, and his eyes never leave mine. He's silent for a heartbeat. Then he reaches across and pinches me.

"Ouch!" I rub the back of my hand. "What was that for?"

"To remind you that it's real."

...

It's evening. The sky is stained the colors of sunset. Food boxes lie at our feet. We got drive-through burgers and returned to the beach. I pick up a fry and chew.

Sitting with Bryson watching the sun go down is one of the most romantic things I've ever done in my life. The thought has me smiling.

"What?" Bryson asks when he catches me.

"Nothing."

"Tell me." He pokes at my ribs with his finger. "Tell me, tell me, tell me."

"Just"—I shrug—"this is kind of romantic."

Bryson sprawls across the sand and rests his head in my lap. "It is."

I reach out and trace his features. This time I'm brave enough to do so. I move my finger across his thick brows and down his straight nose. I hover above his lips, where just last night my own were. Our eyes lock, and electricity sparks between us.

Bryson reaches for my outstretched hand and pulls me forward. He brings our faces together. His lips find mine again. I moan into his mouth as he deepens the kiss.

We stay connected until we're both out of breath. I pull back slightly and hover there, our faces mere inches apart.

"I'm really glad you said yes," I admit.

"And I'm really glad you asked me out in the first place."

Bryson smiles. "When I think back to how you were at the start of this week, I can't believe it."

"Why?"

"You're so open now. So confident."

"Not really," I say. "I'm just comfortable with you. And because of that I'm able to be more myself than before."

"Well, I'm glad I got to see this side of you," Bryson says. "I'm all for it, as long as you never stop blushing. I'd be too sad if that were to stop."

"Just for you, I won't."

We fall into a comfortable silence. Bryson closes his eyes and starts to hum a song by the Graces. I eat the rest of my fries and listen to not only the sound of the ocean, but also my boyfriend's incredibly bad humming.

"Are we dating?" I ask.

Bryson stops humming and his eyes open. "What?"

"Uh . . . we haven't really spoken about it."

"I didn't think we needed to," Bryson says. "I figured I lost the dare when I kissed you."

"So today was our first day as a couple?"

"Yes." Bryson sits up and looks at me. "You, Kai Sheridan, are my boyfriend for real."

I lean in and kiss him. Bryson laughs against my lips, and I try to catch that sound with my mouth. By the time we pull apart, I am breathless and perfectly content.

"We should go home," I say, now that the sun has set completely.

Bryson stands and offers me his hand. I let him pull me up and dust the sand from my clothes. We clean up our makeshift picnic. I'm the first to head back to the parking lot. There's a third car in the parking lot now. Someone climbs out from the car.

It's Dustin.

23

"What do you think you're doing?" Dustin demands. He's looking at me. No, correction: he's glaring at me.

"Dustin?" Bryson asks when he comes to stand next to me. "What are you doing here?"

"You called me."

"Earlier, yeah," Bryson says. "I texted you to tell you I was fine. Kai came."

"I was out with Brittany," Dustin says. "It's why I didn't hear your calls."

"It's no problem, D. I figured you were just busy." Bryson smiles. He walks over to the trash can and throws away the burger boxes. Bryson's phone rings then. "Hey, Mom, you home? . . . Oh, tomorrow? . . . Yeah, I saw Dad." Bryson moves farther away from us to continue his conversation with his mother.

"Why are you here?" Dustin asks. His voice is low and dangerous. I take a step back, putting some distance between us.

"What do you mean? Bryson called me." I make a move toward my car, but Dustin grabs my arm. He jerks me to a stop. His grip is tight—too tight.

"Hey!" I try to pull my arm free, but he refuses to let go. Our eyes meet, and I see more than anger . . . maybe even hatred.

"You shouldn't be doing this," Dustin says. "It's not okay." Dustin tightens his grip, if that is at all possible.

"Let me go."

"What's going on?" Bryson asks. He runs toward us and grabs hold of Dustin's arm, forcing him to let go.

"Are you siding with him?" Dustin spits.

"About what?" Bryson asks. "I don't even know what's going on. Why are you so mad?"

Dustin shoves his phone at us. I peer over Bryson's shoulder. It takes a moment for me to see what I'm looking at. Like my brain refuses to subject me to what it knows I can't handle. Slowly, it all comes into focus: it's a picture of me and Bryson from earlier, and we're kissing.

Eyes wide, I look up at Dustin.

"You took a picture?" Bryson demands.

"You better stay away from him," Dustin says to me. His voice is low, and his eyes are cold. "If you don't, I'll release this."

"And now you're threatening us? What the hell, Dustin?" Bryson says.

"You're mad? This isn't right. I'll fix this." Dustin turns to me. "You need to stop this."

"Stop what?" Bryson asks. "What does Kai need to stop?"

"Making you gay." Dustin looks at his best friend. "This isn't you. You're like a brother to me, BK. We know everything about each other. I was there when your dad first left. You were there for me when my mom got sick. I know you, Bryson. And the Bryson Keller I know is not gay." Dustin looks between the two of us. "You're not a f—"

My fist moves without thought. I've never been in a fight before, but I've also never been this angry, either. And it sure as hell feels good when I'm able to stop Dustin from using *that* word.

I hit him in the jaw, and he stumbles back. Dustin is hunched over. He looks up and bares his teeth.

"Being gay isn't a disease, asshole!" I spit. "You can't catch it. It isn't contagious."

Dustin's lip is busted, but I don't care. He spits blood and tackles me. I hit the asphalt hard and blink away stars. Bryson is quick to react. He grabs Dustin and pulls him off me. Dustin elbows Bryson in the mouth and charges me again.

I roll over to cover my face. Dustin is bigger than me, years of sports giving him muscles that I don't have. Even so, I don't just lie there and take it. I struggle against him, kicking and punching for all I'm worth. It doesn't make much difference. Dustin has the upper hand.

Bryson saves me. He tackles his best friend and they roll across the asphalt. Bryson pins Dustin. Bryson doesn't want to fight; he just wants to stop him.

I sit up and bite back my groan. I refuse to give Dustin the satisfaction of hearing how much pain I'm in, how much pain he's caused. I've always been an angry crier. Tears sit unshed in my eyes, not from the pain, but from the anger that burns within me like a thousand suns.

I exhale and stand.

"What the fuck is wrong with you?" Bryson asks Dustin.

"He hit me first but you're mad at me?"

Maybe throwing the first punch wasn't the smartest move, but at the time it seemed like the only thing I could do. I never want to hear that word. There isn't ever a reason for it to be uttered, and yet people like Dustin Smith think they can just go around wielding that word like the knife it is.

"You're not gay," Dustin says.

"How do you know what I am?" Bryson asks, pain making his voice crack. "*I'm* still figuring it out."

"I would know. I'm your best friend."

Bryson shakes his head. "My best friend wouldn't act like a complete homophobic asshole." He stands. "Are you okay?" He walks over to me and studies me closely. "You might have a bruise."

"I'm fine," I say. I watch as Dustin climbs to his feet. He's glaring at us, and when his eyes land on me, it's like he's looking at a fresh pile of dog shit.

"You better stay away from him," Dustin warns me.

"You better delete that picture," Bryson says. "Or else."

"What, you're going to hit me, too?"

"If you do something to deserve it, I will."

"This is bullshit," Dustin says as he climbs into his car. His tires screech as he pulls out of the parking lot.

Even after he's gone, we both stand and stare at where Dustin once was. Bryson sighs. "I'm sorry."

I turn to look at him. "No, I am."

"I'll talk to him," Bryson says.

"You should go," I say. This is not at all how I imagined our first day as a couple going. "We need to get that picture deleted."

Bryson nods. "Are you okay, though?" He leans toward me to examine my lip. "That needs to be treated."

"I'll take care of it."

Bryson takes my hand in his and looks at my fist. It's bruised from the punch. He brings it to his lips and kisses it. "I'm sorry."

"You said that already." I sigh. "This isn't your fault. This is on Dustin."

Bryson nods. "You should go home." He walks me to my car and helps me climb in. "I'll head over to Dustin's house now."

"Good luck," I say.

Bryson waves and walks over to his Jeep. He honks a goodbye, and I watch as he drives out of the parking lot. I pull down the sun visor and check myself in the mirror. My lip is busted, and already there's a bruise just under my eye. It's clear that I've been in a fight. I groan. This is definitely not going to sit well with Mom and Dad.

I sigh and start the car. Some things are simply unavoidable. It isn't like I can't go home just to avoid the third degree that I know will be waiting for me. As I drive home, the encounter with Dustin echoes in my mind. A part of me is worried about the picture, but the bigger part is angry that such a photo could be used to hurt us. On any given day I can open up my Instagram and see pictures of couples kissing, and yet because it's two boys, it's something to be worried about.

I hate how unfair all this is.

Fifteen minutes later, I pull into our driveway and I'm angrier than I've ever been. I pause briefly at the door to collect myself before entering. I stop to take off my shoes and return Dad's car keys. I head to the kitchen for a bottle of water and find Mom at the fridge.

Mom's eyes widen when they land on me. "What happened to you?" she asks. She studies my face and then my hands. "Were you in a fight?"

"It's nothing," I lie.

"Kai Sheridan, you'd better tell me exactly what happened." Mom reaches out to touch my cheek. I flinch at the tenderness. "You've changed ever since you started hanging out with this Bryson boy," Mom says. Her voice is too loud. "Why are you trying to be so cool all of a sudden?"

I'm not, I want to say. *I'm just trying to live as me. This isn't Bryson's fault. This isn't my fault. It's society and its homophobia.* In the end I don't say any of that. Instead, I make an excuse. "I'm tired, Mom. I just want to shower and sleep. We'll talk later." I meet her eyes. "*Please.*"

She nods and says, "Okay, I'm trusting you. We'll talk later, then."

I head to the fridge and grab a bottle of water. As I walk up to my bedroom, I think that maybe I should tell Mom what happened. Maybe I should come out to her. The thought is fleeting. I don't want to be forced to come out to my parents. I want to do it in my own time, at my own pace.

I want to tell them I'm gay when I'm ready.

And I'm not ready tonight.

24

I stay under the shower until the water runs cold.

After climbing out, I wrap a towel around my waist and move to the bathroom mirror. It's steamed over, so I wipe it. My bruised reflection stares back at me. It feels worse than it looks, and a part of me is thankful for that. At least I won't have to walk around with marks on my body—just my face.

I sigh. I'm too emotionally drained to deal with this—*any* of it. I want nothing more than to jump into bed and dream about Bryson. But in life, we simply don't always get what we want.

I dry myself off and get dressed in track pants and a T-shirt—my usual pajamas. I throw the towel in the laundry and head for my bedroom.

I startle at the sight of Mom standing there. "What are you doing here?"

I don't notice what she's holding at first. She turns then, and that's when I see the strip of photos that I hid in my desk.

Anger blooms in my chest over Mom invading my privacy and going through my things, but it's soon swallowed up by fear. It's the type of fear that seeps down deep into your bones and wraps around your heart.

"What is this?" Mom asks. Her voice sounds hollow. It's like she's trying to make sense of something that she can't really understand.

"Let me explain," I say. My voice is a whisper. My eyes don't leave the photos she holds. Since we took them on Thursday I've memorized every detail of them. "*Please.*"

Mom scrunches the photo strip in her hand. I start to make a move to stop her, but I fight the urge. The photos can't be what's important right now.

I open my mouth to deliver my monologue—the one I've been carefully crafting for years—but end up blurting out, "I'm gay, Mom."

This isn't at all how I imagined it. I'm not ready now. But maybe coming out is one of those things you can never truly be ready for because you can never truly know how anyone is going to react.

Mom stumbles back as if I've pushed her. She stares at me, tears in her eyes. It's almost like she's looking at a stranger. I break then. Tears spring to my own eyes. This is the moment I've been dreading my whole life. This is when everything changes.

"Impossible," she says.

That one word destroys me more than a thousand would.

My knees give out and I sag. If not for the wall at my back, I'd be on the floor—a puppet with my strings cut.

Mom studies me like I'm some riddle she needs to solve. She reaches for the gold cross that dangles on her necklace. I can't see this. I can't watch her pray for me because I'm wrong, because I'm sinning.

I don't want to see any of it. I can't. I grab my phone from my nightstand and turn. Dad's standing at my bedroom door. He reaches for me as I pass him. He places his hand on my shoulder. It's all he can offer me.

And it isn't enough.

I need words and actions to make me know that I'm still loved, that I'm accepted—to know that nothing has changed. I'm still the son that they've raised and loved for the last seventeen years. I'm the same person that they laughed with, that they hugged and kissed, that they cared for when I was sick.

I'm still the same son that an hour ago they were so proud of.

The only thing that's different is they finally know that I like boys. It's a small piece of me, and yet it is all they can see now. It is all they can focus on.

He lets me go and I stumble toward the stairs in a daze. Behind me I hear Mom sobbing. I wipe my tears from my cheeks as I race down the stairs. I leave the house and head outside into the chilly night.

I walk away from the driveway, and that is when it all hits me, crashes into me like a tsunami of emotion. Totally unavoidable.

I can't hold any of it back.

I rip at my seams and everything spills out: all my sadness, all my anger, all my fear.

I cry.

Alone.

• • •

Sometime later, when I've stitched myself back into the shape of a boy, I pull my phone out and send a message to the three musketeers group chat. No one answers, so I dial Donny's number. It rings and rings. I try Priya and get the same response.

Of course they're busy. It's Saturday night. Not everyone's night is a personal disaster. I check my phone again and find there are messages from Yazz and a missed call from Dad. My phone rings and I stare at Dad's photo on the caller ID. It's a family photo of us. In it we're all happy. The sight brings tears to my eyes again. Home is not where I want to be right now.

I start to walk. I'm not sure where I'm going. Eventually I sit down on the curb. No one notices. I'm all alone.

My phone vibrates with a text from Bryson.

I'm sorry about what happened today. I'm worried about you. Are you okay?

Through blurred vision I type: *Can you come get me?*

His response is instant. My phone lights up with a call.

"Kai? What's wrong?"

"I need you," I say. My voice sounds as hollow and empty as I feel.

"Where are you?"

"Oak Avenue. It's the next street over from my house."

"I'll be right there."

It doesn't take long for Bryson to arrive. He doesn't even bother to turn off the Jeep when he climbs out. "Kai, what's going on?"

Tears spring to my eyes again and I struggle to blink them back. Bryson takes in my state. He studies my clothes, then my tear-streaked cheeks. From the look on his face, Bryson's figured it out. He knows, or at least he has a pretty good guess as to why I'm out here on the street alone.

Bryson doesn't say anything, though. Instead, he simply closes the space between us. He envelops me in a hug. He pats my back to soothe me. Even though my eyes are closed, the tears continue to fall. I cry in Bryson's arms, and it is enough.

As my world burns down around me.

This, right here, is enough.

SUNDAY

25

Morning comes without permission. The world keeps spinning. The sun will keep rising, no matter what, and a new day will begin. Always.

I sit up and blink the world into focus. Bit by bit Bryson's bedroom comes to me. Morning sunlight streams in through the window above his desk. I reach for my phone and find numerous messages from Yazz, Priya, and Donny.

I open up Yazz's chat first.

Kai are you ok?

Where are you?

Kai?

Tell me?

And then a series of question marks. Too many to count.

I'm fine, Yazz, I text. *I just needed space. If anyone asks tell them I'm all right.*

Yazz replies a minute later. *Come home when you're ready. I love you.*

I love you too.

The three musketeers group chat is filled with much the same.

I'm fine, I text them. *I'm at Bryson's now.*

Yazz told us what happened. Are you okay? Priya texts back.

I'm dealing. It's a lie. I'm simply ignoring the emptiness that I feel. Every time I close my eyes I see the look on Mom's face.

Sorry we missed your call, Donny texts. *We're here if you need us.*

Thanks. I'll talk later.

I don't have the energy for any more than that. I turn off my phone and throw it back onto the bedside table. The door to Bryson's bedroom opens and he steps in. His hair is wet and he's shirtless. There's a towel thrown over his shoulder.

"You're awake?" Bryson takes a seat on the edge of the bed, and his expression is serious. "What happened, Kai?"

We've delayed the conversation for as long as possible. Last night all I did was cry. I wasn't able to tell him anything. Bryson comforted me and brought me here. I know that I have to explain what happened. But still, I hesitate.

"It's okay," Bryson says. "You don't have to tell me right now. Whenever you're ready to is fine." He smiles. It's small but no less genuine. Bryson stands and moves to hang up his towel. "And if you never want to talk about it, that's fine, too. But just know that I'm here for you. For whatever."

The sincerity of his words is a fist to the heart. I climb from the bed and close the space between us. I wrap my arms around him. My cheek rests against the smooth skin of his chest. I hear his heartbeat pounding. An echo of my own.

Bryson hugs me back. Warm and solid. We stand like that in silence for a while. Then it all comes pouring out of me. I tell him everything that happened last night. By the end, I'm in tears, but it's okay. He's holding me tighter, if that's at all possible.

Bryson pushes me back slightly so that he can look at my face. "First I think you need a nice long shower, and then I'll take a look at those bruises. I've learned a thing or two playing sports. After that we'll deal with whatever else." He leans down so that our foreheads are touching. "Together."

And then I am blinking back tears for an entirely different reason.

• • •

I emerge from the bathroom ten minutes later. Bryson sits on the bed waiting for me.

As I approach, Bryson holds up a tube of ointment.

"I swear by this stuff," Bryson says. "After matches, I end up with a few bruises sometimes."

"And who said soccer was a gentleman's game?" I tease.

"No one," Bryson says. "That's cricket."

"Oh."

Bryson laughs as I sit down next to him. He's still laughing as he touches his finger to the first bruise—the one under my eye. I'm relieved that it hasn't turned black, but it's no less painful.

I flinch.

And then Bryson isn't laughing anymore. Instead, he leans forward and blows on it.

I shiver. I'm not sure how or why, but it does make it feel better. He moves to use the ointment on my lip, too. Suddenly I'm aware of how intimate this is. Us, alone in his room. His finger pauses, near my lip, as though he's asking permission. I subtly shift forward, giving it.

The ointment stings, but his touch is gentle. Bryson leans forward and, at first, I think he's going to blow on the bruise again, but then I feel his lips on mine.

Just as quickly he pulls back.

"All done."

"You're such a tease."

"I'm a what?"

Bryson tackles me on the bed. He's careful not to hurt me.

Swiftly, he pins my hands above my head. Bryson brings his face closer and hovers there. I strain toward him, but Bryson lifts his head, making the space between us grow.

"*This* is teasing."

We're both smiling and so lost in what we're doing that we don't hear someone enter the room.

"Hey, Bry . . . ," a female voice starts, but tapers out at the sight of us. Bryson and I turn to find who I assume is Bryson's sister standing there. "What's going on here?" Her eyes are wide as she studies us, but then her face breaks into a grin. "Tell me everything."

Bryson and I try to untangle ourselves as fast as we can, which only causes him to fall off the bed. I stand and Bryson quickly scampers to his feet. Belatedly, I realize that he's still shirtless.

Crystal takes a seat and sits cross-legged, analyzing us. The smile has not left her face.

"Uh, Crystal, this is Kai. Kai, this is Crystal." Unlike Bryson, Crystal has flaming-red hair and green eyes.

"Charmed," Crystal says. Her arm is in a cast, but she offers me a small waggle of her fingers in greeting. "I'm so very charmed to meet you."

"Uh . . ." I look from her to Bryson and then back at her. "It's nice to meet you, too."

"What do you need?" Bryson asks. It's the most embarrassed I've ever seen him. I'm pretty sure he's blushing as much as I am.

"That's not important," Crystal says. She readjusts her injured arm. "What is, is this scene before me. One"—she holds up a finger on her other hand—"we have two boys, one shirtless and the other very flustered. Two, they were just minutes ago rolling around on a bed." She holds up a third and final finger. "And three, my baby brother is incredibly embarrassed right now, so there must be something going on."

It's clear from Crystal's face that she's enjoying this— a bit too much, if you ask me. Bryson must agree, because he exhales, casts me a glance, and then smirks. It's the smirk that tells me we're in danger.

He reaches for my hand then and interlocks our fingers. At first I'm too shocked to react, but then I try to pull free. Bryson isn't having any of it. He doesn't let go.

Bryson raises our hands for Crystal to see.

"Kai is my boyfriend." He says it so casually that I gasp. I wait for the fallout to follow, but Crystal laughs. She tries to clap but the cast stops her.

"I'm impressed." Crystal makes a show of uncrossing her legs and stands. "He's cute," she says, looking at me. The lightheartedness disappears. "Kai, did your parents do this to you?"

That she even needs to ask such a question breaks my heart.

Gay or straight, everyone has heard the horrors that some kids endure when they come out. It isn't just warmth and acceptance for everyone. Sometimes it's a real goddamn nightmare. It's the reason the closet exists. And why it will keep existing.

"No," I say. "I got in a fight."

"Really?"

"Yeah." Bryson runs a hand through his hair. "I was there. Don't tell Mom."

"You might have to. Mom called to say she's almost home. Her flight arrived early, so she'll be home for brunch. It's why I came here in the first place." Crystal sighs. "I came with nothing but leave with so much." She smiles and then leaves.

And that's it.

Bryson has just announced our relationship to his sister, and yet it all ends not with a bang but with a fizzle.

I finally remember to breathe.

"What just happened?" I ask. We're standing, holding hands, staring at the spot where Crystal just stood.

"I think we're now *official* official," Bryson says. He looks at me. "You okay?"

"I'm okay." I turn to him. "But are you okay? Isn't this too fast? I mean, you just came out to your sister."

Bryson smiles. It's the tight-lipped one that means he's nervous. "It feels weird how sure I am about you."

I blush. "No pressure."

Bryson laughs. "Not to add to that, but it's almost time for you to meet my mother."

And suddenly I'm not okay anymore.

26

We're all currently seated in the family room. Bryson and I are sitting on the two-seater. All morning he hasn't left my side. His presence is calming, especially considering that I am about to meet his mother—I am about to meet my boyfriend's mother.

The unbelievability of the thought does not escape my notice. I steal a glance at him. Even his profile looks sculpted by the gods. We're sitting so close that our thighs are touching. We're both silent, me from nerves and him . . . I don't know. Is he worried about his mom finding out about us? That thought takes me back to my own mother and the mess that awaits me at home.

I sigh. I wish this day could last forever and I would never need to go home.

"There's no pressure," Bryson says to me. He gives me a smile. "You can relax."

"Are you going to tell her?" I ask.

Bryson shrugs. "I don't know." He chews at his lip and runs a hand through his hair. "This coming-out business is weird."

I snort. "Tell me about it."

Crystal lounges across one of the large leather couches. She's watching some reality program on TV. The front door opens and Bryson's mother saunters in a handful of panicked heartbeats later.

She is the picture of elegance. Wearing a casual blouse and faded jeans, she has her red hair piled up into a messy bun. She looks just like an older version of Crystal. Bryson's mother smiles. My breath catches because it's one that I recognize. Her son has the exact same smile. It's the type of smile that can make a heart race, or even stop it altogether.

"Hello, everybody."

"Mom, this is Kai," Bryson says.

"Nice to meet you, ma'am."

"Please, call me Hannah. It's nice to meet you, too, Kai," Hannah says.

"How was your trip, Mom?" Crystal asks.

"Fine, until I heard my precious daughter was hurt." She crosses the room to Crystal. "Are you okay?"

Crystal gives a thumbs-up with the hand in the cast. "It's just a fracture."

"And yet she made me miss school to babysit her," Bryson says.

"We're family, it's what we do," Crystal says.

"You must be hungry," Bryson says to his mom. "I'll cook

something. Come on, Kai." Bryson leaves the family room and I follow him to the kitchen. Even though I've seen it before, the opulence amazes me all over again.

"Have a seat," Bryson says. He taps the barstool before heading to the oven to preheat it. Bryson then moves to the large double-door fridge and opens it. He peers inside for a while. Then he carries an armful of ingredients to the counter before returning for more. I watch as he works. He rinses the vegetables and starts to chop them.

"What are you making?" I ask. I swing from side to side.

"A bacon breakfast casserole as the main, something with greens, and then something sweet for you." He taps the waffle iron.

"For me?"

"Yeah. You said you like sweet things."

"You remembered?" I ask.

"Of course," Bryson says. "I always pay attention to you."

I feel my face start to redden, and to distract him I ask, "Is there anything I can help with?"

"Cute." Bryson laughs. "Just sit there and enjoy the show."

And so I do. Never before did I think cooking could be sexy, but watching Bryson work changes my mind. Judging from the happiness that he radiates, it's clear that he loves cooking.

"Maybe this can be your new dream?"

"You haven't tasted my food. How do you know it's any good?"

I shrug. "You just look so happy. So I figure if it can make you *this* happy, then it should be your new dream."

"I'll take that under advisement."

Bryson and I continue to talk as he cooks. And it is effortless and easy when my life feels anything but.

Eggs crack, bacon sizzles, and time passes. Soon the kitchen is filled with an aroma that makes my stomach growl. Bryson must hear it, because he smiles.

"Come here and try this," he says. "It's scrambled eggs with green peppers and mushrooms." He blows on the spoon before holding it up between us. I lean forward and taste it. Flavor bursts in my mouth.

Bryson's mother enters the kitchen when we're standing like that. She barely offers us a glance, as if it's the most ordinary thing in the world.

"He's a really good cook, isn't he?" she says. She leaves with the bottle of water that she came for.

I pull back—startled.

"I think she knows," I whisper.

Bryson studies my mouth. He reaches for it and wipes away a bit of egg. I feel his thumb dance across my top lip, and I freeze. Later, I will recall this moment and relive it in vivid detail, but for now I am simply numb.

Hannah reenters the kitchen. Like a breath being held, everything stops. Bryson's mother looks at us before picking up an apple from the fruit bowl and leaving again.

"She most definitely knows," Bryson says. He sighs, but it

doesn't hold any fear or sadness or anything. It's a simple *Oh well*. He leans down and gives me a peck on my lips before starting to stir the pot once more.

I can't help but feel envious and think about how different our situations are. Bryson's family has barely batted an eye at us. In comparison to the disaster that was last night, this feels so strange. I sigh. Why couldn't my parents have been this chill?

"You're not allowed to think about anything bad today," Bryson says. He bumps me with his hip. "Try to forget for a bit."

I exhale, releasing the bad thoughts. Bryson's right. Today I just want to relax and enjoy myself. I just want to enjoy one day before I have to go face the storm.

I return to my seat and watch as Bryson mixes the batter for the waffles. When he's done, I help him set the table. We carry over the freshly baked casserole, the scrambled eggs, and the waffles with whipped cream—the only thing that's store-bought. Soon we're all seated and ready to eat.

"It looks so good," I say.

"If I'd had more time, I'd have properly planned a menu." He offers me a tight-lipped smile. Is he nervous to have me eat food he's cooked?

"My brother has skills to pay the bills," Crystal says as she digs in. "So good."

"Thank you for the food, son," Bryson's mother says before she, too, starts eating.

I take my first bite and savor the taste.

"How is it?" Bryson asks me.

"So good."

"Really? I'm glad you like it." Bryson's smile grows now. He shows off the dimple that has become one of my favorite things about him. I mirror him.

"It's so cute I might die," Crystal teases. She's stopped eating and is watching the two of us.

"Crystal, behave," Hannah says. She cuts into her casserole and takes a bite.

"Yes, Crystal, behave," Bryson echoes.

Bryson's mother turns her attention to me. "What do your parents do, Kai?"

"Mom owns an accounting firm and Dad's in IT."

The conversation flows from there, and I find myself relaxing and opening up. We eat and we talk and I forget. And it feels nice. . . . It feels normal.

"Dad called me this morning," Crystal says, and everyone tenses.

"Crystal."

"It's okay, Mom. Kai knows." Bryson smiles at me.

"It was ridiculous to me when he made someone who is two years older than me my stepmother. But now she's pregnant. I'll be twenty-four years older than the baby." Crystal shakes her head. "Does this make sense?"

"Whether you agree to see him and spend time with him is a decision that I'll leave up to you two," Hannah says. "At the end of the day, he will always be your father, and he's at least trying to make an effort now."

"I suppose it beats him trying to buy our love."

"I had my eye on a Louis Vuitton bag," Crystal says. "He's free to buy my love, thank you very much."

"Crystal, please."

"I'm kidding, Mom," Crystal says, but she shakes her head at me as she does so.

Hannah sighs, but there's a smile dancing at her lips, too.

"Oh, did you let your professors know about your accident?" Hannah asks.

"Yes. I'm sure Professor Bartley was more than thrilled to hear I wouldn't be there to ask him questions."

"Crystal studies at UCLA," Bryson whispers to me. "And Professor Bartley is her archnemesis."

"It's truly impossible for me to explain how much I loathe that man," Crystal says. "Just thinking about him gives me a headache."

"What are you studying?"

"Psychology."

"For now," Bryson says. He turns to me. "She's changed her major more than a few times."

Crystal looks at us, and her face is dead serious. "Bryson, I just met Kai. Don't make him have a bad impression of me. These impressions matter. How will I face him at Thanksgiving or Christmas?"

I blush at her words.

"Oh. My. God," Crystal says. "That is the cutest."

Bryson smiles. "I know, right?"

"Kai, please forgive my children."

"We're not that bad, Mom," Bryson says.

"We're practically angels," Crystal adds.

"Whatever helps you two sleep at night." Bryson's mother puts her cutlery down.

At the end of the meal, Bryson says, "Since I cooked, Crystal has to do the dishes." Bryson grins in that way of his that tells me he's really enjoying this moment. "Fair is fair."

"I literally have a cast on my arm. Do you want me to lick them clean?" Crystal asks her brother.

"I'll do them," I offer.

"Fine, I'll help," Crystal says. She stands and looks at her brother. "Prepare for your ears to itch because we're so going to talk about you." She looks at me then. "Let's go, Kai."

I stand and follow Crystal into the kitchen.

27

"So, how did you two meet?" Crystal awkwardly scrapes left-overs into the trash can. I offered to do it for her, but somehow she's managing. "I mean, I know you go to the same school, but how did you two start going out?"

"I asked him out." It feels so weird to be talking about this openly, especially with Bryson's sister. It's weird, but not at all uncomfortable because I can tell that she's genuinely curious without any hidden motives, agendas, or judgments.

"And he said yes?"

"Well, it's part of his dare." I scrub a plate clean as we talk. "You know about the Bryson Keller dare, right?"

Crystal groans and rolls her eyes. "Dustin told me about it when it first happened. I've even clicked on that hashtag a few times." She shakes her head. "It's good to know Fairvale Academy doesn't change. And it doesn't surprise me in the least that Bryson is at the center of something so absurd."

"I'm not complaining about the dare," I admit. I would

never. It's how this all started with Bryson. I wouldn't be here without it.

Crystal shivers. "You just gave me goose bumps." She studies me. "You're so whipped." Crystal hands me a plate and I wash it before placing it on the dish rack to drip-dry. "Do you kids even say *whipped*? Everything changes so quickly, it's hard to keep up with what's in these days."

"You're not that old. Why are you acting like you are?" Crystal and I turn to find Bryson standing at the kitchen doorway.

"It's rude to eavesdrop," Crystal says. "So, is the dare over?" She looks from Bryson to me. "Did he lose?"

"Yes," we say at exactly the same time.

Crystal clutches at make-believe pearls. "Oh, the drama . . . the scandal . . . the romance." She brings the back of her hand to her forehead and performs a fake swoon.

"You're insufferable," Bryson says to her. He looks at me. "If you're done, I'd like to take my boyfriend and leave."

Warmth spreads up my neck toward my face.

"Where are we going?"

"No meal is complete without dessert," Bryson says.

"Bring me back something nice," Crystal calls out as we leave the kitchen.

"No, buy your own."

"Rude!" Crystal shouts back. "You better sleep with one eye open tonight."

I laugh. The relationship between Bryson and Crystal

is surprising. I don't know why, but it is. Maybe I just never thought of Bryson Keller as someone who would be close to his sister. He just didn't seem the type. I don't know what made me judge him in that way, but I'm glad that I got to witness this. I'm glad that I got this window into Bryson's life.

"What are you smiling about?" Bryson asks as we head to the Jeep.

"Just thinking."

"About?"

"You."

Bryson stops walking, and I do, too.

"What's wrong?"

"You can't just say things like that," Bryson says. Dread starts to grow as I think I've done something bad. "You'll make me fall for you harder than I already have." I exhale a sigh of relief, then smile.

We climb into the Jeep, and after a stop for gas, Bryson drives us toward a famous ice cream parlor in town. Because it's a Sunday afternoon, Swirl It Up is filled with families. A pang shoots across my chest at the sight of all the happy little families. In the past, my family often stopped here for a Sunday treat after church.

"What are you having?" Bryson's question pulls me from the past and grounds me in the present. The girl behind the counter looks up from what she's doing and her eyes snag on Bryson. She doesn't look away from him. I can relate, because sometimes I, too, find myself staring at Bryson Keller.

"I'll have the three-scoop Berry-Berry Delicious," I say.

"And I'll have the Mega-Choc," Bryson says. His dimple is showing. He's clearly very pleased at the idea of three large scoops of chocolate.

We wait for our orders and then head back to the Jeep. Bryson drives us toward Melody Beach.

"I hate that Dustin's ruined this spot," Bryson says.

"The good outweighs the bad," I say, and open the door. "Let's go."

We walk down to the beach and sit side by side. We eat our ice cream in silence, both perfectly content with just being next to one another.

"You know, I don't have any photos of my boyfriend," Bryson says after a while.

"You keep saying that," I say. "'Boyfriend.'"

"Why?" Bryson asks. "You don't like it?"

"No," I say. "I really, really, really like it."

"Good." Bryson smiles and leans toward me. "Boyfriend . . . boyfriend . . . boyfriend." He punctuates each word with a kiss to my cheek. On the last one, though, I turn so that our lips meet.

"I also really, really, really like my boyfriend," I say.

"He really, really, really likes you, too."

We kiss.

When we pull back, we're both breathless.

Bryson reaches for his phone. "I was being serious earlier. I really want photos of you."

Bryson opens his camera and leans in to pose next to me. We take a few selfies of us just smiling or making funny faces. Then he leans in and kisses me on the cheek. He takes a picture of us in that position. It is almost an exact mirror of the one we took before, in the photo booth. The one that my mom destroyed.

"This one can't be ruined," Bryson says as he studies it. It's like he's read my mind. As I stare at him I wonder how I got so lucky. How the stars aligned so perfectly to lead me to this moment. I don't wonder too hard, though. I simply accept it.

"Send them to me."

"Will do."

Bryson swipes through the pictures that he's taken for a while. Then he opens the camera again. He takes my hand in his and interlocks our fingers. He holds them up toward the sky so that they are framed by the sunset. He takes a picture. I watch as he goes about setting it as his wallpaper.

"You're so extra," I say.

Bryson smiles. "I'm romantic. There's a difference."

"Uh-huh."

We sit like that, watching the sun go down in our own little piece of the world. Both Bryson and I know what has to happen next. This has only been a short reprieve. It's been perfect, sure, but perfection has a nasty habit of not lasting very long. Most times it's simply an illusion and not reality.

"I think we should go now," Bryson says. His voice is soft and soothing.

"I know." I sigh, dreading what waits for me when I go home.

Bryson stands and dusts the sand from his shorts. He offers me his hand and pulls me up. But he doesn't let it go. Instead, he leans down so our foreheads are touching.

"Do you want me to go with you?" he asks. "I can."

"I think I have to do it alone," I say.

If I were in any physical danger, I would have said yes. I know what awaits me at home isn't fists or physical abuse. It's disappointment and words shaped by religion and tinged with prejudice.

Bryson leads me to the Jeep and then we're on our way. We reach home too fast. I sit unmoving and stare at my house. Both Mom's and Dad's cars are in the driveway, which means everyone is home. It's Sunday evening, so of course that's the case. Belatedly, I wonder if they went to church as they normally do. Did they go and try to pray the gay away?

Bryson lifts my hand to his mouth and kisses it. "I wish there was more I could do," he says. There isn't. It's now or never. I reach for the door handle.

"Call me if you need me," Bryson says as I open the door.

"Will do."

I climb out of the Jeep and step firmly into reality.

"Thanks for today," I say. "And for last night."

"Anytime," Bryson says. And I can tell that he means it. He will be there if I call, when I call. I don't have a Prince Charming on a white horse. Instead, I have one in a white Jeep.

I stop before the front door and turn to look back. Bryson

is still there. Somehow this feels a little easier knowing that I have him. I'm not completely alone.

I wave, and he waves back. Then I turn to face the door that I've never before dreaded entering like I do now.

I close my eyes and turn the handle.

I step inside and shut the door behind me.

28

"I'm home," I announce to no one in particular. I figure it's the right thing to do. Despite everything, they are my parents, and I hope that they will always love me. That they will always care about my safety.

I pause to take off my shoes. Yazz runs down the stairs and barrels into me. I barely manage to keep us both upright.

"If you ever make me worry like that again, I'll kill you myself," Yazz says. She pulls back to study me. "I'm too young to get gray hair. Think of my beauty."

I smile. "Thank you, Yazz." She nods and lets me go. "Where is everyone?" I whisper.

Yazz shrugs. "This is the quietest our house has ever been."

"Sorry."

"It's not your fault."

She's right, but it still feels that way. I walk up to my bedroom and close my door behind me. I turn on a playlist and hit shuffle. The music blares around me as I sit on my bed.

This isn't what I want. I don't want my family to be this way just because I'm gay.

I'm not sure how long I sit there and stare blankly ahead, but eventually I get up and change my clothes. My phone lights up with a text. I open the three musketeers group chat.

How is it? Donny asks.

Are you okay? Priya adds.

Yes. It's scary quiet though.

Should we very naturally come over? Priya asks.

Yeah. It can be totally like, oh hey we wanted to visit. Nice to see you again. Totally normal, Donny adds.

I don't know if that will make it better or worse, I say.

My phone vibrates with a call. *Kelly* flashes on-screen. I swipe to answer it.

"Hello."

"Kai, are you all right?"

"No," I say. "I'm not."

"Should I come over?"

"No, it's fine. I'm fine. I'm in my bedroom."

"What did your parents say?"

"Nothing. I haven't seen them."

Bryson gets quiet. "Are you sure you don't want me to come over?"

"This is enough," I say to him. "Can we just stay like this for a while?"

So we stay like that. Not talking. Just listening to each other exist. I let three songs play before I break the silence.

"I'll call you if anything happens," I say eventually.

"Okay. I'll see you tomorrow."

"Bye."

We hang up. There's a knock at my door and Yazz pops her head in. "Dinner's ready."

"I'm not hungry."

"Even if that's true, you have to do this," Yazz says. "Never cower in front of the enemy."

"Enemy? They're our parents, Yazz."

"Right now they are the enemy." Yazz grabs my hand and yanks me from my bed. "You can do this. Say what you need to say. It's not healthy to keep stuff bottled inside."

"Are you sure you're thirteen?"

"Maturity has nothing to do with age." She pulls me out of my bedroom, toward the bathroom. "Wash your face."

Yazz waits for me while I follow her instructions. I stare at myself in the mirror. My face looks pale, making the faint bruises stand out, and my eyes look lost. I take a calming breath, but it fails to do anything. Eventually I give up and leave the bathroom behind.

Yazz leads me down the stairs. When I get to the dining room table, Mom and Dad are already seated there. Dad looks up at me and our eyes meet, but I look away. Mom keeps staring at her plate of food. She's fiddling with her gold cross pendant.

I'm about to turn around and run from the room, but Yazz takes my hand in hers and guides me to a seat. She slides into the seat next to Mom, and I take the one Yazz usually sits in.

"Let's say grace," Yazz says. She holds out her hand and I place mine in hers. Yazz glances at our parents. "Well?"

Mom places her hand in Yazz's and takes Dad's. He holds out his other hand to me and I take it. Dad squeezes it twice. I look up but find his eyes already closed. I'm pretty sure I imagined it, but then Dad opens his eyes and offers me a small nod.

Yazz starts to lead us in prayer. "Our Father, we have come together to share a meal. Thank you for providing this food and for allowing us to gather as a family. Bless us, O Lord, and bless the hands that prepared this meal. . . ." The prayer starts off the same as the one we say before eating any meal, but soon Yazz alters it to deliver a different message. "And, Father God, help this family now. We stand at a crossroads, and I pray that you guide us to take the right path, heavenly Father. You created Kai in your own image, and only you can judge him, Father God. I ask that you remind everyone of that fact. Heavenly Father, I ask that you show us all that love is love and that a family cannot call itself that when there is hatred and unacceptance," Yazz says. "And, Father, help Kai say what he needs to say. And help my parents listen to him as he does this very scary and brave thing. I ask this all in the almighty name of Jesus. Amen."

Yazz opens her eyes and looks around the table. "Let's eat."

Misty-eyed, I stare at my sister. I'm not alone in this house. One by one, we all start to eat. The sound of cutlery is all that can be heard. Yazz looks from me to my parents. She sighs. "Kai, there was something you wanted to say?"

I shake my head. Dad stops eating and looks at me. "Say what you need to say, son."

I meet his gaze and Dad nods. I appreciate his effort.

I clear my throat. This is it. My voice is nothing more than a whisper.

"Mom and Dad, this is the moment I've feared since I was ten years old. I was that young when I first started to think I was different from the other boys. It wasn't because I felt any different, but rather because everyone around me kept insisting that I'd be different if I was gay. That I'd be sinning because of who I am." My voice gets louder now. I almost sound like myself, except for the tears that I'm trying to blink back. "But I knew that my being gay was unchangeable. It was just like the color of my skin. Something that was a part of me and made me who I am. I'm the same Kai that you know and love. Dad, I'm the son you shoot hoops with and take to the barber to get his hair cut. Mom, I watch those old rom-coms with you and help you solve the crosswords in the newspaper. I'll always be the Kai Sheridan that you made all those memories with.

"I'm still me. Nothing's changed. I know that for certain. Yes, I'm gay, but I'm still me. I know what the Bible says, Mom, but I'm asking you to put your faith in me. I'm asking you to put your faith in your son. I'm not any different just because society wants me to be. I'm the same. So please, Mom and Dad, love me just like you always have? *Please?*" My voice breaks on the last word. I look up to find both Mom and Dad blinking back tears.

I'm hopeful. For one solitary heartbeat, I see a light at the end of this dark and lonely tunnel, but then Mom gets up. And without a word, she leaves the table.

Dad reaches for my hand. He looks at me. "I love you, Kai," Dad says. He gets up and follows Mom. "I'll talk to her."

Yazz and I are left staring at each other. She pushes up her glasses. "You did well, Kai. Now it's on them."

I swallow the lump in my throat. I make to move my plate to the kitchen, but Yazz stops me. "Go. I'll do this."

I nod and leave the dining room behind. I head up the stairs, and as I do, I try to choke down the sound of my crying.

I enter my bedroom and fall face-first onto my bed.

I cry myself to sleep.

MONDAY

29

I roll from my bed and flinch. My body is sore, but it feels a lot better since Bryson applied ointment to my wounds. As soon as I open my eyes, I text Bryson.

Bryson being so worried about me only adds to the feelings I'm developing for him. What started as simple like and attraction is growing and changing into something more. It both scares and thrills me.

The three musketeers group chat lights up.

Are you coming to school with Bryson or do you need me to fetch you? Donny asks.

Bryson.

Okay. We'll see you in the parking lot.

I cross my bedroom and open the door. I peek my head out, but no one is around on the second floor. Down below I hear Mom and Dad clattering. They aren't speaking, though. It seems that the house is still under a spell of silence.

I dash to the bathroom and take a shower, then brush my teeth and shave. Once I'm back in my bedroom, I start getting dressed. I have time to kill seeing as how I'm actively avoiding the kitchen.

Eventually seven o' clock comes, and I grab my school things and dash for the door.

"I'm leaving," I shout, again to no one in particular. I pull the door open to find Bryson standing there. His finger is raised to ring the doorbell.

"What are you doing?" I ask as I close the door behind me.

"I was worried," Bryson says. He grabs me by the shoulders. "Are you okay? Did anything happen?"

The door swings open and Yazz steps out. She's dressed for school. Yazz goes to the same public middle school I did, so she doesn't wear a school uniform. I must be dreaming because never before has Yazz been ready for school so early.

"Hey," Yazz says. "Could I get a ride to school?"

"What are you doing?" I ask. "Mom usually takes you to school."

Yazz looks from Bryson to me and stares at his hands on my shoulders.

"I'm protesting," Yazz says.

"What?"

"I don't like the bullshit in this house, and I refuse to be a part of it."

"Language," I say, but I don't really mean the reprimand, because my heart is melting.

Bryson holds up a hand and Yazz gives him a high five. "You're officially my hero, Yasmine," he tells her.

"It's Yazz, and I take it that's a yes to the ride?"

"It's a yes to whatever you want," Bryson says. He leaves me standing there and trails after my sister. I blink at the sudden turn of events.

"What are you doing, Kai?" Yazz calls out.

"Yeah, Kai, what are you doing?" Bryson echoes. Bryson helps Yazz into the back seat of the Jeep and then looks at me. He cocks an eyebrow as if to ask, *Well?*

"Did you tell Mom you were getting a ride to school?" I ask when I've climbed into the Jeep, too.

"I left a very angrily worded letter," Yazz says.

Bryson and I share a look. He can't fight the smile on his lips, and neither can I.

"Let's eat," Bryson says, which earns him a cheer from Yazz. We head to Glenda's and we both allow Yazz to order whatever she wants.

After breakfast, we drop Yazz off at school before racing toward Fairvale Academy. The unplanned detour has made us later than usual, but neither of us complains. Both of us haven't stopped smiling.

"Your sister is amazing," Bryson muses. He grabs my hand and places a chaste kiss there.

"I've always said she could rule the world if she wanted to."

With ten minutes left until the start of the day, we pull into the parking lot. Bryson parks the Jeep and we get out. I spot Shannon standing far from the crowd, at the stairs leading inside. She's looking down at our cars, at us. It's surprising that she isn't waiting for Bryson. Given her actions last week, I assumed she'd be first to ask him out today. Before I can question it further, Priya and Donny rush toward me.

"Are you sure you're okay?" Priya asks.

"Jesus. Your face."

"It looks a lot better than it did," I say to Donny.

"Hey, Bryson," Priya says.

Bryson waves. "Hi, Priyanka, Donny."

"You can call me Priya."

"What, really?" Bryson smiles. "Well, I'll leave you guys to talk. See you later, Priya, Donny," Bryson says. "I'll see you in drama, Kai."

Bryson doesn't get very far, because he's soon surrounded by girls. We watch as Louise Keaton steps up to Bryson. The look on her face is one of pure determination. "Date me, Bryson Keller!" she says.

Bryson looks from her to me. "Sorry, but I'm already dating someone."

"What! Who?" Louise asks. She scans the girls at her back, searching for any sign of smugness. When she finds looks of dismay on their faces, she turns to face Bryson.

"I was first," Louise says. "So whoever asked you out did it before you arrived at school. That isn't fair."

Bryson shrugs. "No one's actually asked me out today."

"Then what are you talking about?" Louise turns to us. "Kai, do you know what he's talking about?" It seems the chance to date Bryson Keller is enough to make my ex-girlfriend forget that she vowed never to speak to me again.

"Uh, no." Maybe someday soon I'll be able to answer her honestly, but for now I lie.

"So, what's up?" she asks Bryson.

"Just that the whole dare is over," Bryson says. "You should tell as many people as you can. I lost. After spring break, I'll be taking the bus." He casts a mournful look at his Jeep but smiles when he turns to me.

"Over! What do you mean, over?" Louise asks. Her face is a mask of horror. It's like she can't believe this is happening.

All this is giving me a headache. "Let's head inside," I tell my friends.

We're walking toward the school building when Priya suddenly stills. "This bitch."

Donny and I both stop walking and look at Priya, but her eyes are on her phone. We move to stand at either side of her. Priya has the latest issue of the *Fairvale Academy Herald* out.

The headline reads *Closet Case: What It Means to Be a Gay Teen Now.*

"You know nothing," he said to me once. And through my investigation I realized that his words were true. I do know nothing—about him or the situation he faces. To most of us, coming out is an abstract notion, but to some, it is a life-or-death moment. The thing that defines them. And in high school, where labels run rampant and everyone wants to put everyone else into a box, gay teens are forced to conform to what society deems the norm.

I skim the rest of it, but my eyes snag on the parts toward the end.

Eric Ferguson, founder of Fairvale Academy's very own

LGBTQ club, had this to say when I questioned him about what it means to be gay in this day and age: "That we even still need to come out annoys me—no, it angers me. Straight people don't have this fear. They're free to just love and be who they are. We, on the other hand, are forced into the shadows, and when we do step into the light, we're shunned for doing so. Yes, we have taken great steps, but we still have a far walk to go until we are truly treated as equal."

I hadn't thought of this. But Eric's words are backed up by the fact that the subject of this article has had to hide and keep to the shadows, only truly being himself in a different city, and far away from high school.

Two pictures follow. The first is of me in line for the Graces' concert. In the background, there's a group of men being affectionate with one another. They don't look like strangers; they look like a group I'm a part of. It must have been taken while I was waiting for Bryson. A picture is worth a thousand words, and this one is telling a story of its own.

For those in the closet, it's all about hiding, it's all about keeping up the facade that you're normal. . . . But what does normal even mean? Who decided that? And why are gay teens still forced to keep secrets and live double lives?

The second photo is of me kissing someone who is clearly a boy. It's the photo that Dustin took, but Bryson's been blurred out. I'm the only one on show for the world to see.

Whatever relationships develop either have to happen in the spotlight, much like Eric Ferguson said, or have to be kept in the shadows, rendezvous in secluded areas. It's unfair, and until this *article I didn't realize it was still this bad. I can see now that we still have a long way to go.*

"*I don't know, maybe if you looked beyond all that you'd get to know the real me,*" *he said to me in what sounded like a desperate plea. It was truth so loud that I found that I couldn't ignore it. So I want you to know that we see you, Kai Sheridan. We support you. Live your truth.*

The words start to blur into each other. My face is a flaming mess. The sound of blood gushes in my ears. Everyone in the parking lot turns to stare at me. Then the whispers start.

I go numb.

I feel nothing.

I hear nothing.

Donny grips me to hold me up. I'm sure without him I'd crumble.

This secret that I've tried my hardest to protect is now out there.

Coming out is supposed to be by choice.

It isn't meant to be like this.

Never like this.

30

My numbness doesn't last long. Soon I am filled with pure, undiluted rage. I've never before had strong enough feelings to say that I hate someone, but I'm pretty sure that what I feel toward both Dustin and Shannon right now is hatred—the bone-deep kind.

If they were trapped in a burning building, I would hesitate to save them.

In the end, though, I would because I'm not a goddamn monster. But with the article, it's clear that both Shannon and Dustin are. They set fire to my house while I was locked in the closet.

"Kai, are you okay?" Priya asks.

I can't speak.

"Where's Bryson going?" Donny asks. "It looks like he's going to murder someone."

I look up and watch as Bryson storms into the school building. The start-of-day bell rings.

"We should get out of here," Priya suggests.

"Yeah, let's go," Donny says. He reaches for his car keys.

"No." I start walking to assembly. I won't run away, even though I really want to. I have done nothing wrong. I will not let Shannon and Dustin win. I walk into the auditorium. I try my hardest not to care about the pointed stares and fevered whispers.

The fifteen minutes of announcements drag by, but I focus on every word the principal says. I ignore everyone around me whispering about the article . . . about me. Donny and Priya stick close to me. They become my shield. I offer them a small smile. It's all I can afford right now—a token of my appreciation.

The bell rings and everyone leaves the auditorium. I keep my head down and wait for drama to start. I feel the weight of eyes on me. It makes my skin crawl. Blood rushes to my face. Not because I'm embarrassed that I'm gay, but because I hate the attention. I hate that who I was born to love is now the latest gossip within Fairvale Academy. It shouldn't be sprawled on the front page of a newspaper. My being gay isn't news. *What the hell was Shannon thinking?*

I stand and take a seat away from everyone else. I pull my play from my bag and stare at a random page until Mrs. Henning arrives just before the start-of-period bell rings.

"Good morrow, my thespians." She scans the class as she comes to a stop in the center of the stage. "Where are your plays? Why are we so distracted today?" Mrs. Henning claps.

"Please, everyone, work with me." She sighs and opens up her playbook. "Shall we cast the roles for today?"

Not me, not me, not me . . . It becomes my mantra. Maybe even a prayer. Each time a role is assigned without my name being mentioned is a blessing. I am able to breathe.

"Now, for the role of Juliet?" Mrs. Henning looks up from her own play, searching for a volunteer among the sea of students.

"Yes, Isaac?" Mrs. Henning calls when she notices a hand waving in the air. "Would you like to read?"

"No," Isaac says. "But I think Kai might. I think he'd be perfect for the role."

I startle at the mention of my name. And it hurts more because it's him. The snickers start then.

"What's so funny?" Mrs. Henning asks. "The roles of women were often performed by men. Kai, would you like to?" That she doesn't get it makes this worse. Her question is another jab to the heart. I can't think. I can't speak. I can't breathe.

Everyone is watching me, judging me. I want to crawl out of my skin. I want nothing more than to run from this room and never come back. I swallow and lean forward. Do I do this? Do I give everyone the satisfaction of performing as Juliet, like they want? Or do I ignore it?

"I'll do it." Just like last Monday, Bryson walks into drama late. His voice is loud and clear. Everyone watches Bryson as he makes his way to the stage. I don't. I can't.

"You're late, Mr. Keller," Mrs. Henning says. "See me at lunch."

"Yes, ma'am," Bryson says. "But even so, please let me read the role."

"As you wish."

Bryson sits. I want to ask what happened, where he went, but I'm in no position to do so. Instead, I turn my attention to the page in front of me. I stare at it right until the bell rings.

I don't wait for anyone. Not even Bryson. I'm off the stage and out the door even before the bell finishes ringing. I walk-run toward my next class with my head down. It is my sole focus. I realize too late just what hell awaits me next.

Fairvale Academy is on a two-week schedule. So every two weeks the same timetable is followed. Last week, I didn't have PE second and third period, but now I do.

It's well after the changeover has ended, and I'm standing and staring at the doors to the gym. I'm trying to convince myself to enter when someone comes to a stop next to me. In a daze, I turn to find Bryson there. His chest is heaving because he ran all the way here, ran after me. We're the only two in this hallway.

"You don't have to do this," Bryson says. "I'll take you home."

"Go to class," I say. Bryson doesn't have PE with me. "I don't want to be the reason for you to be outed, too. I refuse to let them do it to you, too."

Before we're seen together, I head into the gym and walk

toward the locker room. I can hear the other boys already in there. Dread turns my blood to stone. The door swings open and everyone stops to stare at me.

"I think you're in the wrong room," one of the boys says. "The girls' locker room is next door." I flinch. The words are like rocks.

Anyone who thinks that homophobia doesn't exist in this day and age has never been the gay boy standing in a boys' locker room. I should say something. Defend myself. Make a quip or a joke or something. But I don't. I can't.

The door swings open behind me. Briefly, I hope that it's Bryson. That he didn't listen to me, and he's come to defend me, to save me yet again. I know it's unfair to expect that of him, but my heart doesn't care.

"I warned you."

I turn to stare into the face of Dustin Smith. He has a freshly busted lip, but he looks smug—happy, even. Rage floods my whole being. I turn to him and grab him by the shirt. Dustin is everything I thought he was before. . . . No, actually, he's worse. "I told you I'd use the pic. I was going to delete it, but I saw you yesterday at *his* house. You don't listen. I figured Shannon would know what to do with it. I didn't realize she'd been working on an article all along. I guess it all worked out, huh?" Dustin says.

"How could you?" My voice is low, but somehow everyone in the locker room stops what they're doing and watches me.

Dustin smirks. "Listen, Kai, I'm flattered and all, but I really don't like dudes."

The boys at my back snicker. This is all funny to them. It's like they haven't realized they've changed my life forever.

I step back, dumbfounded. Dustin isn't sorry about this at all. I retrace my steps until I'm outside the gym.

"Kai, are you okay?" Tears blur my vision, but even without being able to see him clearly, I know that it's Bryson. He hasn't left. He was waiting for me. "I don't like seeing you like this. Let me help you. *Please*."

The sincerity of his request is like a tidal wave crashing into my resolve. I almost give in—*almost*. I study him. Bryson's uniform is untidy, and his fists are bruised. Is he the cause of Dustin's freshly busted lip?

"I want to be alone," I say. I turn to walk away. Bryson calls after me, but I ignore him.

I need to think.

I need to feel.

I need to break.

And I need to do it all by myself—I need to do it alone.

31

I walk with no real direction, only the will to leave this place and never come back. My feet carry me, and I follow them without argument. Those students who linger in the halls stop and stare, but I don't care. I've shut down from the hurt.

My house is ten minutes away from school by car, but today I walk. By the time I reach our street, my feet ache in my shoes, and I'm pretty sure that my socks are wet with more than just sweat. Again, I don't care. I feel too empty to do so.

I'm so lost in my own thoughts that I barely take notice of the things around me. I don't notice Dad's car in the driveway, and it isn't until I'm through the front door that I realize he's working from home today.

"Kai, what's wrong?" Dad, without any hesitation, crosses the room and hugs me.

My tears start then. He pulls me to his chest and holds me as I release everything I am feeling.

Dad has never shied away from showing me affection. He's never believed that boys shouldn't be hugged, kissed, or loved. And so Dad stands there holding me tight while I sob.

Between my sobs, I tell him everything. I unload about everything that's happened at school. And even when the words stop and all I have left are my tears and snot, he holds me.

"Everything's going to be all right, Kai," Dad says. His words are what I need right now. "I'm sorry, and I love you. I always will." He holds me at arm's length. "How about I make you something to eat?"

I follow him to the kitchen and take a seat. I watch him work in silence before he clears his throat.

"I want to apologize," he says. "Mom and I messed up on Saturday." Dad's grating cheese onto a plate but stops to look at me. "I'm sorry for how much we must have hurt you. I know nothing can make up for that, but I'm sorry anyway."

Dad's sincerity is like a balm to my raw emotions. For the third time today, I feel myself on the verge of crying.

"I didn't choose to be this way," I say.

"I know, son, I know." He moves around the island and comes to hug me again. "It must have been so hard for you to carry this all alone."

I nod. "I wanted to be the one to tell you, when I was ready."

"I'm sorry that it happened this way. But I'm not sorry that we know." Dad bends down so that we are standing eye-to-eye. "I want to tell you that I love you and that I accept you."

"I'm scared, Dad," I admit. "Everything's changed now that people know. I'm not just Kai Sheridan anymore. I'm Kai Sheridan—the gay one."

Dad sighs. "It's going to be tough, but I want you to live your life for you from now on. You deserve to be happy. You deserve to love and be loved."

"What about Mom?" I ask. "Will she ever be okay with this? Okay with me?"

"Of course," Dad says. And he sounds so sure that I find myself wanting to believe him with every fiber of my being. "I know it might be unfair to you, but give Mom some time. She loves you, and nothing is ever going to change that. Nothing could ever." Dad sighs again. "I think it's just the shock of it all that has us acting foolish. That isn't on you, though. I want you to be happy."

I want that, too. I want to be happy. I want to live—it's all I've ever wanted.

Dad returns to the cheese. He finishes grating, gets bread, and starts to make a grilled cheese sandwich. I watch as Dad butters both sides before placing the sandwich down in a piping-hot pan. It sizzles. Dad's making me my favorite.

I smile. Though things are uneasy between us, I can tell that they will get better. Nothing ever stays the same.

As I start to eat, Dad leaves the kitchen. He returns with his laptop and sits down next to me. We don't talk. We don't need to. Just having him next to me helps. Dad places a folded piece of paper in front of me. I open it and read it:

Dear Mom and Dad,

    I have never been this disappointed to be your child before. I hope you're aware that your treatment of Kai was totally unacceptable, and you should both be very ashamed of yourselves. I understand that we grew up religious and I know our faith matters, but does it matter more than the happiness and safety of your son? No one is asking you to not believe in God. You can do that and continue to love and support your son. The two are not mutually exclusive. Please reflect on what you have done and make amends. Until you do, I, Yasmine Sheridan, will not be speaking to you both.

    It is with a heavy heart that I have written this letter, but it was necessary. I hope to see some improvement in your behavior soon. Please do not disappoint me again. Even though I am angry at you, I still love you both.

—Yazz

I choke back tears, but I'm also smiling. My sister is amazing.

"It's true when they say that children aren't born with hate or prejudice," Dad says. "It's us who teach them those things. I'll never stop being sorry to both you and Yazz, Kai." Dad pats my shoulder. I turn to look at him and find that he's blinking back tears, too. I reach for him and hug him. Dad hugs me back.

"Here." I hand the letter back to Dad.

"You should keep it," Dad says.

I nod.

· · ·

I'm at the sink washing my dishes when I hear the screech of tires. The front door opens with a bang and Mom storms into the kitchen.

"I got your text. What's wrong?" Mom asks Dad. I don't look at them, focusing all my attention on the dishes. Dad tells her what's happened with the *Fairvale Academy Herald*.

"What?" she shouts. Mom spins on her heel and races out of the room.

"Honey!" Dad calls out. He's stopped her at the front door. "Where are you going?"

"I'm going to deal with those fuckers." Mom's swearing causes me to drop the plate. It shatters, but I don't move to pick it up. Instead, I turn to look at my mother.

Mom never swears.

That's when I realize that Mom may not understand me quite yet, but she loves me regardless. I am her son. It doesn't make up for how poorly she handled my being gay, but I feel my heart mend just a little bit. Actions speak louder than words, and right now Mom is showing me that she will always love me.

Mom leaves Dad standing there, and a moment later, he runs out of the house, too.

I run to our front steps. Dad is chasing after Mom. By the time he gets her to stop the car, she's already in front of the neighbor's house. I think that Dad is trying to convince her to come back home—to talk things over. But instead, he climbs into the car, too.

I watch as my parents rush to Fairvale Academy.

As they head into battle for me.

TUESDAY

32

I've barely slept at all. My mind races with all that's happened. I reach for my phone and find it dead. I haven't bothered to charge it. I haven't bothered to do much of anything aside from lying here and staring at the ceiling.

It's fast approaching midday and I'm still in bed. Beneath these covers, the world outside ceases to exist. I'm happy to pretend. Or at least I would be if I wasn't starving.

Last night I heard Mom say she would work from home today. It's another reason for me to not want to leave my room. There's still an awkwardness between us. I sigh. I'm curious to know what happened yesterday, but when I close my eyes, I can vividly recall the hurt. It hasn't scabbed over yet.

There's a knock at my door and I pause. I even go as far as holding my breath.

"Can I come in, Kai?" Mom asks. Her voice is soft and unsure. I wait for the turning of the door handle, but it doesn't come. Instead, she stands and waits.

"Uh . . . sure." I sit up and run a hand through my bedhead curls.

Mom enters my bedroom like it's her first time doing so. She looks around before her eyes settle on me.

She exhales. "We need to talk."

I nod. She crosses the room and takes a seat at my desk. Mom's hands rest on her knees, and she's gripping them tightly. She seems nervous. I am, too. The last time we spoke in this room it did not go well. I hold my breath and wait for her to start.

"I'm sorry," Mom says. She looks me straight in the eye when she says it. "I messed up and I hurt you and I'm just so very sorry." Mom shakes her head. "I was selfish. I thought only about my feelings and not about yours. I can't imagine what you've had to go through. When I think about those assholes at school I just get so angry, but then I remember that I was one of them."

Tears spring to her eyes, and Mom tries and fails to blink them back.

"I hurt you, that I know. Saying sorry doesn't feel like enough, but it's all I can do. I failed you, Kai. But I promise to try, to keep trying so that it never happens again."

"I'm sorry that I disappointed you," I say. Tears are streaming down my own cheeks.

"You didn't, Kai. You're perfect just the way you are." Mom buries her face in her hands. "My son is perfect just the way he is." She sounds as if she's talking to someone else.

I stand and close the distance between us. I only hesitate

once before hugging her. Mom's arms wrap around me instantly. She clings to me. We stay like that until both of us have stopped crying. Mom pulls back and reaches for my face. She cups it between her hands and uses her thumbs to wipe away my drying tears.

"You're perfect, Kai Sheridan," she says. "And I love you a whole lot."

"I love you, too."

"You should get washed up," Mom says, looking at her watch. "Then come eat breakfast. Or lunch. Your dad cooked it. I'm just in charge of reheating."

"Thank God," I say, and we both laugh.

"You're insufferable," Mom says. She stands up and leaves me alone in my bedroom. I close my eyes and bask in what just happened. Piece by piece I feel my heart retaking shape.

When I open my eyes, I notice that Mom has left two things on my desk. The first is the photo strip of Bryson and me. It's crinkled but intact—a lot like me. I pick it up and study those perfectly captured happy memories. I miss him.

The second is a large envelope from Tisch. With my heart in my throat, I rip it open. I only look at the first lines:

Dear Mr. Sheridan,
Congratulations . . .

I scream and I hear Mom laugh behind my door.

I rush to charge my cell phone. When it's powered up, I

clear all the messages and notifications without reading them. I open my camera and take a picture of my acceptance letter. I text it to our group chat.

Oh my God! Priya texts back. *This is amazing! I'm so happy for you!*

Donny sends a celebratory GIF.

I open a new text to Kelly and pause. I tap the edit button and change the name to Bryson. I want to share this news with him, but I don't know how. I look at the strip of our photos. We look so happy and hopeful.

We should talk.

I delete it.

Can we meet?

I stare at those words for a while before deleting them, too.

I miss you more than I thought possible.

I snort. There's no way I'd have the confidence to send that. Annoyed with myself, I throw my phone on my bed and head downstairs to celebrate my good news.

• • •

Later, we're eating dinner. Dad wasn't in the mood to cook, and so we ordered in. We're celebrating my acceptance—both of them. After Saturday night, I thought a dinner like this would be impossible, and yet here we sit Tuesday night. It almost feels normal.

"How was school, Yazz?" Dad asks.

Yazz sighs heavily before she begins to list all the things that annoyed her at school today.

"So, was there anything that you liked?" I ask.

Dad and Mom laugh. Yazz fixes me with a blank stare.

"I'm going to let that slide because I know you're going through a hard time."

"I appreciate it."

"Oh, Kai, you need to see Ms. Coleman when you get back to school," Mom says. "But there's no rush. You can go back when you feel ready to."

I sigh. "No. I'll go back tomorrow."

"So soon?" Dad asks. The worry is etched on his face.

"I don't want them to think they've won, that they've chased me away. I won't give them the satisfaction."

The doorbell rings. We all pause and look at each other. "I'll get it," I offer.

When I pull the door open, my heart soars at the sight of Bryson standing there.

"Who is it, honey?" Mom calls.

For a second, I think about lying. But I'm done with the lies, done with the hiding.

"It's Bryson."

I step out of the house and pull the door closed behind me. The chill night air greets me. I'm oddly nervous to see Bryson. I don't know why he's here, but a large part of me is glad that he is, happy that I get to see him even for a little bit.

"What are you doing here?" I ask.

"You sent me a text and then didn't reply afterward. You ignored my calls, too, so I had to come."

"What text—" I start to ask but stop. Horror dawns on my face. I feel the blood rushing to my face.

"This one." Bryson holds up his phone toward me.

I miss you more than I thought possible.

My words. My confession. Oh God! It went through.

Bryson pushes his hoodie down, and for the first time I get to see his face. It's bruised. Without thinking, I close the distance between us and reach for him.

"What the hell happened to you?" I am both angry and worried.

"Dustin and I needed to talk."

"You shouldn't have done that," I say. "I don't want you to get into trouble for me."

"A three-day suspension isn't so bad," Bryson says. "It was worth it." He still sounds like he doesn't quite believe it. "I'm sorry he did this to you." Bryson blinks back tears. The betrayal is a fresh wound to him. He's hurt just like I am. And I am powerless to do anything to help him, because right now I can't even help myself.

I realize that I'm cupping Bryson's face. I move to pull away, but Bryson grabs my hand and pulls me to him in one full movement.

"I missed you," he says as he hugs me. "I've been worried about you."

"I'm sorry," I say. My arms are at my sides. I want to hug him so bad, but I think that we need time apart. I need to deal with the mess that is my life before I can drag him into it.

I step back, and Bryson reluctantly lets me go. He studies my face and he must see what I'm going to say as if it's already written there.

"You need time?"

"I need to deal with everything," I say. "I'm sorry."

"Don't be. I don't like it, but I get it." He smiles then. It is small and timid. Bryson heads back toward the Jeep. He pauses at the door. "Call me if you need me. Anytime and anywhere." He gets in and rolls down his window. "I'll wait for you, Kai Sheridan."

I watch as Bryson drives away.

I am both happy and sad. I want nothing more than to chase after his disappearing taillights, but I know that I shouldn't. I can't right now. I will not out another person against their will. Maybe when everything dies down, we can go back to how we were.

I sigh and walk back inside.

Mentally and emotionally, I start to prepare myself.

Tomorrow I go to war.

WEDNESDAY

33

Mom is driving me to school. It feels strange not to be in Bryson's Jeep. I've grown so used to our routine. The school day has already started, but Mom doesn't seem to be in much of a rush. We even stop for coffee at the drive-through before heading to school.

"Call me if anything happens," Mom says. She's idling in front of the building.

"I'll be fine."

"Even so."

I nod and climb from the car.

"I love you, Kai."

"I love you, too."

Because of my late arrival, the halls are empty. Ms. Coleman is the guidance counselor, and while I've been to her office a few times, I've never been there with an actual honest-to-God problem. I knock.

"Come in," Ms. Coleman calls.

I enter the office and find her seated behind her large desk.

She offers me a warm smile and points at the empty chair opposite her.

"Have a seat, Kai."

I do.

Ms. Coleman hands me some pamphlets. I read the first one: *It's Okay to Be Gay*. Then the next: *My Sexuality and Me*. And the final, and maybe my favorite, one: *Gay Means Happy, Too*.

I flip them to the back to see who wrote them and try to hide my surprise when I read *Denise Coleman*.

"Uh, thanks," I say awkwardly.

"Of course," she says. "If you have any questions or need anything else, my door is always open." Ms. Coleman reaches into her drawer and places a handful of condoms before me. My eyes widen in horror.

"Always practice safe sex," Ms. Coleman says. "Gay or straight, remember there should always be no love without a glove."

I want to hide my face in shame. I want to evaporate and be reborn as rain falling two weeks from now. I want this torture to end.

"Be sure to share those with your boyfriend, if you have one," Ms. Coleman adds. I'd be surprised if it's possible for my face to get any redder than it is right now. "Is there anything else you wanted to talk to me about?"

I shake my head.

"Well, as I told your parents on Monday, Fairvale Academy

does not tolerate such nonsense," Ms. Coleman says. "This matter will be dealt with severely, and the *Fairvale Academy Herald* is under review. We're questioning the editor and have called in her parents, but she refuses to reveal if she had any help with the article. She claims she's protecting her source." Ms. Coleman clicks her tongue. "I can't believe stuff like this is still happening."

And that's the truth of the matter. A lot of people believe that this stuff doesn't still happen . . . but it does. There are still people who have to fight just to exist, just to love. Just as there are still people who will go out of their way to make that very simple human right something unattainable.

"Dustin Smith sent her one of the photos. I'm not sure about the other, but I think that was her doing," I say. I don't feel bad about "outing" Dustin. Fair is fair, after all.

"Hmmm. He's already been suspended for fighting." Ms. Coleman makes a note. "But I'll pass that along to Vice Principal Ferguson. We'll talk to him and his parents when he gets back." She looks up. "Hang in there."

Feeling exactly the same as I first did when I walked into her office—if not more embarrassed now that I have a pocket full of condoms—I leave. It's ten minutes to lunch, so I decide to waste time while I wait for the bell to ring. So far, I haven't encountered anyone, but I know what awaits me in the cafeteria.

I pull out my phone and open my group chat.

I'm at school. Meet me at Big Bertha.

I head toward the vending machine. I kick Big Bertha and

bend to pick up my soda. While I wait for lunch, a freshman runs past. She almost crashes into me, and I barely manage to avoid a repeat of last week. I chuckle.

The bell rings. Donny and Priya arrive five minutes later. Priya rushes to hug me. I laugh. Donny doesn't hesitate to join in.

"I'm proud of you for coming back," Priya says.

"I didn't have much of a choice. I need to graduate."

"You could have taken the rest of the week off," Donny says. "No one would have blamed you."

"I'm tired of running away." I finish my soda. "This is me. It's out there, so I might as well face it head-on."

"Well, you have us," Donny says.

"All for one, and one for all," Priya chants.

I smile. We start walking toward the cafeteria but stop when Shannon comes into view. She sees us at the exact same time but continues as if she will just walk right past us. It pisses me off.

"Aren't you even going to apologize?" I ask. The students in the hallway all stop and turn to look at us.

"Apologize for what?" Shannon asks. She crosses her arms. "I did my job, reported a story—that's all. I think I helped you."

"The *Herald* isn't some tabloid," Priya says. "I thought you wanted to be a real reporter."

"It got the most views of any story this year. I call that a success."

"And that makes you proud?" Priya asks.

Shannon fixes Priya with a look that should kill. "Why are you talking to me? This has nothing to do with you."

"That's the thing with you, Shannon. You're never really sorry when you hurt someone," I say. "You always have excuses, always have your reasons. And they always matter more than the hurt you caused. That's what makes you a bad person."

Shannon rolls her eyes. "Save your speech, Kai. Nothing you say is going to make me feel bad. I did what any reporter would do."

"I really want to punch her in the throat," Priya says. "Just right in the jugular."

"She's not even worth it," I say. I meet her gaze. "Do you really think a story like *this* is going to get you off the waitlist?"

"Shut up," Shannon says. She looks around.

"Wait . . . you're waitlisted?" Donny asks. "You told me you got accepted to Stanford when I did."

"Oops." I bring my hand to my mouth in mock apology.

Donny throws his arm over my shoulders. "You should know that my parents love Kai. When I told them what happened, they were very upset. Dad even offered to call the chairman of the school board himself. They go golfing every Sunday afternoon." Donny smiles at me. "Let's eat. I'm hungry."

The three of us leave Shannon standing there with her mouth hanging open. When we're out of earshot, I whisper to Donny, "Did your dad really say that?"

"Yes," Donny said. "He's calling your parents today to set something up. I'm pretty sure Shannon has written her last story at Fairvale Academy. And I'm pretty sure she can kiss being valedictorian goodbye."

"I wish something worse would happen to the wench," Priya says.

"Wench?" Donny asks.

"I'm trying to use alternative curse words where she's concerned. The normal ones have stopped feeling good."

I laugh. We enter the cafeteria, and it's like all at once everyone notices us—notices me. I can feel the blush rise on my cheeks. I've never heard the cafeteria so quiet before. It lasts a few heartbeats before the whispering starts. I can't do this. I'm about to backtrack, but Priya links her arm in mine.

"You can do this, Kai," Priya says.

"We're right here with you," Donny adds.

Everyone is watching, but Priya and Donny don't seem to care. I find that comforting, and soon I am mirroring them. We sit down at our regular table and have a perfectly normal lunch. The people who matter to me most accept me for who I am—100 percent. And there is power in that. It is my shield and my armor.

"You know, your mom went on a rampage on Monday," Priya says. "It's no wonder she and my mom get along so well."

"Was it embarrassing?"

"A parent standing up for their child should never be embarrassing," Priya says.

"It was totally embarrassing," Donny adds.

"Shut it, Donald." But there is no malice behind Priya's words. Donny simply smiles and dips a fry into ketchup.

I laugh.

Thanks to Priya and Donny, I survive my first lunch back at school. People continue to talk about me, but I choose to ignore it. I go through the day with blinders on. The end-of-day bell rings and I make my way to the parking lot to wait for my friends.

I'm standing next to the Quackmobile when Eric approaches me.

"Hey." He offers me a smile.

"What's up?"

"I just wanted to check how you were doing." Eric shakes his head. "I didn't know that my quote would be used for that. I'm sorry."

"It's not your fault."

"Screw Shannon. I want you to know that Mom's upset. She says she's going to punish everyone who was involved in this."

"Really?"

"Of course. Outings are not news. They're a violation. And they're something that should never happen at Fairvale Academy. This has given the LGBTQ club a new mission." Eric shifts on his feet. "You know, you're always welcome to come to a meeting if you want. We more than just fight for rights and talk about serious stuff; we also just hang out and have fun. Sometimes it's nice to spend time with people who get it."

"I'll think about it," I say. "Thanks."

"No problem. Let me know if you ever need anything."

"Ooh-la-la," Isaac says as he's passing by. "This is romantic."

"Grow some brain cells, Isaac," Eric says with an eye roll. He offers me a parting wave. I watch him leave before turning to look at Isaac.

"You're such an asshole," I say.

"What?"

"Did making that comment make you feel better? Did it make you feel cool?"

"What are you talking about?" Isaac asks. "It was just a joke."

"Jokes are meant to be funny, you jackass." I cross my arms and stare him down. "That one wasn't."

Isaac shakes his head. "Loser."

I watch him walk away. This will be my new normal now that I'm out. There will always be someone like Isaac waiting in the wings to say or do something homophobic. It isn't right and it isn't fair. But it is life.

I will be happy despite the hate and the homophobic assholes. And if I fall down and stumble, I know that I'll have people to pick me up, to support me.

My coming out might have been less than ideal, but even so, I know I'm one of the lucky ones.

I will survive this.

FRIDAY

34

I've made it through yet another day of school. Thursday passed by so fast that it felt like I skipped it altogether. Today was the easiest so far. But even so, I am exhausted. It feels as if I could sleep for a week. Instead, I turn up my music and open my homework.

I check my phone for any messages. Bryson hasn't texted since we spoke outside my house. It makes me sad even though I know I'm the one who asked for time. I type a quick response in the group chat and put the phone down. Just then, there's a knock at my door and Yazz pops her head inside.

"Are you busy?"

"Why?"

"I have something for you."

"For me?" I turn on my desk chair to face her. She holds up her sketch pad. "What is it?"

"I figured you might need it."

I open the pad to find Yazz's very first comic book. It's about a gay superhero. One who looks an awful lot like me.

"When did you start this?" I ask. There's no way Yazz could have completed this since Saturday night.

"Last week," Yazz says. "After I figured out what was going on with you and Bryson."

"What? How?"

"I've suspected it for a while, to be honest," Yazz says. She pushes her black-rimmed glasses back into place. "But it was confirmed when I saw a message on your phone. Kelly is Keller, right?"

"How did you know that?"

"I'm smart," Yazz says. "Plus, I know you, Kai. The smile you had when reading those messages was a dead giveaway. I don't think I've ever seen you that happy—that free."

"So you knew even before?" I ask. "And you kept it a secret?"

"Of course." Yazz shrugs. "I knew you'd come out when you were ready. But it made me happy that you had someone like Bryson in your corner when you did."

I page through the comic book, admiring not only my younger sister's talent but also her thoughtfulness. This without a doubt is the best gift I've ever received.

"I love you, Yazz."

"Yeah, yeah, yeah," Yazz says. "Let's not get carried away." She looks at me. "Is Bryson still your boyfriend?"

"Of course."

"Then start acting like it." Yazz sighs. "You know what trope I really hate is when the main character decides to give up on the person they love in the name of protecting them." She fixes me with a stare. "That's what you're doing right now.

You're trying to protect Bryson, but you don't realize you're hurting him instead."

"It's more complicated than that," I try to argue.

"Really? Do you not like him anymore?"

"It isn't that. Of course I like him." I chew at my lip. "A lot."

"Then why aren't you seeing him?"

"Because I want to protect—" The words die on my lips. "Oh."

"Exactly." Yazz shakes her head in exasperation. "Sometimes I really worry about you. The advice is free this time, but next time it'll cost you." Yazz stands and heads for the door.

I pull my phone from my pocket and open Instagram. I click on Bryson's profile. He's uploaded something new. I hold my breath. It's a picture of us, one we took on the beach last Sunday. He's leaning his head close to mine and I'm smiling in a way I've never seen before. I look happy; we both do. But even more than the picture, the caption catches my eye and makes my heart race.

It was real then. And it's real now. I'm using my wish now. I wish you were here. I miss you.

Already it has 219 likes and just as many comments, with the number growing as I watch. I study the picture once more. There's no denying that it is a couple photo. This is Bryson Keller coming out . . . for me. I open the comments and scroll through them:

OMG. IS THIS REAL?!

Is Bryson dating Kai?

THEY LOOK SO CUTE!!!!!!

Is the dare really over?

I ship it!

Seriously? I can't believe this.

I sit and stare without seeing. My sister is right. I have been an idiot. I've pushed Bryson away to protect him, but I haven't asked how he feels about everything. Now I'm looking at the answer to my unasked question. This photo reminds me that it isn't just about me. There are two people in this relationship.

I stand and grab my wallet and phone before running out of my bedroom.

My phone buzzes with a text. It's the three musketeers group chat.

Romeo, Romeo, where art thou?

I exit the house to find Donny and Priya standing next to the Quackmobile.

"Your chariot awaits," Priya says. She dramatically motions to the car.

"What are you guys doing here?"

"What do you mean?" Donny asks. "We obviously came to help our best friend get his man."

I look between them . . . confused.

"Yazz texted us, telling us she was going to kick your ass into gear," Priya explains. "So we came to play our part."

I look back at the house, where my mastermind sister is. Amazing.

"Plus, we saw Bryson's post. It seems the King has a romantic side after all," Donny says.

"I can't believe Bryson just came out. This is awesome," Priya says. "Let's go. We're wasting time."

Donny nods and climbs into the driver's seat and Priya opens the passenger side to get in. I jump in the back.

Priya fiddles with the radio and settles on a love song. Satisfied with her choice, she turns the volume up.

"Where to?"

"Melody Beach," I say.

Donny puts the car into gear and we speed off. As we drive to the beach, I hope that Bryson is still there. The photo was posted fifteen minutes ago. If he's not at Melody Beach, I'll call him. I will meet him today. I will fix what I've ruined.

We arrive fifteen minutes later, and it feels so much longer than that.

Priya twists in her seat and looks at me. She offers me a big smile.

"You can do this, Kai," she says.

"We'll be waiting for an update in the group chat," Donny says.

I nod. "I'll tell you everything." I climb from the car. "Thanks for this."

Priya rolls down her window. "Also, tell Bryson that tomorrow we're having a double date. We still need to judge him."

Donny sticks his head out the sunroof. "We also need to ask him what his intentions are with our sweet summer child."

"Please don't embarrass me," I whine. "I've been through enough this week."

"We would never do such a thing," Donny says.

"Never," Priya adds.

I laugh and turn away. I'm relieved when I spot Bryson's Jeep in the parking lot.

I approach but find it empty. He isn't at the basketball court, either.

In the distance I spot him. Bryson's standing near the surf with his back to me, staring out at the setting sun.

He hasn't noticed me yet. When I near, I reach for his hand, a balled fist at his side. Bryson startles at my touch and turns to me. He looks from my face to the hand that I'm holding. This is the first time I've reached for him.

"Am I dreaming?" Bryson asks. The sea air has playfully tousled his hair. He has a slight five-o'clock shadow, as though he couldn't be bothered to shave. I want to run my finger along his jawline.

Instead, I draw him close and pinch him. "To prove it's real."

His lips twitch. "What are you doing here?"

"I came to see you."

"Why?"

"Because I need to tell you that I've been an idiot."

"What do you mean?" His blue eyes darken with confusion.

"I'm sorry I asked for time. I was only doing it because I didn't want you to get hurt because of me."

"You should let me decide that," Bryson says. He smiles and his dimple shows. "I already have."

"I know," I say. "I saw." I can't help but smile, too. Even so, I ask, "Are you sure?"

Bryson lightly grips my chin. "Yes." He rests his forehead against mine. "This was my choice. I know what I want, and I want to be with you," Bryson says, "regardless of what anyone else has to say. I like you, Kai Sheridan. I like you a lot."

I didn't think I could cry anymore after this week, and yet here I am crying again. It's totally embarrassing. Bryson laughs, and I smack him on the chest.

"Shut up," I say. "That was sweet."

"I know." Bryson winks. He reaches up to wipe away my tears with his thumbs. "You're lucky you have such a sweet boyfriend."

"Yes, I am."

Bryson kisses me then, and I deepen it. Just like I wanted to before, I trace his jawline. Bryson bites at my bottom lip and I moan. Our mouths move against each other, and that becomes the only thing that matters.

I don't know how long this will last, but I choose to focus on the here and now.

I choose to be happy.

Because I can be.

Because I deserve to be.

Gay means *happy*, too, you know.

Author's Note

Telling this story was both the scariest and the most thrilling thing I've ever done. I've never before written a story so personal, so very tied to my own lived experience and history. There are many bits and pieces of me in this book. Some are big—like Kai's anxiety and blushing, my thoughts and feelings on coming out, growing up in a religious household, and being mixed race. Others, small—like Kai's list of hates, his taste in music that distances him from his cousins, the lunchtime detentions and the blazer rule, and even the text-message flirting with someone you probably shouldn't flirt with (ooh boy, that's a story for another day).

When I sat down to write this book, I sought to tell an #ownvoices story for the LGBTQ+ reader that exists firmly within the LGBTQ+ narrative. I wanted a story that touches on the troubles and tribulations that many gay teens still face. But more than that, I wanted to tell the reader that despite those trials and tribulations, there is hope, that we have worth and deserve to be happy.

I know I'm not the first to tell a gay love story, but I've always believed that more than one story of a certain type can exist. We need more representation all around. We shouldn't settle for just one thing, because we are not just one thing. Our race, culture, geography, sexuality, and experiences make us different. These things shape our stories, our lives. These things become the themes that we explore in the stories we tell. I hope that after reading this book, you can see my heart and my thoughts—that you can understand my inspiration a bit better. And if teens—or any readers, for that matter—see themselves in this story, in these characters, then I'll consider my job done.

The guidance counselor in this book was purposely written to be hopeless at her job. If that feels true to life for you, and you're looking for something more helpful, I urge you to read "Coming out of the Closet: Some Resources to Aid the Process" (huffpost.com/entry/coming-out-resources_n_4085658). James Nichols and the rest of the team at Huffpost Queer Voices wrote this wonderful article and compiled numerous resources not only for LGBTQ+ youth but also for parents and allies. Please remember that coming out is totally up to you. *You* get to decide when you want to.

Coming out is an important decision—life-changing, even—which is why I wanted this book to be more than a love story with a happy ending; I wanted it to be a coming-out narrative. I'm a firm believer that stories of this nature will always be needed because there will always be a teen faced with the daunting task of coming out. I'd love for a teen like that to pick up this book and feel seen—feel understood.

For so long, gays have been banished as background characters or cast as the main character's best friend for comedic relief. And when I think back to the rom-coms I grew up on around the late nineties, most of the characters were White and heterosexual. Those movies made it seem as if only people who looked like that or loved like that deserved love stories. So I wanted this book to show that a lead who is gay and of mixed race can have a love story that could be described as epic.

I'd like to end this note by thanking those who've inspired me in the writing of *Date Me, Bryson Keller*. These authors, filmmakers, and other creators are crafting diverse stories about teens, sparking ideas, and inspiring a new generation of writers to tell stories with authentic representation. Such stories are woven into the tapestry of this novel. I owe a great debt to all of them, including the Norwegian web series *Skam* (particularly season 3), *To All the Boys I've Loved Before* by Jenny Han, *Simon vs. the Homo Sapiens Agenda* by Becky Albertalli (as well as the film adaption, *Love, Simon*), the manga *Seven Days: Monday–Sunday* by author Venio Tachibana and illustrator Rihito Takarai, and the '90s rom-com *She's All That*. *Date Me, Bryson Keller* is my #ownvoices take on these prior works.

Representation matters, and to all those who have inspired me, I thank you from the bottom of my heart.

I hope this book can inspire another writer to tell their story—to write their response. We must continue to push forward, to demand that our stories be told with authenticity and care. The readers of the world deserve it. Children growing up deserve to see themselves as heroes, whether slaying dragons, saving the world, or simply falling in love.

We deserve to be loved, supported, and accepted.

We deserve to be happy. *Always.*

Acknowledgments

Writing a book should be considered a team sport. As such, I have so many people to thank. Forgive me if this section runs long, but having the opportunity to even write this feels surreal. I've always loved reading acknowledgments, and I can't believe I'm sitting down to write my own. Be warned: I will repeat the words *thank you* no less than a bazillion times, and it still may not be enough. I will also mean it. Every. Single. Time.

First and foremost, thanks go to Mom and Dad, the best parents ever! Thank you for believing in me and for encouraging me to chase my dreams, no matter what anyone else said. Your unwavering support and love have made this book possible. I truly lucked out in the parent lottery.

To Shane, the best big brother in the world: Thank you for always having my back. I'm pretty sure you'd help me bury a body, too. To Charné, the best sister-in-law in the world (seriously, you're practically just my sister at this point): Thank you for the encouragement and for always being willing to read everything I write. Thank you for helping me fancast my books too. To my nieces and nephew, who are too young to read this: Just know that I'm thankful to you, too. I love you so much more than words can say.

Thank you to the rest of my family—those still here and those who have passed. You've witnessed me chasing after this dream for years. Thank you for your words of encouragement. It took me a few years to get here, but thank you for always believing that I would.

To my best friend, Naadira: When the expression *ride or die* is thrown around, I think of you. We've been friends now for close to a decade, and I've loved every moment of it. Thanks for the laughs and the memories. I know that without you my life would be dull and incomplete. You're my first fan, always willing to read my books—thank you, thank you, thank you. Long live "Kevra."

To Saira: You know I can't call you my best friend because your sister might smack me, but know that I have loved spending every moment with you, too. Your wit and honesty are truly highlights in my life. And to the rest of the Moodley family: Thank you for being a second family to me. When I say I'm part of the furniture, we know that I mean it.

To the Fourth-Row Rejects—or whatever we're calling ourselves now: Thank you for being weird and wonderful with me. Temara Prem, Allan Convery, and Darren Jayna-rayan, film school and my life would be a lot less meaningful without you. I can't believe our group chat has been active since 2013. I think that's when we met. (Is that right? You know I'm bad at math.) Special thanks to Allan for the deep-cut convos and for being my buddy in misery and hope. Here's to us adulting and figuring stuff out! We got this, friends!

To Christopher Schelling: Thank you for taking a chance on a twenty-one-year-old writer with a dream. You taught me so much about writing and the industry. I'll forever be grateful.

To Beth Phelan: Thank you for creating #DVpit. Without this spectacular program, I would not be living my dream right now.

To my writer friends—and I truly have met so many of you, and I am thankful to each of you, too. Lucky 13s—Julie C. Dao, Jessica Rubinkowski, Heather Kaczynski, Mara Fitzgerald, Rebecca Caprara, Austin Gilkeson, Jordan Villegas—I would be very lost without our email threads. You were there for me for the ups and downs, and the in-betweens, too. Your faith and support made me keep going, and I can't thank you enough. Special thanks to Jessica for the pep talks and for pushing me to pitch this book in the first place.

To June Tan, Deeba Zargarpur, Emily A. Duncan, Rory Power, Christine Lynn Herman, Rosiee Thor, Emma Theriault, and Alexa Donne: Thank you for the support and chats. You make being a writer a lot less lonely. Special shout-out to Alexa Donne for being amazing and always willing to talk. Your advice and insights have been priceless. I'm blessed that I get to call you my friend.

To Gwen Cole: Thanks for being the best critique partner. Your support, insight, and enthusiasm are truly invaluable to me. I'm a big fan of you and your stories!

To my Author Mentor Match mentees, Alexandria Strutz, Daniel Voralia, Debra Spiegel, and Joanne Weaver: Thank you for the support and trust. Alex, thank you for the chats and for fully understanding my love of not only BTS but also SHINee. The CDs you sent are among my most prized possessions, as are the photo cards. Next time, though, I will get the flaming charisma that is Minho. Thanks, friend!

And to Daniel, user of terrible fake accents and holder of an amazing British one: Thank you for the chats and, more often than not, for getting me. I can't thank you enough for being the first reader of this book, and for offering brutally honest notes on those early chapters. They were just the kick I needed to get my confidence back, and I am forever grateful.

To the rest of the Author Mentor Match family: Thanks for the support. It means the world to me.

To my editor—and magical human being—Chelsea Eberly: Your insight into this world and these characters has truly been invaluable. Thanks to you, this story is much stronger. You pushed me further and further with each draft, and I am grateful that you did. From the moment I got your first edit letter, I knew that you understood Kai and Bryson and the rest of the cast. That you believed in this story with all your heart. Thank you for making this debut experience one I can look back on fondly. Thank you for making an offer and turning my dreams into reality. Thank you for loving this book as much as I do.

To Polo Orozco, thank you for your wonderful insight, and for getting me and this book across the finish line.

To everyone at Random House Children's Books: Thank you for the support and the work you've put into this book. Regina Flath, my book designer, you designed the most amazing book cover and jacket ever. I seriously get chills when I look at it. Howard Huang and the cover models, thanks for the photographs and for playing a part in creating something truly spectacular.

To Robert Guinsler—agent extraordinaire, and quite possibly superhero: I don't think a paragraph is space enough for me to tell you how grateful I am to you. Thank you for telling me to send this book to you. Waking up to your email the next day felt like a dream, and it was the start of this magical journey. You understood this book, and more important, you understood me. When you said I'd have a book deal by Christmas, I thought you were lying. Thanks for giving me the best Christmas present a writer could ever dream of. I'm still in shock at how far we've come, and I know that none of this would have been possible without you. Thank you, thank you, thank you! Onward and upward we go!

And to everyone else at Sterling Lord Literistic, Inc.: Thank you from the bottom of my heart. I appreciate everything that you do for me and this book behind the scenes. Danielle Bukowski and the rest of the foreign rights team, thank you for making the most impossible of dreams come true.

Finally, to you, dear reader: Thank you for picking up this book and giving it a chance. I hope that you liked it and that you love Kai and Bryson as much as I do.

A thousand thank-yous and more!

About the Author

Kevin van Whye is a writer born and raised in South Africa, where his love for storytelling started at a young age. At four years old, he quit preschool because his teacher couldn't tell a story. Kevin's love affair with stories led him to film school to study script writing. *Date Me, Bryson Keller* is his first novel. Kevin currently lives in Johannesburg, and when he's not reading, he's writing books that give his characters the happy rom-com endings they deserve.

kevinvanwhye.com